Praise for *Then Came the Evening*

"All the elements are in place for an inspirational, heartland-America redemption story, but Hart taps into his characters' fears with gritty lyricism and noirish repartee that subvert any feel-good temptations."
—*New York Times Book Review*

"Hart's clipped prose mirrors the stark Western landscape . . . A solid, original work that defies convention."
—*San Francisco Book Review*

"Tragic and gorgeous . . . Gritty and poignant . . . In Hart, there is an echo of Cormac McCarthy's resolute yet restrained capacity for tragedy and violence. Yet there's something here that is all Hart, something we should all look forward to seeing again. —*Missoula Independent*

"Hart's evocative debut traces the long descent of a tragic Western figure straight out of a Sam Shepard play . . . Desiccated descriptions of a long-fallow landscape and the author's ability to conjure up the ghosts of a low man's past further enrich this heartbreaking, convincing drama." —*Kirkus Reviews*

"*Then Came the Evening* is an edgy and affecting debut from a writer already bursting with promise and achievement. Brian Hart's narrative voice is as tender as it is unflinching—and his novel of love squandered and oh-so-nearly retrieved is a triumph."
—**Jim Crace, author of** *Quarantine* **and** *Being Dead*

"The story . . . resonates with power and potential. Idaho can be a stark state, battered by the elements that mark northern climes. In *Then Came The Evening*, Brian Hart turns this circumstance of geography into a fresh tale of family breakdown and self-examination."
—*Petoskey News*

"Like the characters in this quietly exceptional début novel, the author is an Idaho native, and an astute observer of the transitional Western landscape." —*New Yorker*

"This novel's finely detailed episodes of physical and emotional violence bring to mind the works of Larry Brown, while its lyrical descriptions speak of landscape and rural community life like the books of Robert Morgan. Hart explores, with brutal honesty and a delicate respect for the strength of the individual spirit, the human needs for love, for continuity after death, and for redemption." *—Booklist*

"*Then Came the Evening* is an important book, a novel of raging velocity and blazing empathy, a mature achievement. Brian Hart knows everything about his rural western setting, everything about his short-on-luck characters, and everything about making a reader turn the pages. This is a first novel written with a master's skill."
—**Stephen Harrigan, author of** *The Gates of the Alamo*

"Most impressive is Hart's ability to conjure rich and conflicted characters in an uncommon situation; his handling of the material is sublime." *—Publishers Weekly* **(starred)**

"It takes a rare writer to be able to convince a reader to follow a group of bad-news characters to such bleak places, but Brian Hart's prose makes the story enjoyable, even when the events it describes are not. In *Then Came The Evening*, Hart has achieved a consistency of tone, a concision of description, and an intensity of focus that make for a satisfying drama." *—New West*

"The unforgiving rural landscape of Idaho is the perfect backdrop for first-time novelist Hart's poignant story of three misfits . . . Hart refuses to tie up everything neatly, and that's what makes this novel so appealing. Highly recommended." *—Library Journal*

"Brian Hart's considerable genius is that he sees what the rest of us are unwilling to see and says what we are unable to say. *Then Came the Evening* is both harrowing and haunting, hypnotic and exhilarating. Hart can flat-out tell a story. He's savvy, insightful, and fearless. What talent, what nerve, what an achingly beautiful and astonishing first novel."
—**John Dufresne, author of** *Requiem, Mass.*

THEN CAME THE EVENING

A Novel

Brian Hart

BLOOMSBURY

New York   Berlin   London   Sydney

Published by Bloomsbury USA, New York

All papers used by Bloomsbury USA are natural, recyclable products made from wood grown in well-managed forests. The manufacturing processes conform to the environmental regulations of the country of origin.

LIBRARY OF CONGRESS CATALOGING-IN-PUBLICATION DATA

Hart, Brian (Brian Woodson)
    Then came the evening : a novel / Brian Hart.—1st U.S. ed.
        p. cm.
    ISBN: 978-1-60819-014-0 (hardcover)
    1. Families—Fiction.   2. Idaho—Fiction.   3. Psychological fiction.
I. Title.
    PS3608.A78396T47 2010
    813'.6—dc22   2009016969

First published by Bloomsbury USA in 2010
This paperback edition published in 2011

Paperback ISBN: 978-1-60819-469-8

1 3 5 7 9 10 8 6 4 2

Typeset by Westchester Book Group
Printed in the United States of America by Quad/Graphics,
Fairfield, Pennsylvania

For my family

Chapter 1

THE BURNING SEASON

THE CABIN WAS DARK then a light flickered inside. Flames filled the windows and wormed at the sash; the glass blackened and shattered. Smoke poured out and drifted over the fields, the marshlands, and the creek and formed a dark ribbon at the base of the three hills that separated the Dorner land from the main road. Sometime after midnight the wind picked up and the trees on the mountainsides whispered and bent to it. The smoke was pushed beyond the hills and settled against the walls of the Finnish church and in the small graveyard nearby, but by then the fire was only a flicker, and the cabin was gone.

Bandy Dorner woke to a fogged windshield, cracked and spattered with mud and grass, the watery shadows of two policemen banging on his car hood with their fists. He opened the car door with his shoulder and fell into the canal. The shock of the water stole his breath and when he went to stand the strong current knocked him down. He dug his hands into the mud bank and pulled himself up to flat ground and stood dripping. The fog was nearly as dense outside of the car as it was within and it took him a few seconds to orient himself. The barbed wire from the fence he'd driven through was tangled up in his rear axle and strung across the field with some of the posts still attached.

"You can't prove a thing," Bandy said. He knew the two policemen and didn't like them. Turner was the tall man's name; Meeks was the shorter.

"I care about proof," Turner said.

Meeks took a toothpick from his breast pocket and slipped it into his mouth. "We got your bed ready in town. It ain't even pissed in. Yet." He smiled and the toothpick pointed skyward.

Bandy slapped the water and mud from his pants. "Go on, leave me alone. I'll fix the damn fence. It's not like I hurt anybody. Yet." He smiled and went toward them and they stepped aside and he walked between, a few inches taller than Turner.

"Go up there and load yourself into the backseat of that car and we'll be fine," Turner called after him. "We ain't wrestling with you again."

Bandy ignored him. Dead grass snared his boots and made him stumble. He didn't feel well. He touched his back pocket to see if his wallet was there and it was. He didn't bother taking it out and looking inside because it was empty. He'd have liked to get home before Iona woke up, but it didn't really matter. He could do as he pleased. They'd argued before he left for the bar. Going home was exactly what he'd been avoiding.

He walked through a dense belt of fog into a lesser pocket and saw his father standing in the ditch bottom with his fists clenched on the top wire of the fence. On the road behind him the haggard ranch truck that Iona usually drove was parked in front of the police car, but she wasn't there. He didn't see her. The gumdrop light turned and sounded out the closeness of the fog. Meeks and Turner followed Bandy at some distance and spoke quietly to one another; what they said he couldn't hear.

It occurred to him that he'd been dreaming of the mill fire before the police woke him. He'd been a boy when it burned and hadn't seen the actual fire, only the aftermath: the slow collapse of the town. In the dream, the fire raged in the mill and the ripe colors of the flames danced in the night and painted the glass surface of the lake. There was the sound of snapping cables and creaking timbers then the tower tilted and fell to the ground with such force that a single wave left the shoreline, only a few inches high, but it lifted the logs in the booming grounds one after the other and ran across the water with the silent determination of a falling star.

The fence wire was loose and the staples half pulled in the crisp and rotting posts. Bandy spread the wires and ducked through but he was too big and a barb tore the back of his shirt and gave him a rosary bead scratch just above his belt. Jack Dorner stayed fixed as a statue and watched him. He looked tired, like he'd been up. Bandy wanted to be easy with the old man but the tension was there always and had been getting worse. He pointed at the ranch truck. "How's Iona supposed to get around if you steal her rig?"

His father drew back a little as if he'd seen something terrible over his son's shoulder. Bandy turned but it was only the policemen and the fog behind him. "What's wrong with you?" he said to his father. "You don't like my shortcut?"

The old man's eyes dulled and he shook his head. Bandy picked up a stick from the ditch and carefully made his way up the steep bank onto the road. Black, gummy hunks of mud fell from his boots with every step. He hopped onto the hood of the cop car and dented it and fuck their car along with them. He crossed his legs and held onto his boot with one hand and rooted the mud out with the stick. His father still hadn't moved.

The cops took turns holding the fence wires for one another like they were cocking a crossbow. Their shoes were slick-soled and it took them several tries to make it from the borrow pit to the road. The old man followed them, mechanically kicking the toes of his boots into the soft earth for leverage. He made it to flat ground and touched his forehead and brushed his hand across his chest then looked at Bandy.

"It's my car and I crashed it," Bandy said to him. "There's no reason for you to be out here. This is a young man's game."

"Some game."

Bandy smiled at that and finished with his boots and threw the stick over the fence into the field. "Nothing for you," he said, blinking. "God, I'm still drunk." He turned and noticed the rip in his shirt and touched it, held up two bloody fingers. "Cut myself. You see that? Sonofabitch." He smeared his blood on the cop car, made an X.

"I sent for these police," his father said.

Bandy looked at the old man, not really believing him. "That's a rotten thing to do. Even to me."

Jack Dorner showed his teeth, not a smile. "You certainly pick your days." He poked a finger into the corner of his eye then held it out and looked at it, at Bandy. "Son, last night, out of all of them, you should've been at home."

"Well, I'm headed there now. That'll have to do."

"It's too late." The old man retrieved his pink, once red, kerchief from his back pocket and wiped his hands then stepped back and waved the cops in. "Go to it," he said.

Meeks stayed where he was while Turner circled around. Bandy scooted off the hood and the blood went to his head, his whole body felt unstable and hollow.

"I'm doing you a favor," his father said. "Someday you'll realize that."

"I don't need your favors."

"You go with these two and you might avoid doing any real harm. To anyone. You're going to need time to think, Bandy-boy."

"Don't call me that. I ain't a boy," he said.

Meeks spit out his toothpick and took a few herky side steps then stopped when Bandy looked at him. Turner was in a wrestling stance, slowly making his way forward. Bandy was ready for it: He wanted a fight.

Jack Dorner shook his head, blinked. "Does it even matter what I call you? You don't ever listen." The old man folded his kerchief and put it in his back pocket. "There was a fire," he said.

"What fire?"

"It was the cabin. The cabin burned down while me and your mother were in Boise. We didn't get home till late. We must've drove right by you out here. We didn't see you. It was pretty much over by then anyway. Nobody could've done anything." He slumped his shoulders and made a dismissive gesture with his hand. Bandy suddenly understood what it all meant, his father, the police. He wondered if it was the smoke from the cabin that had gifted him the dream of the mill fire.

"Her rig was there," his father said, thumbing at the pickup behind him. "She might be gone."

A deep, buried fear came up from the ground through Bandy's feet and it was like watching the guts drop out of a strung up animal, standing there realizing that she'd burned and I was in the bar while she burned then sleeping, drunk in the car sleeping while she burned.

"She wasn't with me," Bandy said. "I wasn't with her."

Turner caught him by the wrist and startled him. Bandy snatched his arm free and hooked the cop in the stomach, threw his weight into him, and knocked him to the ground. Meeks came forward and Bandy lunged and struck the smaller man in the jaw and sent him stumbling backward down the embankment into the ditch bottom. Bandy's father was saying something but Bandy wasn't listening. He wanted to kill somebody; the urge filled him and carried him on. He went and stood over Turner and without thinking anything besides don't break your hand, he held him by the back of his collar and punched him over and over in the back of the head until he quit struggling then he grabbed him by the hair and ground his face into the dirt and felt the pop of his nose as it broke from the pressure.

When he'd finished he stood and leaned back and looked into the white of the fog and the low torn clouds like ghosts. The dream of the mill entered his mind: the wave and the smoke.

Meeks made his way back up from the ditch and stood with his pistol drawn and told Bandy to get down on the ground. The old man told him to wait, to just hold on a second. "Put the gun away," he said.

"Look what he did to my partner." Turner wasn't moving. "You be good, you big bastard," Meeks said to Bandy. "Or I'll shoot. I swear I will."

Bandy looked at the pistol and at the cop's eyes and he didn't care. He crossed the distance in three quick steps and palmed the gun and wrenched it away and it went off. Meeks fell to the ground with a hole in his shirt above his liver. Jack Dorner caught his son by the shoulders and tried to pull him away but Bandy turned and pushed the old man in the chest and he fell back and rolled to his side as stiff as a length of kinked wire.

"You want to shoot me too?" he said, righting himself.

"No." Bandy held the familiar weight loosely in his hand. He couldn't meet his father's eyes. He turned to Meeks on the ground and he could see the silver and gold fillings in the man's teeth as he yawned for breath. He had vague thoughts of mercy and compassion, but it was over. He lifted the gun and shot the policeman in the forehead. The man snapped to attention then went limp. The shot roared and faded.

His father hacked out a series of thick, cancerous coughs as he got up from the road. He went toward his son with his arm outstretched for the pistol but Bandy wouldn't give it to him. "I meant to help you. I meant to keep you safe." He turned up his hands then squatted down on his heels and rested his elbows on his knees.

"You did your best." Bandy tipped the gun and studied it, looked at his father. "Is she really gone?"

His father nodded at the road.

Bandy dropped the gun at his feet. There was nothing to be done.

Behind him Turner opened his eyes and wiped the gravel from his mouth. He lifted his head, blood poured from his nose. He got to his knees and brought up his pistol, leveled it and fired. That shot and the next were wild, but the third ripped through Bandy's shoulder as he was reaching for the gun on the road. The bullet buried itself in the meat of his chest and he fell to his knees then slumped facedown in the gravel.

Jack Dorner knelt between the dead policeman and his son. The sun burned through the fog. The new light went down the roadway and on like a cracked door against the pastureland hills. Fool's gold scales glimmered in the wet dirt, sparking like ocean swell. And there was the graveyard in the distance with its lowly stones and across the road the one-room church, freshly painted, as white as the fog had been, whiter: fog manifest.

"Look what you did," the old man said, and at first it seemed that he was talking to the dead man. "Look what you finally did."

Iona told Bill to stop the truck alongside the cold ashes of the cabin instead of parking up near Jack and Maude's. Bill did what she asked. He didn't argue. He was her new man and she was leaving with him. He switched off the engine. She made no move to get out of the truck. Somebody had been after the debris with a tractor; they'd pushed in the edges and burned it all. The soil itself was burnt and looked ruined.

Bandy had hauled the cabin down from the Stibnite mine on a borrowed lowboy soon after he and Iona had met. Their cabin, along with dozens of others, had been sold at auction. The complete apparatus of the company town was taken away on lowboys and flatbed trucks. There were whole neighborhoods in Lake Fork composed of mine cabins, sometimes several cobbled together to make a more substantial home. Miner mansions, they were called. Bandy had settled the cabin within cold-night earshot of his parents' house, fifty yards, a little more maybe. It had all been too close for Iona, every part. She'd remained after he joined the army and went overseas, had fought the urge to leave nearly every night. That she stayed as long as she had now seemed laughable.

The dirt in the driveway was torn up from the tractor tires, the grass rutted, a flowerpot smashed. She imagined that there had been volunteer firefighters and all kinds of strangers there to watch and wonder where she was, if she had burned. She got out of the truck and smelled the dead smoke, acrid, somehow telling of things lost.

"I guess you should've taken your stuff," Bill said. He lifted his bag of tobacco and his papers from his breast pocket and began twisting a cigarette. His deep focus betrayed his simplicity if not his kindness. The metal of the truck door was cold in Iona's hand and she caressed it with her thumb and the coldness faded. It was all very unreal, the whole scene. When buildings burn they really do just go away, she thought. She looked right through where the front door used to be at the fields and the creek and the hills beyond. "I need to at least leave them a note."

"You could send a letter."

"We're already here." She flipped the visor down; a notepad and a pen dropped onto the floor. Bill looked at her and smiled and she thought maybe someday she would love him. He'd said once that he was a fan of adultery as long as he was the one doing the committing. Iona had to remind him that she and Bandy weren't married, not by a church or a judge, only by common law. Bill was no longer her shadow man; he was in the light. Bandy was in the dark. She didn't think Bill would leave her, not now, not after what had happened. She bent at the waist to grab the notebook and felt the sickness come over her again. She'd already thrown up twice at Bill's that morning. She suspected she was pregnant and at some point she'd have to go to the doctor to be sure but now was not the time. She stood up straight and tilted her head back and looked down her nose because that seemed to help. And there was Bandy's car covered in mud parked next to the corral with a tow chain coiled on the hood.

"You gonna be all right?" Bill said. He lit the cigarette with a strike-anywhere off the dash and pitched the match out the window.

Iona nodded. She pushed her hair behind her ears. It was black and shiny and warm to the touch. The note she wrote to Bandy's parents was an apology and nothing more.

Jack and Maude, I'm sorry. Iona

"I'll only be a minute." She walked toward the house with the note in her hand. She was sick with guilt, sick all over.

"I ain't in a hurry," Bill called after her. "Take your time."

The house was newly painted and sturdy looking. The yard was mowed and raked clean except for a chain harrow rusting under the eaves, slowly being swallowed by rye grass. Jack had his tractor lifted onto a pair of homemade jack stands in the driveway. The rear axle was beside it hanging from a cherry picker and safety-blocked with railroad ties. Scattered around there was an open toolbox and a milk stool, Jack's coffee cup and thermos, oil rags, a five-gallon can of oil with a red funnel turned up on it like a dunce cap. Iona knew that Jack needed Bandy's help to fix the tractor and now he wouldn't have it. The curtains on the front windows were drawn, and she was thankful for that.

The mudroom door was propped open with a fist-sized rock shaped like a hog's head that at some point Bandy had scrawled DAD on with red keel. Iona went in and quietly opened the screen door and slipped the note under the front door then let the screen door close. She wasn't ready to face Maude, or Jack. Two pairs of muddy boots, one pair larger than the other, sat side by side under the bench in the mudroom. She went back out.

The dog was sleeping beneath the weeping willow in the yard. The tree had grown around a length of barbed wire that had years ago been strung through its crotch. Iona had looked at it before and she went to it now and plucked it. The dog looked up at the sound and she squatted to pet him. His fur was stiff and jagged, stinking of pond scum. She wondered if the wire was still silver and new inside of the tree. The dog took deep, whistling breaths, its eyes opened only a slit, briefly.

The front door then the screen door slammed and she turned and watched Maude Dorner pull on her boots. Bandy's mother fixed her eyes on Iona and stood up easily with a straight back on strong legs and came outside.

"We didn't find any bones," she said. "We figured you were someplace else then we heard. Somebody called and told us they saw you." Her face was without its usual robust color and she had dark circles under her eyes.

Iona pressed her hand to the rough bark of the tree and tried to hold back the nausea. "I'm sorry, Maude."

"I read the note." Maude seemed to wince at her own unfriendliness. "Do you want to come in for coffee? I just made a second pot."

"No. Thanks. Bill's in the truck."

The old woman looked at the ground. "Just like that. Off like a shot."

Iona wiped her hand on her jeans. Maude walked from the shade into the sun of the driveway and Iona followed her. They stood beside the tractor and the axle.

"He's got a part coming from Oregon to fix it, a gear of some sort. I don't know what." There was a drowned grasshopper in Jack's coffee cup.

After a long silence Iona said quietly: "What would you have done?"

"I couldn't say. I guess if you had to leave—"

"Jesus Christ, Maude."

"Don't swear at me."

"I didn't want this to happen."

"Then you should've told him yourself that you were leaving. You could've knocked and come inside. Slipping notes under doors, sneaking around. You're a grown woman." Her eyes widened and she bobbed her head. "Things won't be mended till you face them. They never are."

"I don't think I believe that, Maude. I think sometimes walking away is best." Iona swept her foot across the driveway weeds. She thought of the bitter taste of dandelion milk, seeds on the wind, killdeer running and crying and making a show of their deceit. The old woman stooped to pick up a cigarette butt and walked over to the coffee can by the front door and pitched it in then reached in the mudroom and grabbed a grizzled broom and swept the single concrete step. The Dorners' four horses came around the side of the barn and gathered at the fence and one of them, a muddy appaloosa, began licking the paint on the roof of Bandy's car.

"Tell Jack I said bye, all right?"

"He's inside with the paper."

"I don't want to bother him."

Maude half smiled at that. "Sweetie, at this point I think he's officially bothered."

A bank of thunderheads sent a cold breeze over the ranch and Maude's flower print dress was blown against her stout legs and the heavy folds of her stomach and breasts.

"You know he came back different," Iona said.

Maude fixed her stare on Iona, her dark eyes as hard as marbles, Bandy's eyes, and Iona thought maybe in Maude's opinion I'm just one more big mistake in Bandy's life, maybe the biggest yet, bigger even than joining the army and going to Vietnam. The old woman nodded slightly. "J. D. says he didn't come back. Someone else, he says. Whatever that means."

"I know what it means. So do you."

The old woman covered her face with her hands for a moment then lowered them, balled them into fists so tightly her knuckles went white. "Everybody blames the war for everything. I'm sick of it."

"It's no accident."

"No, it's not, but what happened with Bandy started before he left. It started when Neil Guntly was killed. He changed then. I saw it happen. The light just went out."

"I don't get to go back that far, Maude. That was before we'd met. It would mean I never knew him, and I know him. I know why I left."

"I'm sure you do."

Iona breathed hard through her nose so she wouldn't cry. "He never said anything to me about that."

"Why would he?"

"I don't know, because I cared, because I stuck around."

Maude shook her head. "We're not bad people. We're good people."

"Maybe you are. I'm not so sure about me."

"Pity."

"What?"

"You're pitiful."

"Maybe so. I'm going. I meant what I said: I'm sorry about the cabin, everything." She turned and kept walking and didn't look back.

"Honey, wait. We don't care about the cabin," Maude called after her.

Iona stumbled then walked on, faster now.

"Iona, stay for a little while. Don't go yet. You're part of this family. We need you here now."

Iona raised her hand to wave but didn't look back. She reached for the door handle on Bill's truck and couldn't hold it any longer. She threw up and got it on her shoes and the cuffs of her new blue jeans. She turned with her hair in her hands and saw Maude coming toward her and opened the door and climbed quickly into the truck. Everything tilted then righted itself. Her eyes watered.

"You all right?" Bill said.

"Drive," she said. Bill took a last drag off of his cigarette and stubbed it out in the ashtray then started the truck. They backed out of the driveway while Maude walked toward them. Iona was crying and she couldn't help it.

"Wait," Maude yelled, walking as fast as she could, arms swinging. "Iona, wait."

"Don't you fucking stop," Iona said to Bill.

At the end of the driveway Bill swung the truck around and roared out onto the county road. When Iona looked in the side mirror she couldn't see Maude for the dust. They crossed the creek bridge and the three hills then slowed at the graveyard and the church and turned north toward Bill's. There were men in the field mending the fence that Bandy had driven through.

Any map of the Long Valley would show that Bill McKinley's house wasn't more than a mile or two from the Dorner place, but if you drove it, it was nearly seven. At the end of an unpaved mountain road, shoved back into a dark, windless gap among the lodgepole and black pine, Bill's tar-paper and scrap-wood A-frame sat like a pouting child. It was surrounded by scattered wads of dusty huckleberry and buckbrush, pine needles mounded up from runoff, thistles purple and green, snakegrass and skunk cabbage. The land was grinding through a transitional phase somewhere between solid rock and sand: dirtless, organized rubble.

Iona got out of the truck and watched Bill hoist grocery bags from the bed. She liked Bill's house at night because it was warm and quiet and dark; it reminded her of childhood hiding places, but in the light of day it scared her. The witch-hair moss hung from the straight, unmoving pines like torn fabric or flood debris, the pale gravel and sand stripped naked, ferrous granite rusting, bleeding away in streaks on the cliff walls and weeping from the boulders. She'd tasted it in the tap water, the stink of sulfur. She knew when winter came, if they were still here, they wouldn't see the sun until June and they'd have to walk up the hill from where the plow stopped and trudge. Like the Donner Party, she thought, like goddamned cannibal pioneers into the dark woods, doomed. Last year the fences had stayed buried all winter. In February the snow had drifted up to the eaves on the back of the cabin and opening the curtains on the lone bedroom window was like looking into the dead eye of a giant.

Iona went inside empty-handed and stood in front of the sink and looked out the dirty kitchen window at the tree trunks and the amber pitch frozen mid-ooze on the bark. Spider webs shone in the setting sun, the dusty light, like cracks in glass. The window wasn't trimmed yet and Iona could see the shims holding it in place and she held her hand up and through the rock wool stuffed there she could feel the evening breeze.

It took Bill three trips to bring all the groceries inside. At Turnery's, Iona had slouched low in the truck with Bill's fishing hat pulled over her eyes. Bill worked as the butcher there and had lots of friends while Iona was only a part-time checker and rarely spoke more than a few words at a time with any of her co-workers. She wasn't going back to work; she wasn't ever setting foot in that store again. They needed to leave town. Bill was younger than Iona so it was embarrassing on top of everything else, on top of being tragic and wrong. Everybody knows everything now, she thought. News travels fast in a town with dirt roads.

Bill kicked the front door shut and came inside and put the last of the bags on the counter. Iona turned and watched the final dance of the fall-time, tree-filtered sun cross the untreated floorboards. The shadow of the ladder to the sleeping loft made bars on the floor, a skewed rail track on the wall. Then the sun went and in an instant the room felt cold. It struck her that she and Bill had just made some kind of promise.

"We can't stay here," she said.

"We can't leave without money. We need some time to save up."

"I don't need time, I need a drink."

Bill kicked at the paper sacks until he heard the bottles clink together. They squatted down and Bill caught Iona by the wrist and kissed her and they pushed the bags apart and curled up together on the floor like lost children. She wouldn't let him undress her; she pulled his arms around her and she could feel his heart beating against her back. Terrified, she thought. He's just as scared as me. She felt part of something. She brought his hands to her face and covered her eyes with them.

Chapter 2

THE CHILD

THE YEAR WAS 1990. Iona wrote Bandy a letter saying that their son had just celebrated his eighteenth birthday. It was a simple letter drafted in black ink on yellow notebook paper. He smelled it and it didn't smell like anything. He'd been transferred back to Idaho the year before when the new Indian Creek Correctional Facility was completed: a new prison in his old state. He reread the letter. He was in a room they called the Educational Center, the EC, and he thought that was maybe true like the way the eardrum is still part of your ear or the bones of the foot were still part of your foot. It's all educational, the whole place, is what he thought, and this sure as hell wasn't the center.

There was adhesive tape stuck to the tabletop and he picked at the tape and fumbled with his stob of a pencil. He was uneasy to be in Idaho again. He'd been in New Mexico and before that Texas, a place called the coop. It was a hard labor and road-crew place but a good prison, if that was possible. He'd had friends there, other vets. These new prisons were worse than the old ones, the raw light and plastic, the lack of history. Spaceman prisons, his cellmate called them. Lunar lockups.

"Send me a picture if he's mine," he wrote on the three-by-five card the trustee had given him. He studied his handwriting and

17

the words on the card then turned the card over and looked at the blank side and thought about asking Iona how she was doing. Where have you been? All these years and you pull up the gates on something like this. Like it isn't hard enough being here, or being someone's kid with your father locked up. He knew plenty of convicts with kids on the outside and none of them, not on either side of the wall, seemed better off for having the other. They followed each other like satellites. Why would she do it? Even if it is true. He flipped the card over and underlined the word *mine* and put the card in the envelope and turned away from the men at the table beside him and ducked his head and licked the envelope and sealed it. He held it up and the trustee took it.

The boy arrived two weeks later. He was brought into the opposing room at the Visiting Center, a wall with four alcoves and four windows separating them. There was only one chair in either room and they were alone except for the COs. The boy smiled for a moment then his features went neutral. His hair was black like his mother's. He was as tall as Bandy but thinner: more cat, less bull. He had a heavy brow and Bandy's broad nose. Physically he mirrored Bandy in his youth, but his eyes were pale blue instead of brown. Bandy tried to remember what Bill McKinley had looked like, if his eyes were blue, but he couldn't be sure. It still got his pulse going a little to think of Bill. Then he remembered he had an uncle, long dead, his mother's brother, Saul, who had had blue eyes. Bandy wanted to believe he had a son and that surprised him. He studied the boy, there was no mistaking, really there couldn't be, their shared blood. Look at him. Look at him: a normal, grown kid. He tried to keep calm, but outside of his lawyer a long time ago in a different lockup, he'd never even had a visitor. He'd never allowed his parents to see him.

"Sit," he said. The boy sat down. "How do you know?" He stretched his neck and kept his eyes on the boy.

"She told me."

"That's it?"

"What else is there?"

"What's your name?"

"Tracy. Dorner. Ma made me keep your name. She took McKinley."

"You always had my name?"

"That's what it says on my birth certificate."

"You didn't try and find me before?"

"No, I didn't."

Bandy caught his own reflection in the glass, scarred and pounded looking, an eyetooth missing. His greasy brown hair was combed straight back and held there with spit, his comb tucked into his shoe, pressed to his ankle. He'd cleaned up for this. "Is she still married?"

"Bill died," Tracy said. "Me and my mom moved to Spokane to live with my aunt. We'd been in Coeur d'Alene before that."

"Is that where you live now? In Spokane?"

"That's where I drove from. It's where I've been staying."

"How long did it take you?"

"I don't know, seven hours. I left at midnight last night, slept in my truck for awhile when I got here. Spokane's a shithole. I don't plan on going back."

"Is she here?"

Tracy wiped his nose with his thumb and forefinger, shook his head.

"Don't fuck with me."

"No, she isn't here. I came by myself."

"You're alone?"

"She isn't here. She told me you might have a house in Lake Fork so I came to see you. She called somebody and checked."

"Who'd she call?"

"The police. They said my grandparents were dead and the house is there and as far as they know it's empty." He narrowed his blue eyes. "I got some carpentry tools that Bill left me. Maybe I could fix up the place, take care of it for you."

"Your grandparents," Bandy said. "Your fucking grandparents. Christ." He paused and let the significance of the words settle in. "There's more than a house and a barn, ya know? There's land. I don't think a hammer and saw's gonna do you much good with that."

"I'll bring a shovel." The boy smiled again, blinked. He had kind, vulnerable eyes. "I need someplace to go, but I don't want to make this into a big deal. I was just asking. If you can't help me out, it doesn't matter." He slid his chair back from the counter. They looked at each other for a few long seconds.

"Tell anyone who asks—who's just asking—who you are. If they don't believe you, tell them to write me." He allowed himself to smile a little. "The place is probably in the dirt by now. You might take one look at it and go the other way."

"No, I won't."

Bandy watched the boy, the halving of himself and Iona into a person breathing and talking, and it was a two-parted anguish that he felt: first, that it had been allowed, then that it had been kept from him. But there was joy in it too; deep in it there was something warming him. "This is a hell of a thing," he said. "Your grandparents. You said that: my grandparents. If they could see you—things would've been a whole lot easier on them if they had." Bandy stood and the CO stepped forward from the wall where he'd been leaning. "I don't want you to come back here," he said to the boy. "You can write me, but don't come back here."

Tracy nodded. "What should I call you?"

Bandy looked hard at the boy before answering, trying to scare him, waiting for him to look away but he didn't. "We don't know each other. There's no reason to pretend like we're something we're not. We can use first names. I don't want you calling me Dad or fucking Pop, if that's what you mean."

"That's not what I meant." He gave Bandy a knowing, slightly cruel smile that seemed to be something he'd inherited from his mother, then he stood and without saying anything else, went out. Bandy watched him walk away and his mouth went cotton dry. The CO grabbed him by the arm. "Don't do it." The guard let go and gave Bandy a cockeyed nod and held his hands up at his waist. "You goddamned know better," Bandy said. The CO gave him room and they walked back to his cell, the CO a few paces back.

The bumper of Tracy Dorner's pickup tapped the heads off of Canadian thistles when he pulled onto the faded traces of the driveway. Fences, wooden and barbed, peeked out from the tall grass. He parked the truck and got out.

The barn was small and the color of dried blood with a gambrel roof and an L-shaped pole fence corral. There were two shed-roof outbuildings that were open on two sides to the weather, meant for wood or equipment, Tracy didn't know, nothing remained. One of the large sliding doors on the barn had pulled loose from its rollers and was flopped on the ground like a door to a storm cellar.

The house was dingy white and simple looking, taller than it was wide, nested in rye grass and creeping, ragged bushes. It was two stories and had twin dormers, a brick chimney, and wood siding. A giant weeping willow in the yard blocked the house from the morning sun; its branches and shoots poured from the triple forked bole like a fountain. He couldn't believe the place was his. He'd never even had an apartment. It seemed fated that he was standing where he was. He wondered, on a blood level, how much do you get from one parent and how much do you get from the other? Standing on Dorner land, his life suddenly seemed full of dark possibility.

He stepped over a fallen tree branch beneath the willow and looked up and saw the jagged nub from where it came. It smelled like a freshwater spring in the shade of the tree. Squawking birds were hidden in the leaves and branches. He stood and listened to them and the sound fell down on him and froze him there for a minute, then he kicked around in the grass for a rock and found one and pitched it into the branches without bothering to aim. The birds scattered in a wave, the whole noisy bunch, starlings, enough to startle him a little, several dozen, fifty maybe, suddenly in the air and flying west in a swarm.

After that it was quiet. The flock dodged and bolted senselessly across the sky until they were out of sight. He had the feeling that he'd disrupted something that had been going on for a long time, and in a small way he wished the birds would return. He looked over the fields to the south. Beyond them there was a house on the hill backed up to the tree line, the windows burned with reflected sun. His mother hadn't mentioned neighbors—hadn't told him much at all—but of course there would be neighbors.

He turned and studied the mountains, near at hand to the east, far and hazy to the west. The Long Valley. LAND OF MANY USES, the Forest Service sign outside of town had said. Boise, two or three hours to the south, nothing to the west really, nothing east: wilderness. The fields all around were filled with mustard and oxeye daisy, and in the driveway there was chamomile and bindweed and dandelions a foot high, more thistles.

He walked around to the side of the house and waded into the tall grass, held his hands out to touch it. In places it was up to his stomach. He stepped carefully, moving slowly, smiling. The paint was peeling from the siding and showed bare wood in places but not much rot. A few nails to suck it in where it sagged wouldn't hurt. He went back to the front of the house and noticed that the big picture window, which had been blocked by the willow, had a jagged hole in it about the size of a human head. He felt something behind him and when he turned there was a fox and it stopped and squatted and lowered its ears. It was mottled gray and red, ragged with molt. Tracy thought it was ugly, for a fox. He whistled at it and it darted under the corral fence and disappeared into the weeds. A moment later he heard its claws hit the gravel road that led up the hill.

He turned again to his new home and watched the second-story windows for the sign of movement but there was none. He was alone and he knew it as surely as he'd ever known anything. It put him on edge, having absolutely nothing familiar to scare him. He smiled to prove to himself that he wasn't afraid, but he was afraid. He was on his own.

The front door was open. Inside, it smelled like rotten lawn clippings. There were drag marks on the doorsill where things had been hauled from the house. The walls were ripped open and the wiring and the plumbing had been torn out. A chainsaw had been used to cut the wood paneling between the stud bays to get at the wiring and between the floor joists to get at the plumbing. There were beer cans and under a pile of splintered lumber a rusted chainsaw chain coiled in a lopsided figure eight: infinity. There was no furniture.

He could imagine how whoever had done this had worked. He could see where their sledgehammers came down and where their wrecking bars had punched in and levered back. The trespass felt personal, as if they knew he was coming and what his plans were. He kicked a beer can and it banked off of the wood stove and disappeared into a hole in the floor.

He opened drawers and the cupboards and found mouse shit. The cabinets were empty except for a yellowed cookbook that had apparently come with the woodstove, a stack of red-and-white-checkered place mats. He looked again at the hulking woodstove then back at the front door and figured they would've taken the stove too if the house hadn't been framed around it, or at least the mudroom added after it was brought in. He lifted one of the circular covers on the top of the stove with the handle he found on the shelf and looked inside but it was just black and he couldn't see anything.

He went through the barren living room and the downstairs bedroom and bathroom. The tub remained but the toilet and sink had been plucked, harvested along with the faucets and the curtain rods. He climbed the stairs and looked in on the three upstairs bedrooms and the second bathroom and it was the same as the one downstairs: tub, no toilet or sink. The bathroom fixtures, light fixtures, carpet, window and door trim, everything had been taken.

He collected a pencil and a notepad from his truck and went from room to room making notes and a rudimentary materials list. He did this somberly, as if in memoriam.

In the morning he sat up shirtless in the back of his truck. The sun hadn't reached the driveway yet and he could see his breath. He pulled his sleeping bag up to his armpits. The evening before he'd driven to town and ordered a hamburger and fries from the drive-thru. He drove to the park by the lake and ate, watched people, his new neighbors. Nobody seemed to notice him, which was good and not good. He called his mother from the gas station on the highway on his way home. She told him to be careful out there in the sticks. She sounded drunk. He could hear his aunt yelling in the background. It was strange but he missed them both. He'd been restless and paranoid all night out in the open and thought fondly of the couch he used to despise.

He scratched at himself and spit the bad taste from his mouth and let the sleeping bag fall. He touched his stomach when it growled. There was a sound in the distance getting louder, like a plane or a motorcycle. A man on a four-wheeler appeared on the road. He slowed as he approached and turned into the ranch. He parked next to the pickup and hit the kill switch like a judge passing sentence. Tracy sat scratching at his arm. The man was very old and wore dark blue coveralls and a light blue mesh hat that said SILVER FOX on it, a greasy gray ponytail hanging out the back.

"Morning, squatter," the old man said. He swung his legs sidesaddle on the seat. "You sleep good?"

"Yeah, except for that last part when I got woke up." He slid out of his sleeping bag and put on his shoes, shivering a little tying his laces. The old man watched him. Tracy finished and found his shirt underneath his pillow and pulled it on and hopped down out of the truck bed. He stood and stretched his back. Fucking cold, he thought. "Goddammit," he said, and undid his pants and pissed loudly on the front tire.

"You moving on or am I going to need to call somebody?"

"I'm not trespassing. Call who you want."

The old man got to his feet and peered into the truck window at the tools stacked in the cab. "If you came to salvage and steal, I think the other vultures already beat you to it."

"I got permission to be here." He buttoned his jeans and wiped his hands on his shirt. "Who did that to the house?"

"Some dopes like you, I'd say. Pilfering turds. On whose permission?"

"You got a mouth, don't you? How would you like it if I came and woke you up and started calling you names?"

"You'd have to get up pretty early, but I'd be fond of the attention if you did." The old man lifted his hat and the ponytail went with it, like there was a wig inside of the hat.

Tracy couldn't help but smile. The old man's real hair was short and bristly. "What'd they call you?" Tracy asked.

"Good-looking mostly." The smile turned off. "You first, usurper."

"Dorner," Tracy said. "Tracy Dorner."

The old man took a step back and lowered his chin to his chest. Tracy looked away from the searching eyes. "Iona's boy?" the old man said.

"Yeah. What the hell's a usurper?"

"Never mind. You're not Bandy's boy?"

"I said Dorner, didn't I?"

"You did. Holy hell. Well—" The old man seemed truly stunned. He stood and kind of huffed for a few seconds then smiled broadly. "Well, let's go meet the rest of the natives. I'll buy you breakfast."

Tracy nodded. "All right." He held out his hand.

"Wilhelm," the old man said. "Guntly. I knew your grandparents. We were friends." He looked at the ground then looked up with a slightly menacing expression. "I know your old man. Your mom, too." He paused. "Let's get these tools put away."

They unloaded the tools from the truck into the barn and the old man climbed in the passenger seat and pointed up the hill. "We'll get my mule later." He smiled and looked at Tracy and smacked his hand off of the dashboard. "I thought they quit making Dorners."

Tracy didn't know what to say. He shut the door in the old man's face and walked around and got in the truck.

"They sure chewed up that old house, didn't they?" Wilhelm said.

"You don't know who did it?"

"No. One day I drove by and the window was broke and I stopped to look at it and that's all that was wrong. Then I noticed some tire tracks later in the week and when I went back to check it was like it is now. Ripped to the framing. I called the sheriff but they didn't do anything since it's abandoned. Since it's your dad's place now."

"I knew it'd be in bad shape."

"Bandy told you that?"

"Yeah."

"He'd know," Wilhelm said. He was being sarcastic but it burned and faded and was simply true.

The Guntlys gave Tracy a place to stay while he worked on the house. They told him what they knew about the Dorners from the first ones that settled in the valley all the way up to what Bandy and his mother had been like when they were together and young. They omitted some things of course, public knowledge and private domain. The Silver Fox's wife's name was Ellen. She was a bird-thin old woman with white hair and sharp gray eyes. Their children were grown and gone, one dead in a car crash; they didn't say anything more than that about it and Tracy didn't ask. There were at least a dozen fat, pink grandchildren in embroidered picture frames on the mantel. Their house was all wood, stained dark and clean. The wall clock was the only noise. Tracy fit into an empty place in the couple's life like kindling in stacked cordwood.

Chapter 3

DEEP WATER

IONA'S SISTER, FAITH, got her the cashier job at the truck stop. She worked all through the spring and summer. A heat wave came and went and came again. She stole cigarettes and ate jerky straight from the tub. It was busiest in the afternoons. People incessantly complained to her about the state of the roads, the potholes and construction projects. Some of the truckers said she and her sister looked alike and offered her money to go out into the parking lot with them. Days, the hue and bustle, often seemed to eerily repeat themselves.

Then it was her birthday and she was sitting at a picnic table on an overwatered patch of grass near the truck wash having a cigarette. It was her lunch break. She rolled the cigarette between her thumb and forefinger and looked at it. The truckers that drank Mountain Dew always smoked. Truckers that drank bottled water never did. Truckers who snorted crank had rotten teeth. Iona had a rotten tooth. She sucked air over it until it hurt. The sleeper cabs in the semis were bigger than she would've imagined; they were like little apartments. This is a one-time deal, she told herself the first time. After that she just didn't think about it. She was lonely and sometimes it helped. It could've been about the money if she'd let them pay her. They gave her drugs. She thought of herself as being picky and having good taste and discovered that she could maintain that attitude as long as she never slept with the same man her sister did.

She took one last drag on her cigarette and put it out then lit another. The smell of diesel was strong. She smelled her shirt and her shirt stunk of it. She decided not to go back to work. Faith was there and she could handle it. Faith was there and she could go fuck herself.

Iona snuck into the pay showers in the truckers' lounge and stole a towel from behind the desk. She turned on the water as hot as she could stand and stayed inside the stall until her skin was welted looking and her fingers were pruned and dead white. She avoided looking at any part of her body except her hands. After she got out and toweled off she discovered that someone had stolen her shoes. Her purse was on top of the lockers and the shoe thief hadn't found it. She dressed and went through the lounge barefoot. A trucker sitting on one of the couches called her Sacagawea and asked her where her moccasins were. Iona told him to get fucked. The trucker's friends all laughed.

Faith took off her apron and shoved it into Iona's hands and walked out the door without saying a word. She hadn't even noticed that Iona was barefoot. Then it occurred to her that it could've been her sister that stole her shoes, but she would've taken the purse too. She opened her purse; her wallet was empty and her cigarettes were gone.

After work, as she crossed the parking lot to her car, she cut her foot on a small shard of glass. She bled on her gas pedal and rubbed it on the floor mat while she was stopped at the lights.

Faith wasn't home when she got there and it was a good thing because Iona was mad enough to hit her. The apartment they shared was dark and cluttered with yard-sale junk. The living room and the kitchen were in one room and there were two small bedrooms off of the bathroom.

She rinsed her foot off in the tub then stood in front of the bathroom mirror and looked at herself. The mirror was pitted gold around the edges and one of the corners was cracked where someone had tightened the mounting bracket too tight and dog-eared it. Before she'd left for work she'd cleaned the toilet and the tub, and the smell of the heavy-duty cleanser she'd stolen from the truck stop was still strong and it left her nostrils feeling bored out. She spent a lot of time in the bathroom because there was a lock on the door.

She took down the shoebox from above the water heater in the bathroom closet and put it on the sink. She usually kept an extra pack of cigarettes there, along with all of her dead husband's hospital bills. The cigarettes were gone and it was only the bills in the box, years of them stacked on top of each other. These are the reasons why I no longer have a home, a place for Tracy to stay. He had to leave, though. He would've gone regardless. He's an adult. I didn't make it easy for him, Faith didn't; and now he's met Bandy. She had no idea where that could lead. She'd considered writing Bandy a long letter explaining why she hadn't told him sooner, but she didn't have any real reason except that she couldn't. She'd told herself it was all about protecting Tracy but that was probably a lie. There were a lot of lies and they were piling up. She threw the shoebox on the floor but it landed flat and didn't spill. She kicked it over and kicked it again.

"Bullets are cheap," she'd said to Bill at the hospital. The words had seeped out and he'd heard her and they'd argued before he died. That's real guilt, she thought. The kind that gets shellacked onto your soul and turns yellow and kills you. She hated herself and felt there was nothing to change it. In the mirror her eyes looked back at her from someone else's head. The sink never stopped dripping. This is hell, she thought. She twisted the knob until the name of the manufacturer was impressed into the flesh of her palm. It never stopped.

She gathered up the papers and envelopes and put the shoebox back on the shelf and went to the kitchen and opened one of her sister's beers and drank half of it then made a peanut butter and maple syrup sandwich because there was no jelly. Her foot was still bleeding a little and she left blood splotches all over the floor like mouse tracks in the snow. Twenty-two steps to make a peanut butter and maple syrup sandwich and open a can of beer, she thought. Eleven spots, two feet. Linoleum bingo squares. Her whole body ached. She rubbed her feet on the greasy carpet on her way to the couch and it felt good. There was a postcard from Tracy in the ashtray on the coffee table.

A water skier sliced a deep blue mountain lake—THERE'S NO PLACE LIKE HOME LAKE FORK, it said. She flipped over the card. Miss you ma, it said. She held the card close to her face and studied the photograph. There were new buildings all along the lake and a new system of docks where before there'd been only the one and everything on the hill had been painted and given new roofs. The vacant lot where the city and county road crews and everyone else had always dumped the concrete and asphalt debris from foundation repairs and road construction, like some kind of jetty for the waves that never came, was now a park with a beach and what appeared to be volleyball nets and barbecue grills.

The lake looked the same as ever. Iona remembered when scientists came from the University of Idaho and tried to find the bottom but failed and were informed by the local mackinaw fishermen that it was goddamn deep and they didn't need a degree or fancy boat to tell you that. She hoped they never found the lake bottom and if they did that they had the sense to keep it to themselves.

A drip of maple syrup fell onto the top of her foot. Cars drove by outside the apartment and the windows bulged slightly from the wind. She put her sandwich down on the table and went into her bedroom and found a half pack of cigarettes and a lighter on the floor and was about to light one but she crumpled the pack instead and went outside, barefoot still, gingerly across the parking lot and threw them into the otherwise empty dumpster. It was an easy thing and probably hollow but it left her feeling uplifted. She had to get better. She had to try and get better. This was no way to live. She wasn't naïve enough to think that quitting smoking would change anything but she had to start somewhere.

She went into her bedroom and lay down with the postcard. When she heard Faith come in, she switched off the light. Her sister wasn't alone. It would be another long night. Faith knocked on her door. "Don't open it," Iona said.

"Lame bitch," her sister said, and banged on the door one more time. Iona didn't sleep. Neither did Faith or her friends. Later, Iona got up and joined them. She didn't know what else to do, and what did it matter. She was forty years old.

Chapter 4

LOW STATES

WILHELM GUNTLY HAD RETIRED from his job as an electrician fifteen years ago but he still kept in touch with people in the trades, so when Tracy started looking for work Wilhelm made a couple of calls and found him a job framing houses for a man named Dan Cole, Cole Construction. Dan was tall with ropy muscles and a bulging Adam's apple like he'd swallowed the head of a doctor's reflex hammer. He kept a neatly trimmed mustache and an outdated haircut that he combed often. He said he remembered hearing about Bandy when he was a kid. He told Tracy some stories but it all sounded like thirdhand bullshit.

They finished the ground floor and Tracy rediscovered his fear of heights. He'd hoped he'd outgrown it. He did his best to keep it hidden, but Dan was always watching. Although never called out, the fear was there, and job assignments were shifted. He kept his head down and worked. The situation kept Tracy up nights. He thought Dan was a prick like some of the kids at his high school had been pricks. He thought they were of a breed, like dogs are of a breed: men who seep a low kind of terror at the corner of their eyes as they watch for weakness.

Over time, they came to work without talking and the days went easier. The air compressor and the job radio filled the silence.

They ate lunch together someplace in the shade and it wasn't bad. Sometimes Dan's wife, Sandy, sent cookies with him to share. Tracy thought he was a pretty good guy when his mouth wasn't moving. He knew his business too; he was a good framer and made it look easy. Tracy had to keep reminding himself to learn from him, to take instruction and learn.

In the fall Wilhelm surprised him by buying him a steer at the county fair. He was small and completely black with eyes that didn't seem vacant. Tracy had no idea what to do with him but he spent a lot of time at the corral fence watching him. The steer was curious and sometimes playful, and at times he and Tracy stared intensely at one another and there seemed to be an exchange. Tracy thought perhaps he was a person reincarnated. He didn't know. He'd never been around livestock. He bought feed and a book from the farm service. It didn't cost much and it was nice to have him around, but he discovered that he worried about him when it got cold at night and he'd get up early at the Guntlys and drive down the hill to check on him. He wasn't a very sturdy animal and Tracy knew Wilhelm had picked him up for a bargain because of his diminished size. The winter could kill him. Tracy pieced together the two salvageable doors on the barn with scrap then built a new sliding door out of alder that cost him a week's pay. The door was heavy and too unwieldy to hang by himself so Dan came over with Wilhelm to help.

"The hell're you messing with the barn for?" Dan said. "You planning on living in the house or just strapping on a feed bucket and shitting in the stalls?" Tracy ignored him and watched and worried a little about Wilhelm as he strained beneath the weight, his back straight, knees bent, the tendons rising up on his cross-wrinkled neck: an old man working too hard.

"I don't know why it isn't going," Tracy said. "I know it fits." He also knew that he and Dan had most of the weight but he still wanted to hurry for Wilhelm's sake. They were fighting the door, grunting. Tracy lifted hard and let his eyes linger on the veins and muscles on his arms. He'd been getting stronger working all the time and he wondered if strength always came with a little vanity, wondered if it were possible to have one and not the other. He was pretty sure it wasn't.

"Fucking fuck, you little shit." Dan said. "Did you even fucking measure it?" Tracy watched Dan's fingers as they began to slip on the chamfered edge of the frame, leaving greasy brown stains on the unpainted wood. He feared they would drop it, and then, like it could go no other way, the door settled into place. It rolled back into the pocket framed into the barn. He tested the door back and forth, greased and true, it moved with the sound of stone on stone. The steer was in the corral watching him. He shut the door then opened it. The steer stood rooted in the mud. Tracy stepped back and worked his elbow, the joint felt stretched and coarse. "Now I have a shop for the winter, and I can store all my shit in here while I finish the house," he said to Dan.

"Alder," Dan said. "Probably the first time in history someone's built a barn door out of alder." He tried to dig his thumbnail into the edge but the wood was too hard. "Something wrong with cedar or fir?" he said. "What the hell is wrong with Doug fir?"

"I like alder," Tracy said.

"Compared to what? Balsa? Teak? You don't know what you're talking about," Dan said.

"My book says it's durable."

"Your book says?"

"Don't start," Wilhelm said to Dan, and sat down slowly on a jumble of lumber that used to be a loading chute. His hands were shaking. He wasn't the Silver Fox. Sweat dripped down the sides of his face. "About lunchtime, ain't it?"

"I'll buy," Tracy said, and helped Wilhelm to his feet. "Quit acting old, you old bastard."

Wilhelm leaned into him and smiled, whispered. "I am old," he said. "Old and in the way. Don't tell Ellen, though. She'll leave me."

"If she hasn't found a reason yet," Dan said.

Wilhelm stared coolly at Dan then looked at Tracy. "You better not be taking us to someplace where we eat out of a bag. I need to sit down at a real place."

"Wherever you want," Tracy said.

Wilhelm rode with Tracy, and Dan followed them in his truck. They passed two cars coming toward them with out-of-state plates on Farm to Market and the old man remarked on the traffic. Dan was tailgating and Tracy tapped his brakes to get him to back off. There was the bark of tires and he fell behind then closed the distance and stayed there, only a few feet from Tracy's bumper, closer than he'd been before.

"You couldn't imagine what it was like before the swarms arrived," Wilhelm said. There was something smug in his voice that stopped Tracy from simply agreeing with him. He was oblivious to what was happening behind him, didn't even realize what Dan was doing.

"Swarms," Tracy said.

"People with money," Wilhelm said. "We're being colonized."

"You can't be colonized by people in your own country."

"If somebody builds a golf course within a mile of my house, that's colonization: an act of war."

Tracy thought the old man was being overly dramatic and he laughed a little.

"It's not funny. These developers, these millionaires, they come into town and start barking orders like they're appointed by the king, like we're only here to support their noble endeavors. Last time I checked this wasn't a plantation."

Tracy cleared his throat. "If it was up to me, I'd sell off a little land so I could fix up the house faster."

"It's getting fixed."

"One board at a time. It'll take me years to finish."

Wilhelm turned and looked at Tracy. "You got time. Don't sell that land."

"It isn't up to me. I was saying I might. I didn't say I would."

"Don't. Someday it will be up to you, so don't. It's worth more than money. It's your family land."

"Fine."

"I mean it, it's something you can't afford to lose. And you wait, when the rest of the country goes south into a depression—and it will, because it always does, and we will too—it won't hurt the real rich ones. While we're digging in our easy chairs for spare change and feeding the kids government cheese these bastards'll be buying up all the ground. They'll leave you with nothing if you're ready to sell out. They'll have vacation homes and signs that say private drive. You know what vacation homes look like when you got no home? Like the side of the road. Like a pup tent in the ditch." The old man drummed his finger on the dash. "Speculators. Colonizers. Carpetbaggers riding into the dust of victorious generals."

"You're getting carried away."

"I am not."

"But that's the way it's always been. Isn't that the natural order of things? Towns grow and turn into cities or turn into dust. Places change. The swarms you're complaining about, they've always been coming, and there'll always be more coming. You were part of one of the swarms that came into this valley, you weren't part of the first."

"Nobody living was part of the first. They're all gone."

Tracy eased off the gas and Dan roared past them.

"Why's he always gotta drive like an asshole?" Wilhelm said.

Tracy gave Dan the finger then looked at Wilhelm. "What'd the people who were already here think of you when you showed up?"

"Who?"

"Whoever was here."

"Wasn't anybody out here but your grandparents and a bunch a crazy Finns."

"People were in town though, logging, living on the lake. I've seen the pictures. What'd people say about you out here, building a house and not farming or raising cattle?"

"I was building a house for my family."

"So's everybody."

"It's different now."

"No, it isn't. Same thing."

"They're building to excess."

"They're building as much house as they can, same as you did. As much as they can afford and a little more. Nothing less. I don't think that changes. People find a hill and put a house on top of it, same as you did."

"I built where I did so I'd be out of the way, so they could farm around me."

"You don't like the view from the high ground?"

Wilhelm shook his head and looked out the window and Tracy could sense his frustration. "You're missing the point."

"Yeah, what's the point?" Tracy said.

"The point is: What's sacred if everything's for sale?"

"Nothing. Everything's for sale." Tracy didn't know if he believed that but he liked the way it sounded.

"I'm not, and my goddamn land isn't either."

Tracy felt the smile fade from his face and his mouth twitched and wouldn't settle into its normal position again. "All I know is that rich people always need houses built, Wilhelm." His voice was shaking; his nervous self-righteousness surprised him. "That means work for a lot of people—it means work for me. I'm no farmer, or rancher. I don't live off the land, neither do you. We need these people."

"I don't think *need* is the word. You don't need millionaires or a million people to find a job, and they don't need five-thousand-square-foot homes and golf courses. That ain't need." He paused. "What they can afford. They can afford to be considerate and not eat off everybody else's plate."

"Even if they're paying for dinner?"

"Especially then."

Tracy took a deep breath. His window was cracked and the air smelled like fall, the aspens were starting to change. Wilhelm gave him a couple of sideways looks. "What?" Tracy said.

"You built that door for your cow," Wilhelm said.

"So what if I did? You know Dan would've been an asshole about it if I told him. He's always riding me about something." He looked at Wilhelm. "I wasn't lying, I'll use it for a shop too. I needed the door."

"Sure," Wilhelm said. A few moments later: "You've got a cow palace."

"It'd be better than living with you."

"Cow hotel."

"Shut up."

"Cow resort."

"That's just stupid."

"Cow spa resort hotel. Zone for that, levy taxes on it. God-damn pampered cattle, people too. We're all on vacation," he said. "We're all busy relaxing and throwing money around in our resort paradise."

"Enough."

"It is." Wilhelm was getting red in the face.

Dan pulled over in somebody's driveway and let them pass, then pulled in behind them because he didn't know where they were headed. Town was busy and blocked with road construction. There were new utilities being put in under the street for a thirty-unit condo complex across from the new brewpub. The asphalt had been dug up and put down so many times since Tracy had lived there he thought it would be a smoother ride if they just left it dirt.

Wilhelm pointed the directions to the Mexican place he said he liked. They were the only people there and Tracy thought, this is why he likes it here. For such a talkative guy he'd never met anyone that despised crowds as much as Wilhelm. The waitress came and they ordered and ate then the waitress brought the check and Tracy paid.

They went outside and it was sunny with high, fast-moving clouds tinged with gray but hardly ominous. At Wilhelm's sugges-tion they piled into Dan's truck because it was big and new, and drove out around the lake. They stopped on the way and bought a six-pack of beer. Wilhelm pointed to the deep places where he'd caught mackinaw and to a line of rocks jutting from the water where ski boats always ran aground, where every summer someone died.

The mountains above the lake were all granite, elephant-hide gray, and the evergreens spread thick and reaching away from the water's edge like ink seeping into coarse paper up the drainages until they faded and disappeared at the tree line, strangled by rock and thin air. They parked at a deserted campground on the north side of the lake and got out and walked to the waterline and stood with their cans of beer and stared out over the expanse of water.

As a child Tracy had wandered into the dim lobby of an old hotel in downtown Spokane. It was being remodeled and he'd watched as a group of men unrolled a large sheet of copper onto the lobby floor. They anchored it there with bags of sand then began cutting it into pieces with knives and snips to fit onto the mantel of the large stone fireplace. The workmen moved as deliberately as stage actors under the large unlit chandelier. The lake looked like that, like greased copper, like if you were careful, you could walk on it.

At the shoreline the pine needles and lake scum marked concentrically how fast the water had fallen. It had been a dry summer. In the distance Tracy could see the bent, wormy shapes of the summer-home docks high and dry on the sand and the emerging boulders.

"Feels like winter already," Wilhelm said.

"I'm fucked if it snows," Dan said. "I need another two weeks of good weather."

"Maybe less," Tracy said.

Dan gave him a heavy look. "Maybe more," he said. "You seen this kid do high work?" he said to Wilhelm. "Because he don't.

I've been carrying him since I cut the stairs. He needs to think about finding a new line of work before I fire him."

"Then fire me," Tracy said, and he and Dan looked at each other for a moment and Tracy was afraid of what might happen next. Then Dan smiled; he'd won. He'd hurt Tracy and made him look weak. It was that easy: a good day gone bad.

"I'll fire both of you," Wilhelm said, and sat down stiffly in the sand. He leaned over and smacked Tracy in the back of the knee so he'd sit too. A few minutes later Dan sat down. They watched the sun set. Once the stars began pricking holes in the gloaming they got up and drove back to town and Dan dropped them off at Tracy's pickup and he and Wilhelm drove home under a sliver of moon.

"There's worse things than being afraid of heights," Wilhelm said.

"Not to me." The pavement was rough and Tracy drove slowly toward the darkness at the end of the twin columns of the headlights.

"There will be," Wilhelm said.

All morning it was freezing rain then in the afternoon it began to snow, big flakes falling purposefully. Dan went home with a hangover and left Tracy to dig the footers alone. The snow fell soundlessly. He hacked at tree roots with a double-bitted axe that sparked against the rocks. The holes widened and yawned in the white and he imagined himself a gravedigger. The next time he looked at his watch it was time to go home.

He sat in his truck in the near dark and waited for the defroster to thaw the ice on the windshield. He knew he should just get out

and scrape it clear but his hands were finally warming up and starting to feel the needles and pins. He waited and thought about
weakness and bullies and fear and what he was made of. What,
perhaps, his fear of heights was made of, like it was a physical part
of him that could be removed. He wondered what Bandy was
afraid of, probably nothing.

The heat rolled out of the vents in the dashboard. He switched
on the wipers and the blades pushed the glass clear in a couple of labored passes. Fuck it, he thought. Fuck it. I don't care. He slammed
his truck into gear and spun his tires and railed broadside up the
driveway and heard the mud and snow spatter against the wheel
wells.

As he crossed the bridge into town, the snow fell steadily in
large wet flakes that thudded against the windshield. The street-
lights were up and the few people he saw in the storm were hun-
kered down and slow moving in their layered clothes. He stopped
at the gas station outside of town on the highway to buy beer from
the woman that liked him, that didn't card him. She was old enough
to be his mother but she was still pretty. He'd asked Wilhelm about
her; her name was Vera Meeks. Tracy knew that name from the
newspaper he'd looked up in the library. "Meeks? That Meeks?"
Tracy said. Wilhelm nodded. He was the policeman that Bandy
had killed.

Tracy put his six-pack and his money on the counter. The
woman motioned to the mud and snow on his shirt. "Looks like
you just crawled out of a grave," she said.

"Something like that."

"Well, cheer up. It's Saturday and Sunday all weekend long."
She gave him his change then put the beer in a paper sack.

Tracy flicked a piece of mud off his sleeve onto the floor.

"Can I ask you something?" She nodded. "Is your last name Meeks?"

"Yes, it is. Have you been checking up on me?" She smiled, wrinkles around her eyes.

"I mentioned you to somebody, they told me your name. You know what my last name is? You'd already know if you ever bothered to card me."

"You're plenty old."

Tracy hesitated. "My name's Tracy Dorner. I'm Bandy Dorner's son."

The woman slowly took a step back from the counter, and her face no longer looked pretty enough to fantasize about. "Why would you say that?" she said.

"Because it's true."

"He was my brother. Ben Meeks was my brother."

"I've only met Bandy once. I went and saw him. He's still in prison."

"You're not his son. You can't be." A tear slipped down the woman's cheek and hung on her jaw.

"Would you mind telling me what he was like? What your brother was like?"

"Don't ask me that. I don't know what you're after. I don't believe you."

"I'm telling the truth."

She paused. "You're not lying to me?"

Tracy opened his wallet and passed her his ID. She studied it and dropped it on the counter then looked at him. She was crying. Tracy picked it up and put it away.

"You just came in out of the storm and decided today was the day, huh? That today you'd come in here and knock me down a peg."

"That's not what I meant to do. I'm sorry." But he thought maybe she was right, maybe that was exactly what he wanted to do.

The bells on the door jangled and a man and two young boys came in from outside covered in a smattering of wet snow. The man clapped his gloved hands together and looked at Tracy. "You believe that shit outside?" he said. His eyes were mismatched, one blue one black, and it gave the illusion of one being set deeper in the socket than the other. The man noticed that the woman behind the counter was crying. "You all right, sweetheart? What's wrong?" He looked at Tracy and Tracy looked at the boys. The boys were watching the woman. They were probably eight or ten years old, blond and unkempt, serious looking for their age.

"I'm fine, Regan," the woman said. "Hello young Piatts," she said to the boys. "You been keeping an eye on your dad?"

"Yes," the older boy said.

"He's old, he's supposed to watch us," the younger boy said.

Tracy took his beer from the counter.

"Wait a second," the woman said. "Regan, this is Tracy Dorner."

Regan was headed toward the beer cooler but he turned and came back. He was unshaven and had a surgical scar on his temple that disappeared into his hairline. He seemed too young, too feral, to have the two boys.

"I know that name," Regan said.

"He's my dad," Tracy said. "My family has a place out past the Finn church. I'm fixing it up."

The two boys looked at their father and he nodded to them like he understood. "Is that what made you cry, Vera?" Regan said. "Him coming in here? By God, I'll throw him out if you want me to."

"No," Vera said. She spoke quietly to Regan. "I wouldn't blame your boys for the stupid things you do, would I?"

"No." Regan turned and looked at his boys. Tracy couldn't tell if he was simple or simply drunk. Regan held out his hand. "Good to meet you."

Tracy took his hand and shook it.

"Regan's one of our local celebrities," Vera said. "He raced the giant slalom in the Lake Placid Olympics." She smiled through her tears. "He met Walter Mondale."

Regan's jaw tightened and he winced a little. He went to the beer cooler and stood and assessed his choices. His boys disappeared to the back of the store.

Vera leaned toward Tracy and whispered. "He fell during a race in Italy and hurt his head. His wife left him with the two boys while he was still in the hospital. His parents used to watch them but they both passed away a few years back. Now Regan has them full-time. He doesn't do the greatest job at it but he's better than nothing. Better than some."

"I'm sorry if I upset you."

"It's okay. You just scared me for a minute. I haven't thought about Ben for awhile." She carefully wiped her eyes so she wouldn't mess up her eye makeup more than she already had. "Be safe out there tonight. The roads are only going to get worse."

He went out the door and the cold air and snow was welcome. He looked into the storm as he walked to his truck, and as he drove he found the eye of it; the empty core followed him. He didn't know what he was doing, or why he was in Lake Fork at all. Maybe he should leave. He could join the army. His buddy Jim had joined up after high school. Where was he now? Doing push-ups somewhere probably, marching, shooting guns. "The army's like a recipe," Jim had said. "I'm an ingredient. You could be an ingredient too. Like mayonnaise. You could be the mayo."

Tracy thought he might've signed up with his friend if he and his mom hadn't moved to Spokane in the middle of his senior year. He didn't even graduate. He thought: It's some weak shit to blame your mother for your problems but I do. She started this whole thing. He smiled to himself imagining walking into a recruiter's office. Bandy had been in the army; he'd even fought in Vietnam. Tracy had read that in the paper too. I don't have to be here, he thought, or follow anybody's footsteps.

He drank two beers on the way home then parked in the driveway at the ranch with his headlights on the house and drank the rest. The snow came down. Friday night. Big time on the farm. Another night of jerking off in the tomb that was his bedroom in the Guntlys' house. A grown man holding his breath in the total dark, yanking his dick, trying not to make the bed squeak. Christ, it was fucking sad. He needed to find a girlfriend but all the women in town seemed to either be old or in high school. They didn't stick around if they didn't have to. He wasn't going the statutory route. Since he'd visited his father, the idea of going to jail scared the hell out of him. He thought again of Vera Meeks and absently rubbed his penis through his jeans.

The rusted metal edge of the rooftop loomed in the headlights and snow was beginning to stick to it. At least Bandy did something, he thought. It would be best to do something, to not be a little bitch your whole life. You're just scared of heights, and a lot more than heights.

He opened the door and got out and threw his empty can at the roof. The wind snatched it away and it tumbled into the darkness. He dragged the extension ladder from the side of the house and kicked the feet into the dirt and snow as deep as he could and began to climb the twenty-five feet or so onto the roof. The rungs were like icicles in his hands.

A thin sheet of snow slid from the roof and waterfalled over his shoulders and dumped down his coat. He stopped for a moment and looked at the gray sludge on the ground, his black footprints leading up to it. Snow melted against the skin of his hands.

The step from the ladder to the rooftop would be the worst and when he came level with the eaves he told himself, Don't hesitate, don't slow down. Climb and step onto the roof, away from the ladder. He imagined the move and his body did it. Then there he was, on all fours scrambling, still climbing, crawling up the pitch using the screwheads for traction. The terror built in his chest as he went between the dormers and up until he was sitting on the ridge cap with one leg on either side of the roof.

At this new height the wind was blowing hard and the snow and sleet stuck in his eyelashes. He smiled and blinked, then rubbed his eyes with his sleeves and pushed himself up to his feet and stood in that bowlegged way agawk the ridge like a conqueror and looked into his headlight-lit dome of storm-filled sky. He imagined some other poor trembling jackass standing on some stony precipice looking back at him across the empty world. He took comfort in this then his foot slipped and he sat back down and dented the ridge cap.

It was stupid to come up here on today of all days with the snow and ice and no one around. It's like when a father throws his child into the lake to teach him to swim. This is my lake and Bandy threw me in. He thought of his mother and how pathetic she was, and how she and his stepfather had lived tethered to fear, anchored by it, alone, nearly friendless. They had each other, but that didn't mean anything. Tracy wanted more than one person; he felt he deserved more than that. If I can just do this, then I'll be all right. His hands throbbed with cold. Looking down at the ladder he felt a tightening in his scrotum.

He set his jaw and began his descent. He thought he'd have to stop in the valley of the dormer and ease himself down. He'd hang from the flashing if he had to and lower himself to the ladder, and if he couldn't, he'd go in through an upstairs window. But that would be defeat. No one would have to know, and if they did, they wouldn't care. This battle was small and personal, but he felt that it would decide his future.

Then his foot slipped and he started to slide. He sprawled and looked for anything to grab hold of but there was nothing. It happened slowly; it seemed ridiculous. He thought he'd been afraid of falling but now that he was falling he thought he must be afraid of something else because this isn't scary; it simply can't be happening. And the disbelief continued and time went slower and slower as he gained speed. He slid between the dormers and as he passed he had time to look at both of the darkened windows. He was alone. His boots thudded dully over the screwheads and hunks of rubber were notched from his soles. His hands were slashed and bleeding. It was really happening. Then he was at the edge and he knocked into the ladder and tried to catch it but it fell from his hand and silently tipped away. Below him there was nothing but the ground, the depthless snow, and a couple of long seconds. It happened just as he dreamt it would.

He hit and nothing made sense then he came back to himself. He was hurt. He tried to stand on his shattered ankles and tipped over onto his side and passed out.

Wilhelm found him or he might've frozen to death. There was

already a layer of snow covering his body and when the old man rolled him over his face was pink from the cold. Wilhelm didn't waste any time. He dragged Tracy to the pickup by his armpits and roughly loaded him into the cab. He drove as fast as he dared and mumbled reprimands, prayers.

Tracy woke up in the hospital. A doctor with dark, wooly eyebrows and bright blue eyes was standing over him. Tracy tried to explain how he fell and why but the words he said didn't seem to be doing the trick. He had a catheter and an IV. His left index finger appeared to be broken but no one said anything about that. A nurse approached with a needle. She didn't say anything.

"You aren't cutting off my feet."

"Oh, sweetie. No, of course not."

He didn't believe her. He swatted at her arm and she caught his wrist and twisted it expertly into his body. The doctor and another nurse held him down. He managed to get an arm free and the IV was jerked out. Everything was so much whiter once the blood was on it. Then Wilhelm was there. The old man forced his way in between the doctor and nurses.

"Take her easy, Tracy," Wilhelm said. "You're all right. You're okay now."

"Somebody needs to call my mom."

"Don't worry about that. We'll get a hold of her. Somebody here will track her down."

"What'd I do? What'd I do to myself?"

"You're gonna be okay, son," Wilhelm said.

The doctor reinserted the IV and took the needle from the nurse and gave Tracy the injection. Everything hurt all through his guts and his bones. Tracy screamed and the doctor and Wilhelm held him by the arms. The lights pulsed and a rarefied hum held in his ears. He felt the drugs run through him and clean out the pain like warm air through an empty hallway. The nurse pushed his hair gently back from his forehead. "You'll be okay," she said. "You're gonna be just fine." He closed his eyes and he kept falling, falling.

Chapter 5

REUNION

IONA WAS IN THE KITCHEN scraping the mirror for a final bump before she went to work. Faith was asleep on the couch with her new boyfriend, a Nez Perce guy with a Mexican name, a biker with leathers and no bike. They were twisted together and Faith's shirt was half off, her panties on the floor among the empty bottles. The TV was on and blaring static. The biker's buddy, some nameless lurch, was passed out in Iona's bed. The flickering light of the TV made the dark apartment look strangely like an aquarium.

Last night Faith had announced that she was pregnant with the biker's child. Iona doubted if the child would be Nez Perce or have a Mexican name. She thought for being sisters there was a real lack of love between them, a lack of compassion, but they'd seen a lot together, been through a lot. Maybe that's all we get, she thought, scraping the mirror. She imagined brothers who fought one another during the Civil War or even those who fought on the same side but for different reasons. The distance between Iona and her sister was the distance between stars. The mirror was clean except for a perfect square pile in the very center. The powder smelled of cat piss and her jaw ached just looking at it.

The phone rang as soon as she snorted the line. It was a nurse in Lake Fork. Iona asked the woman to repeat herself then hung up.

Her suitcase was in the closet in her bedroom. The man in her bed was naked on top of the sheets. He had a large tattoo of a cross on his back and it was blue and ugly and scarred. She put the suitcase on the floor and opened it. The smell of the thing brought back a flood of unwanted memories: of Bandy and Bill and unformed archaic thoughts of her mother. She shook them off and loaded her clothes. She was leaving and she wouldn't be back. Her heart pounded in her ears and she took short, erratic breaths. She would never forget the day when Tracy was born. She would never forget today.

In the bathroom she caught her reflection in the mirror: She was a mother. She was the mother. She gathered her toothbrush and what makeup she had and went back to the bedroom and pitched it into her suitcase. The man in her bed rolled onto his side away from her and the mattress groaned. She closed the lid and latched it and hauled the suitcase out of the bedroom. She found Faith's purse and took what cash she had then dug through the biker's pants and found his wallet and took several hundred dollars and a credit card. She picked up the suitcase and left, no note, nothing. She slammed the door behind her like someone was chasing her.

She stopped to fill up with gas and bought two large cups of coffee. The high from the crank was already falling off and she knew that soon she would be very low, unbelievably low, suicide low. She paid and left the coffee on the counter and went to the bathroom. She was getting her period and had to get a tampon from the machine. She could smell the tattooed man on her.

As she crossed the parking lot a blond child with afflicted eyes and a red nose watched her from the window of a parked car. Iona tried to smile but she didn't know what her face actually did; the child pursed its mouth woefully.

She got in the car and propped one cup of coffee against the emergency brake and sipped on the other. She turned the key and eventually her car started. It had been running poorly for the last few weeks. She disliked people that named their cars and talked to their cars like they were people or pets. They were cars and that was all, "But please," she said to her car, "please don't quit on me today."

Above the highway the skies were louring and without definition. Even when she drove fast it felt like she was going slow. The farmlands, the rolling wheat fields south of Moscow, were all stubble and on the hillsides she could see the tire tracks from the machinery that had cut them and they made her think of crop circles and some TV show she had watched at work. Suddenly angry, she reminded herself that Tracy was in the hospital and that is all you get to think about. You are his mother. You don't get to think about crop circles or car culture or anything. Tracy is hurt. Drive.

The tears came self-consciously at first then she kind of broke and her muscles went weak and it came through her like a shock and wrung her out. It was real and it had been a long time since she had cried for real, since Bill. Her nose dripped and tears streamed down her cheeks and her hair stuck in it all. She sobbed and her body shook and she wondered if maybe she should pull over because if it gets any worse I might crash. Drive, she thought. Drive.

She smelled the pulp mill in Lewiston before she saw it. From the top of the grade the valley below looked as flat as slate, the split ribbons of the Clearwater and the Snake hashed by bridges and dams. The road was steep and the guardrails were battered and smeared with paint. She continued down and the pulp mill with its steaming towers came into view. It smells like money, someone had said. Where do you keep your money? was the reply.

Once she crossed the Clearwater the rank smell faded. The rain hit the windshield then weakened and spit. She turned on the radio and listened to an AM talk show about intelligent design. Her high was gone and it came with a price. When she got like this it felt like her heart was pumping oil, dark and irredeemable.

She drove past fields of rapeseed edged with milkweed taller than two men. Grain silos began to appear at the roadside and high on the hills were terraced wheat fields. She was nearing the town of Fern where she'd been born and raised. The rain stopped and the radio reception faded; it seemed somehow appropriate that the host's voice died where Iona's began. The idea of intelligent design struck her as being a unique kind of stupidity that only man could be capable of.

A sign announced Fern and its meager population, an arrow pointed to a one-lane bridge that crossed the river. The pines and cottonwoods concealed all indications of commerce. She slowed when she came to the squat buildings of the old hog farm because it was no longer a farm at all. What used to be clapboard and bare dirt had been remodeled into an antique furniture store with what looked to be rooms for rent on the second floor. It had been landscaped with hedges and grass and crushed quartz walkways. Iona's father used to be employed by Cannon, the man who ran the farm, a red-haired, gray-skinned man who was constantly picking at the frayed skin on his fingers.

"He's coming apart at the seams," Iona remembered her father saying. The hog farmer lived alone in a house upriver from the farm. In his yard he had a lightning-struck cottonwood with a tire swing in it but his wife and children had left before Iona could remember. It had always been Cannon alone with the hogs. She guessed that he must have died by now. Her own family had splintered, come apart at the seams as it were, while Cannon had still worked his farm. Faith had worked there for a summer. Iona had harbored a crush on the man but Faith had acted on it and eventually seduced him, or at least she said she had.

Iona drove for another quarter mile then stopped at the gas station and sat in the car and looked at the cigarette ads, the lottery ads, a yellowed missing-dog poster. She remembered coming here as a child and buying candy with nickels given to her by friends of her father's. She felt the sentimentality creep into her thoughts and it made her shiver. It was a hundred to one, bad times to good. She hadn't been back to Fern since Tracy was a baby. She guessed that no one would remember her or her family.

The door was open a crack and Iona hesitated for a moment before she went inside. A fat, white-haired man was working behind the counter and he smiled at her when she came in. He was eating microwave popcorn from a bag laid out on the countertop. Iona bought cigarettes and when the man gave her the change from her five his greasy fingers touched her hand. Later when she was driving she saw the shine of his fingerprints there and wiped them off with her sleeve.

She passed beneath a train bridge and followed its line to the trestle bridges on the hillsides above. The cuts made in the hills for the tracks were reflected in the timber frames of the bridges below and the two oscillated gracefully, mathematically. She climbed the Winchester Grade and at the top she could look out over the whole valley. Thunderheads were forming to the east, tall and dark, and the haze that Iona took to be rain at first, she realized as she got closer, was smoke from the burning stubble fields. The thunderheads were piled above the flames, tamped down tight and flexing, and when they broke the rain bled into the smoke and the flames, and it appeared that the whole conflicted process was connected by wires, like a giant mobile.

A man and two small boys were walking the burnt fields. The man had three shovels on his shoulder while the boys each carried a gallon jug of water and one of them, the taller of the two, carried a smudge torch. They looked insignificant and lost out there in the burn and they worried Iona with their identical and determined gaits. She watched them until she entered a deep cut in the hills where the road passed through and the stratigraphy revealed rich, nearly homogenous soil unmarked by layers of stones.

The rain chased her south across the Camas Prairie. She climbed the Whitebird Grade in third gear and slowly the rain turned to snow. Fat, dancing flakes caked her windshield and covered her headlights. The wipers could hardly keep up. Her car labored in the slush and she drove cautiously. It had been a long time since she'd driven through a storm like this so far away from home. Twelve years probably, before Bill started getting sick. She thought her life as being divided into pre-, post-, and during-Bill eras synchronized to her age: young, middle-aged, and old.

Once, they'd driven to Yellowstone and spent a week camping as a family: Iona, Tracy, and Bill. They'd watched a black bear climb on top of a station wagon with Iowa plates and shit on the roof. When it was finished the bear ambled down the hood and swiped the antenna to the ground like a willow twig. The people in the car were frozen in their seats until the bear moved safely down the line of onlookers then, after they were sure it was gone, they clapped. The man driving the car got out and picked up the antenna from the road and pointed to the turd on the roof and laughed. The whole family got out of the car to look.

"I got mixed feelings about what they're calling the nature experience," Bill had said. Iona missed Bill and his warmth. He didn't have the capacity for the quick hatred that ran through her, came on like bad weather in Tracy. Iona recalled how difficult it had been to write the letter to Bandy telling him about Tracy and not say anything else, not ask any questions. Without realizing it she let him crowd into her thoughts, let the memory of his hands and his voice take hold of her. It was a memory so old she couldn't be sure they were even his hands; they could be another man's, or an amalgamation of all.

At the bottom of the grade she came to the Salmon River and was glad to see it again. The storm worsened as she gained elevation. The trees were soon white and weighted with snow. Later, she passed tractor trailers pulled over on the side of the highway waiting out the storm. She chain-smoked and filled the car's ashtray. The radio wouldn't pick up any stations any longer and her tape deck was broken. A snowplow must have come from somewhere because the road ahead had been cleared. She hadn't noticed when the bad road ended and the good began. She was the only car on the road. The sign said LAKE FORK 38 MILES. She felt like she was going home instead of leaving it.

A CO named Penry came to take Bandy to use the phone. The big, pale-skinned guard ducked his head and spoke into his radio mouthpiece and stepped back. After a moment the door racked open. It was off hours and Bandy was wary to leave his cell. He hadn't done anything recently to merit any interest, or respect, and this left him in a vulnerable position. Penry had been getting bold. Tracy and the ranch had been occupying Bandy's thoughts and he was often distracted. His silence and inactivity he knew others saw as weakness. Bad things happened when you were taken out alone at odd times but usually it came from Crookshank, the head CO. He had a reputation for handing out beatings, hurting the unruly. Whatever it was, Bandy knew it wasn't good.

"Don't wait on me. I'm always ready." Penry held up a yellow piece of paper with a phone number on it. "Let's go."

Bandy slipped on his shoes and stepped out to the march line and Penry shoved him forward. Morning count was over and chow wasn't for another hour. Some of the cons from Ad-Seg were being taken out for showers and to their state-required visits to the yard so Bandy wasn't the only prisoner on the move. He didn't look at the other men, rattling by all Jacob Marley in full-dress shackles. Penry walked Bandy to the end of the tier and through the open gate. They went down the stairs then down the hall to the sally port and after a short conversation between Penry and another bull they passed through the second door and out to the main causeway. When they reached the Unit Command cage Bandy stood in the box out- side and waited for the grille doors to open.

"Where the fuck do you think you're going?" Penry said.

"You said I gotta make a phone call."

"It doesn't mean I'm walking you all across hell to do it. Get over here." Penry banged on the glass of the UC cage and the CO inside put down his magazine and got up from his chair and came over and opened the small sliding window. "Let this fucker use your phone," Penry said.

"No way. Take him out like you're supposed to. I ain't letting him in here. He's gotta sign for it anyway. Get him the fuck outta here."

Penry looked at the floor then glanced at Bandy. "Don't make me call Crookshank, Stan."

Stan was skinny with sunken cheeks and acne scars. "And tell him what?"

"Maybe I'll tell him what I saw you doing in your car with Owens last week."

"Oh yeah? Go ahead," Stan said, his eyes shining. "And I'll tell him about your thing up there." He pointed up the stairs, in the general direction of Bandy's cell.

"He already knows about my thing, asshole. He loves my thing. I don't think he's gonna love yours." Penry made a circle with the thumb and index finger of his left hand then poked his right index finger through the hole and leered at Stan.

"You're a piece a shit, Penry."

"Go on. Open the door. It'll take a goddamn second."

Stan opened the door and Penry gave him the scrap of paper with the phone number on it. Penry pushed Bandy into the cramped little room and Stan shut the door behind him. There were control panels for the locks on all the cages, closed circuit TVs, several telephones; it felt very sophisticated to what Bandy was used to. He could almost feel the electricity from all the devices on his skin, lifting the hair on his arms.

"Wait." Penry unfolded a piece of paper from his back pocket and slid it through the slot in the door then gave Bandy a pen and told him to sign next to the X so the phone call could be logged in. Stan picked up the off-road magazine he'd been reading from the chair and the cover slid down and underneath was a skin magazine. Bandy signed and passed Penry the pen and the sheet of paper. Nearly half of the TV screens above Stan's desk were black. Stan saw him looking and told him to sit his ass down and shut up. He dialed the phone for Bandy and handed him the receiver.

The phone was ringing. "Who am I talking to?" Bandy said to Penry through the barrier glass.

"You'll see."

The receptionist at the hospital answered and gave the hospital name then her own name. Bandy couldn't think of anything to say so he said his name. "I'm Bandy Dorner." The receptionist put him on hold for a long time then he was transferred to a nurse then the nurse transferred him to Tracy's doctor. After the doctor had explained basically what had happened and how bad Tracy was hurt, he told Bandy to call back next week if he wanted to talk to his son.

Bandy hung up the phone and Stan opened the door and pushed him back into the hallway.

"You fucking owe me," Stan said to Penry.

"Fag," Penry said. "Move it," he said to Bandy. "Walk goddamnit." He shoved him forward on the march line. Bandy walked. They climbed the stairs. "Bad news?" Penry said, laughed. Bandy kept his head lowered and didn't speak. Someone above them called out to Bandy but he ignored them, then someone called Penry an ass eater and dozens of other cons joined in with bull faggot until Stan got on the loudspeaker and threatened the tier with loss of privileges, then it was a general moan and a chorus of fuck-yous. There was nothing of this in Bandy's head. The kid was all he could think about.

When they got back to his cell Penry spoke again into his radio. The door opened and Penry pushed him in and walked away. The door racked shut. Bandy sat down on his bunk and worked his fingernails beneath one another, scraping the grease from the machine shop onto the stained fabric of his mattress. He lay down on his bunk and put his hands over his eyes. He didn't leave his cell for chow.

That night, after lights-out, he woke to a commotion nearby on the tier. He heard his friend Fulcrum scream then batons came down and beat him silent. Bandy stood and went to the door of his cell. He pressed his cheek to the steel grate and he could hear Penry and maybe one or two of the other hacks down the hall joking and laughing.

"Hey, Fulcrum, you okay?" Bandy's voice echoed across the tier.

"Your little butt buddy has been very bad, Dorner," Penry called back to him. "Berry berry bad." The COs laughed. A dull thud, a pinched breath. The batons whipped down on his ex-celly until they stopped then he listened to the COs breathe, laugh nervously, radio static, a door buzzer, footsteps on steel grates.

"You all right?" Bandy said, after it was quiet again.

Fulcrum groaned. "Broke my nose again. Fucking ribs."

Bandy could hear him as he climbed back onto his bunk. Other inmates started talking on the tier, about nothing, about how they never slept.

"My boy fell off a roof," Bandy said.

"B 'n 'E or fucking around?"

"He's straight, I told you. He works construction."

"Yeah, well, somebody's got to."

"What's with you and Penry?"

"How about you leave me alone with my misery?"

"Yeah. All right." He sat in the near dark and concentrated and in his head composed two letters, one to Tracy and another to the Idaho State Board of Corrections.

Chapter 6

THE ROAD USED TO END HERE

TRACY SLEPT UNDER a white sheet and a pale yellow blanket, eyelids shuddering with his dreams. Iona sat with Ellen Guntly at his bedside. They'd been together since Iona had arrived. The old woman spent time praying and Iona watched her pray. Spit in the ocean. She was kind to the point of being annoying or suspiciously fake. Tracy slept and didn't move. The hospital went on outside of the room and the sounds came through the door and the walls and made Iona feel like she was hiding. Maybe she was hiding.

Ellen took a short breath and held it. Iona looked up and their eyes met. "Wilhelm's always joking with him. They laugh all the time, they're like little children." She smiled.

Iona looked away. She needed another hit if she was going to make it through this. She needed to shake it off, the whole mess, like a wet dog; just get it off of her. She couldn't remember Tracy laughing. This man in the hospital bed, he wasn't quite her son. He was like someone seen through a shop window, a reflection across the street. She closed her eyes. This might be it, she thought. This might be when I finally fucking lose it.

"Are you all right?" Ellen placed her hand gently on Iona's shoulder.

"I want him to wake up. I want to see his eyes."

"He'll be sleeping for awhile longer yet. The doctor said six or eight hours with the shot that he gave him."

"When did he say that? How long ago?"

"Not long after you got here. You talked to him. Don't you remember?"

Iona hardly remembered meeting the doctor at all. She definitely didn't remember what time it was when she arrived. It was daylight and it was snowing, she remembered that much.

"It's okay," Ellen said. "Worrying will only age you."

"It's all I can do. I hate this."

"He'll wake up soon and we'll be here waiting. He'll be so happy to see you."

"I don't know about that."

"Don't be ridiculous."

"We haven't seen each other for months. We haven't talked or anything."

"You're his mother, he'll always be glad to see you."

"Our family isn't like that."

Ellen squeezed her shoulder one last time then let go. "I remember when you and Bandy lived down the road on Jack and Maude's place."

"That was a long time ago."

"Yes, it was. I remember the night the cabin burned. I watched it from my front room. I didn't know what it was of course. I thought it was a slash pile until the fire truck showed up. You know how Jack was always burning something, he'd burn anything so he wouldn't have to look at it or move it somewhere. God forbid he'd have to pay to take something to the dump. Wilhelm's the same way."

"I don't want to talk. I don't want to talk about this." Iona was surprised at what she'd said but it was exactly what she meant.

Ellen's mouth set into a thin straight line. "Sometimes you need someone to talk to, or talk at you. Sometimes all you need is another voice."

Pain and frustration washed over Iona in a wave. "I can't do this right now."

"Listen to me, Iona. This is important."

"Please."

"My son, Neil, he was killed in a car wreck. He was with Bandy. Do you remember that?"

"It was before my time."

"But you know what happened."

"Yes."

"I don't know how you ever lived with that man."

"With who, Bandy? How could you bring that up?"

"I'm sorry. I shouldn't have said that. I'm sorry."

"I haven't been back here for almost twenty years. I didn't kill anybody."

"You're right, you didn't do anything."

"I didn't say that. I said I didn't kill anybody."

The old woman stared at Iona. Her face betrayed no emotion.

"What the fuck are you looking at?"

"I want to tell you something."

"Jesus Christ, what? What do you want to tell me?"

"That I left Wilhelm after Neil's funeral. I went to Kansas City to live with my cousin, and when I came back I was in worse shape than you are now. My son was dead. There was nowhere I could look, no sound I could hear, no smell."

"Tracy's not dead. He's not going to die."

"He'll be fine. Listen, while I was gone I did things that I have to live with now, things I can hardly stand to remember. My cousin wasn't a well person. She's dead now, God save her. She went with a lot of men; she was that kind of woman. While I was away I was like her, but nothing I did made me feel better, nothing could make me forget. I know you've lost your husband and now this. I understand what you're feeling. I want to help."

"Then shut up."

The old woman pinched the back of Iona's arm and made her jump. "That's not the way and you know it," she said.

"Don't touch me." Iona's arm really hurt, even after she rubbed it.

"You need to keep your heart well, and open, and it'll get better. Be patient. It's good that you've come back."

"Why won't he wake up?" She grabbed Tracy's arm and shook him.

"Let him be." Ellen gently took Iona's arm and put her hand back in her lap and held it. "I know about bearing burdens, and I'm telling you right now that when you're ready to put yours down I'm here for you."

A nurse came in and asked if they'd like lunch because the cafeteria would stop serving soon, then they'd have to wait until dinner. Iona couldn't imagine eating, couldn't remember the last time she ate. She took her hand away from Ellen and got up and pushed her way past the nurse and went down the hallway. Back in this town. All the doors were closed on either side of her. The exit was directly ahead and the sun shone in the wire-grid windows and down the hall. The door would open and all would go black, all of this would end. No, it wouldn't. She had to get straight, get some sleep. She banged out the doors and the sun blinded her. The snow had stopped. She crossed the parking lot in the white light and it felt as if she was in a dry room waiting on inclement weather, or in inclement weather waiting on an earthquake. She was not safe, something was coming for her. It was her fault, she shouldn't have told him about Bandy. He wouldn't have been here at all, wouldn't have ever been on that roof.

She cleaned the snow off her car and got in and drove. She didn't know where she was going; she was just driving. She was mad at Ellen and knew she had no reason to be, but that didn't change anything. The old woman didn't know what she was talking about. Iona smiled meanly at the idea of Ellen being a slut, a whore in Kansas City. The smile shifted on Iona's face and her vision clouded with tears. It was nothing to laugh about. She knew what it meant to need something and to hate it at the same time. She coughed and wiped her eyes and whatever restraint she had suddenly broke. She screamed as loud as she could and kept screaming until it wasn't a noise at all, only a vibration. Her vision narrowed to pinholes and her body felt leaden as it hung on her soul.

Then it was over. She was still driving and she could see and hear. She needed to find something she recognized, to regain the ground.

The local market where she used to work, Turnery's, where Bill used to work, where she'd met Bill, was gone and one of the chain supermarkets sat in its place. A building at least twice as big as the old one, it was fronted by a sprawling black parking lot so seamless and watertight and connected-looking to the store that the two appeared to have come finished and ready for business in one contiguous piece, and for a few hundred yards downtown there were actual sidewalks. Bandy would never believe it, Iona thought, Lake Fork with sidewalks. The fake little town. The lights had come up: last call in Lake Fork. Why am I thinking of Bandy? She remembered the old town and she would take this new touristy place over the timber and dirt reality of the way it used to be any day.

What will I even say to Tracy when he wakes up? She'd destroyed a whole part of herself since he'd left Spokane. Ellen had seen her for what she really was, and so would he. She was scared to face him, didn't know what she would say.

She parked in an empty lot at the lakeshore, not far from where the mill used to be. The day was windless and along the banks the snow was mounded smooth against the straight edge of the dark water like porcelain cupping black coffee. She opened the door and the cold air swept over her. She considered taking a walk along the shoreline but she didn't have the right shoes for it. She'd need to find some snow boots. In the old days they had to drive to Boise to get things like boots but now with the new stores and everything else maybe she could find a cheap pair. She would ask Ellen. She looked forward to asking, to apologizing.

Across the lake she could see the new, taller buildings that had been built on the lakefront. A resort hotel took up a large section of the shoreline but there was a bar and some shops there too. She'd driven by the Pitcher Bar and it was boarded up and dark and that was fine with her; it was a place she could stand to forget. Near the end, Bandy had been coming home every night drunk and bloody or smelling of other women or all three. She hated that place like it was a person.

She was in the shade and it was cold so she started the car again and pulled into the sunlight and opened her door and let it warm her legs. She leaned out and put her face up to it, breathed in the warmth. She remembered how she and Bandy had once snuck into the old mill site through a hole in the fence and climbed up among the burnt and ruined buildings, emerged covered in ash and soot. This is all too much, she told herself, these memories. You need to stop. She couldn't, the door was open. The sun felt good and cleansing.

Jack Dorner was a filer at the mill but he'd been let go before it burned. After that he traveled to other towns to find work, other mills. He'd kept the ranch, but it couldn't have been profitable. He'd told Iona that when the mill burned he'd watched the glow of the flames from the hillside above his house. There'd been several times when she'd almost gone back to see Maude and Jack but she never had. She tried to make a connection between the fires, but there wasn't one. Things end, she thought. And when they burn someone will be more than happy to watch. Ellen had watched the cabin burn. Iona had a hard time taking that in. She didn't know what it meant.

The story went that a mill worker had started the fire, but Jack said it was the owners that did it so they could cash in on the insurance money before they had to shut the mill down for lack of easy timber. It didn't matter, she thought. The same thing always happens. You run out of trees, you run out of rocks, or you run out of room. It happens everywhere and after everything all that's left are tourists and scenic overlooks: plaques and museums. She was walking through a graveyard now and what she was seeing in the new Lake Fork was simply new graves in an old yard. The real real estate, she thought. Then she thought the same thing could and did happen to people. They died a little and rebuilt and sold off things that mattered in times of want to get by. It had happened to her. She wasn't only walking through a graveyard; she was a graveyard. This line of reasoning led her to take stock of her resources, to see what she could stand to lose. She'd given and sold too much of herself. She imagined herself threadbare and rusted, covered in years of dust.

The mill debris had all been hauled away and where it had been the ground was flat and smooth with snow. Visible between the trees was a sign announcing a city park and further down the shoreline a marina and a boathouse. Iona imagined in the summer there would be ski boats and small sailboats parked where the booming grounds used to be. She thought of the postcard that Tracy had sent her. She closed her eyes and she could see the boats as they cut gently through the slight waves of the lake. Birds, Iona thought, the summers here always had so many birds. There aren't any birds here now. Nothing doing, not even a junco. Not even a raven. Such a quiet day. At the hospital Wilhelm had said something how Tracy had been trying to fly when he fell. "You forgot your wings," he'd said to the sleeping boy.

Iona shut the car door and cried and later when a car pulled in the lot she buried her face in her hands so they couldn't see her. She got cold sitting there and eventually she couldn't cry anymore.

The motel she found was run-down and cheap. She remembered it from the old days. She and Bandy had stayed there on occasion when they got too drunk to make it home. She unlocked her room and put the key in her purse and shut the door behind her. She sat down on the edge of the bed. The room was dark with wood paneling and shag carpet, a heavy wooden armchair shining with lacquer and a table that matched.

She curled up on the bed even though she needed to get back to the hospital to see if Tracy was up. Awake, she needed to see if he was awake. He wouldn't be up. Her body ached from lack of sleep and inactivity. Sitting, she thought. I do nothing but sit, nothing but wait. She closed her eyes and listened to the cars go by on the highway out front, the jangle and thud of the snow chains, the familiar scrape of the plow. It had been snowing on and off and would of course continue. Her thoughts circled in on themselves, her body numbed, her breathing slowed. So close to sleep. This warm place.

This blanket of sleep. She opened her eyes slightly and looked at the ugly orange lamp and the glass ashtray on the bedside table. Her heart beat unevenly in her chest, the speed had finally quit dying; it was dead. She could sleep now if she let herself. She sat up on the edge of the bed then stood. She shouldered her purse and checked to make sure the room key was there and drove back to the hospital.

Tracy's eyes were open when she came in. Someone had brought a tray of food and the room smelled of fried chicken. There were bones on the tray and a dirty spoon. The smell made her slightly sick.

"Ma," Tracy said. He looked bad and his voice was thick and wrong. He had grease from the chicken on his lip and cheek.

"I came earlier. I've been here. You were sleeping."

"Wilhelm told me. Him and Ellen just left. He has a doctor's appointment across the street. You just missed them."

"How are you?" she asked, not knowing what else to say. She sat down in the chair next to the bed.

"Pretty numb." He was studying her. She couldn't bear it; she looked away. "You look like shit, Ma. What's wrong with you? Are you sick?"

"I'm fine. I haven't slept. You scared me. I got the call from the nurse and drove here as fast as I could."

His eyes were glassy and slow to blink. He scratched at his cheek with the pulse monitor taped to his finger and Iona wondered why they had to keep that on him; he wasn't going to die.

"How's Faith?"

"She's fine. Let's not talk about her."

"All right," Tracy said. "They told you everything then, how it happened."

"I don't know why you were up there. You've always been afraid of heights."

"It doesn't matter. I fell."

"You fell."

They looked at one another. Sometimes when she looked at her son it felt as if her heart would be pulled through her chest; she could feel it move forward and beat against her ribs. It couldn't really happen, she knew that, but it felt like it could, like her heart was in a drawer and he opened it and there it was right there, a ball, as if made of string, about to be thrown. He has such a terrible power over me. There is no protection.

"Did you eat?" She pointed to the tray.

"Yeah, they fed me. Maybe we should get you something."

"No, I'm fine." Iona hesitated, then: "Wilhelm and Ellen like you. They've been worried." Tracy didn't say anything; his eyes had gone distant. She wondered where he went. "It's like you have a whole new family here," she said, and it came out accusatory. She reached over and touched her son's hand then leaned down and smelled his skin. He was fine. He was going to be fine.

"I've been writing to Bandy," Tracy said. "He's coming to stay with me when he gets out."

"When?" Iona said.

Tracy pulled his hand away. "I don't know. He said soon."

"You should get to know him before you offer something like that. You have enough to worry about."

"It's his place, Ma. And I do know him. I talked to him, remember? I went to see him."

"Okay."

"I know him."

"Maybe you think you do. No, it's fine. It'll be fine." She took a breath. "How's staying with the Guntlys?"

"Fine," Tracy said, mocking her. He smiled. "But Bandy's

house is almost livable, I'll move in there soon. Me and Wilhelm redid the wiring then I swapped out some framing to a plumber that my boss knows. It's all new."

"It's an old house."

"I know what it is."

"Trace, I can't fight with you right now."

"I'm not trying to fight with you."

"All right." Iona reached out and gently touched the blanket covering his legs.

"Smashed."

"Trace."

"Don't, Ma. I'll get better."

She cried then and Tracy watched her and didn't speak. He didn't reach out to comfort her. After Iona had wiped her eyes and brought herself together, she looked back at her son. His jaw was set, his eyes unblinking. She got up and placed her hand on his forehead. She left without saying anything but against her throat the words: don't hurt me please don't walk on me, child, I am weak. When she left the room Wilhelm and Ellen were standing at the nurse's station and she walked quickly in the other direction so they wouldn't see her leave.

Someone pulled up outside her motel room and the sound woke her. It was early, just daylight, and the room was perfectly still. She'd been up when it was still dark but she'd fallen asleep again and felt more tired now than she had before. There was a vodka bottle on the table below the wall-mounted TV. She'd thought she wanted a drink but the plastic cup and the ice with the holes in the middle didn't make her feel anything except worthless. A car door opened. Iona sat up on the bed. She thought about hiding the vodka but there wasn't anybody that would come and see her.

There was a knock at the door. She didn't move. She waited for it to sound again so she could be sure that it wasn't at a room down the way. The knock repeated, a little quieter this time. Iona opened the door a crack and looked out.

"Morning," Wilhelm said. "Sorry to bother you."

"I'll get dressed."

"I'll wait."

Iona shut the door and put on a pair of jeans and pulled her big T-shirt over her head and put on a sweatshirt of Tracy's she'd found in her car. She straightened her hair in the bathroom mirror then went back and held the door open. The room was tidy but she was embarrassed about the vodka.

"I thought I might get drunk," she said, pointing at the bottle, "but I fell asleep before I managed." She smiled as best she could. "Come on in and get warm." Wilhelm took off his hat. She felt unsavory in front of the old man. The room was nearly filled by the bed. Iona went to the wall-mounted heater and turned it on. She held up the bottle.

"No, thanks," Wilhelm said.

She moved into the shadowy corner next to the television. Wilhelm stayed by the door. "It's about Tracy?" she said. "Everything's okay, isn't it?"

"Sure. Ellen's with him now. He's doing fine."

"What is it then?"

The old man patted his head and the bristly hair made a scraping sound against his hand. "You remember the ranch, Iona? The Dorner place, where the cabin used to be?"

"Of course I do." It was both painful and flattering to think that she could've forgotten.

"I guess you would, and you probably know that Tracy's been working out there too, right? Fixing it up."

"You're not here to try and buy it, are you? Because it's not up to me at all. I don't have any say about that."

"No, hell no. I want to finish the work on the house that he started so when he gets out of the hospital he can go and stay in his own place if he wants. I think it'd be good for him. I came to see if you wanted to come out there and maybe help out a little. It'd get your mind off of everything."

Iona thought of Maude's kitchen and Jack's muddy boots by the front door. She remembered the blue camas coming up in the spring and the irrigation canals sometimes so loud and close it seemed like they were inside her head. Grasshoppers like a plague in summer. She remembered the day of the fire and how she had set out across the field, her shoulder aching as she lugged her suitcase up the hill toward Bill's.

"You don't have to if you don't want to, but I bet between here and the hospital you're about to lose your wits. It'd help to get moving, get something done. I should say too that you have a room at our place. Ellen's going to insist, so you know."

Iona couldn't help but smile. She liked Wilhelm. "I'm not very handy. I'm not like Tracy."

"You'll do fine."

"I might need to be alone for awhile, to stay here."

"I understand that, but Ellen'll argue you into the grave." He smiled. "I used to be four inches taller, you know. She's like the weather, you can't win. It might be easier if you just packed up and followed me out."

Iona crossed her arms over her breasts and lowered her head. She didn't want to but she said: "Could I come out this afternoon? I'd like to see Tracy first."

"Sure. Sure, I was kidding. Come out whenever you want," Wilhelm said. "But don't say anything to him about what we're doing. I want it to be a surprise." It was quiet and strange for a moment in the small room then Wilhelm opened the door. The cold air felt soft against Iona's face. She turned down the heater and stepped out of the shadows.

"He told me that Bandy's getting out," she said.

Wilhelm lowered his head and his face darkened. "When?"

"I don't know. He said he's coming back here. He said it's his house."

"I can't see how that could do anybody any good, and with all the work that Tracy's done, I can't see how it's his house even. Shit, it would've fell down without Tracy."

"It's legally his, though."

"Ellen's my wife, it doesn't mean I own her. I own her. Iona. Doesn't mean Iona." He smiled and Iona laughed.

"You still want me to come out?"

"In my mind Tracy's the sole heir."

"Is that a yes?"

"It is. You come and stay with us. There's no reason for you to be paying for this motel." He paused. "You don't need to be alone, even if you think you do, you don't."

"Thanks," she said. Wilhelm touched her shoulder and got in his truck. She stepped back inside and shut her door. She opened the bottle of vodka and took a quick sip then capped it and set it down. She looked at the clock. It was time to go back to the hospital.

Chapter 7

CLAY EATERS

BANDY'S DOOR CLANGED OPEN. He slipped on his shoes and wrapped a blanket around his shoulders and stepped out of his cell onto the line. He'd been sick for the last month or so. He was losing weight and his skin had gone ashen. At first he thought it was the flu, but it didn't go away. No one else got sick. He couldn't remember being this skinny. The doc had him on some medication but it didn't seem to be doing any good. They didn't even know what was wrong with him yet. More tests were being scheduled, but nothing wanted or needed ever happened quickly inside.

Inmates and convicts watched him and the other sickies as they walked the short line. He looked in on Fulcrum but he wasn't moving, a twisted lump under his blanket. In other cells men sat on toilets and on their bunks and did push-ups and hung on their cage doors with their hands above their heads like they were food lying on a grill. A halfwit named Pettigrew was sitting on the floor Indian-style masturbating with a confounded and serious look about him like he was working and working hard but was worried that he might be doing it all wrong and for no good reason. Bandy made a face at him and kept walking.

They had the med table set up downstairs at the UC where Stan the hack had let him use the phone. The doctor shined a light in his eyes and squeezed his throat then motioned him toward the trustee down the line. Bandy signed his name on the printout and took the pills he was given. They repeated the trip back up the stairs and he was locked down again. He sat on his bunk and probed his swollen liver. He'd held cow and deer and elk livers before and he could imagine holding his own. Something was wrong with him; he felt it in his bones.

An hour later the buzzer sounded for chow and this time all the doors on the tier jolted open at once and men came out and stood and talked with their neighbors, much like shopkeepers would, bargain sellers of wholesale time. He checked over his shoulder for who was watching then strayed from the line and leaned against the chain link that blocked the handrail from the big jump. From there he could see Penry standing at the tier gate blowing on his hands, rubbing them together. The furnace had been malfunctioning for the last few weeks; it was either on full blast or it was off. Bandy was glad the snouts had to bear up to it, too, Penry especially. The men on the tier below weren't visible except for their fingers, knuckles clutching the chain link like fleshy growths on a steel trellis. The common area in the center of the unit was empty and the men on the far side were still in their cages because they ate in shifts. Across a canyon, they seemed very far away.

All the cages cleared and Fulcrum still hadn't come out. Penry would lock him in; he didn't care if Fulcrum ate or not. The line sensed that it was almost time to go and straightened out and got ready. Bandy went and stood in Fulcrum's doorway. "On your feet," he said. "You think you're resting, but you're just getting stove up."

Fulcrum pulled back his thin blanket, revealing his scrawny bruised torso, his stained underwear. He grabbed at himself. "I'll show you stove up," he said, smiling.

"Come on, I'll help you." He took Fulcrum's hand and pulled him to his feet. Once standing, Fulcrum climbed into his jumpsuit then crouched down and pulled on his shoes. The splits and bruises on his shaved scalp were crusted red and yellow and purple and irregular like a child had drawn them on.

"Why's Penry been cranking on you all of a sudden?" Bandy said.

Fulcrum looked up and said seriously, "You have to act to avoid being acted upon."

"Bullshit. You acted stupidly, now your stupid ass is getting beat for it. You burned Penry on something, and that means Crookshank's only a couple steps back. You don't want any part of him, and you been here long enough to know it. You hear me?"

Fulcrum ignored him. "My jaw's all unhinged," he said. "My ears pop every time I open my mouth." He opened and closed his mouth like an animal dying. "You can't hear that can you?"

"No."

"It's loud."

"I can't hear it."

"Seems that loud, like you might."

"It's in your head."

"Really."

"Fuck you."

"Really, it's in my head?"

"Quit complaining," Bandy said.

"You try living in this train wreck for a day and we'll see how much you bitch."

"I'd trade with you."

Fulcrum looked like he'd say something, like Fulcrum always

had to say something, but this time he didn't. Bandy wasn't well and his friend knew it.

Penry yelled for everyone to get on the line and the grille door opened. Bandy put his hand in Fulcrum's armpit and helped him onto the catwalk and they moved out at the front of the line. Men pressed in behind them, all of them of a basic description: eyes sleepy, unshaven, stinking of sweat in their jumpsuits and slip-ons, felony fliers. Dangerous men shuffling. Bandy kept an eye over his shoulder to see who was close. A lop was being worked on by Hinton and Perez, the local arm benders. They were crowding the new guy, whispering in his ear. They'd have him by dark.

"Heard any more about your boy?" Fulcrum said to Bandy.

"Nothing," Bandy said. Fulcrum moved carefully down the stairs. Penry watched them from the landing, his bald head shining like he waxed it. Someone from the back of the line called out for Bandy and Fulcrum to hurry the fuck up.

"We're all in a big hurry," Bandy said to Fulcrum.

"Top speed, brother," Fulcrum said.

Someone, Hinton or Perez, pushed the lop from behind and he stumbled forward and fell against Fulcrum's back. Bandy let go of his friend's arm and the newbie apologized and tried to get away with his eyes rolling and there was true terror in them and Bandy grabbed him by the throat and slammed him against the fence and held him and he would've hit him because he had to, because it was required, but Penry smacked his baton against the handrail at the bottom of the stairs. Bandy stopped what he was doing and let the man go.

"Holy shit," Penry said loudly. "It's the dawn of the living dead peckerwoods." The CO smiled, a mouthful of crooked teeth. "You go on and flex, Dorner, get able. Pretend you can still lift your own dick, sick as you are." Some of the men in the line laughed. Bandy grabbed Fulcrum's arm again and tried to hoist him along but he wouldn't go.

"Penry, you fucking narwhal-headed faggot, I ain't scared a you," Fulcrum said.

"You better be."

"Why don't you eat some shit and leave us the fuck alone?"

"What'd you say?"

"You heard me, you shinehead cocksucker."

Penry quit smiling and started up the stairs. He pushed Bandy aside and grabbed Fulcrum by the arm. "We're walking, shitbird. Time to go to the limbo room." He rabbit-punched Fulcrum and his legs went out from under him.

"Come on, Penry," Bandy said. "He was just talking. He didn't touch you." The CO looked up then let Fulcrum fall onto the stairs. The men behind them in line were moving back up to the catwalk. There would be more COs coming. The lop was pressed flat to the fence half grinning at Bandy with wet, brown eyes.

"Dorner," Penry said, and wrapped his baton around Bandy's neck. He got behind him and pushed him down onto the stairs then he and Fulcrum were facing each other. Fulcrum was smiling like an idiot and Bandy couldn't help but smile back at him.

"Don't fucking bleed on me, Dorner," Penry said. "I'm not catching whatever that crap is you got." He jacked his knee into Bandy's spine. The metal of the stairs was cool and sharp against the side of his face. His arms were pulled behind him and his wrists zip-tied. Fulcrum lifted himself up while Penry was bent over Bandy. The stairs vibrated with footsteps. The plastic of the zip tie cut into Bandy's wrists. He rolled over in time to see Fulcrum and

Penry tumbling down the stairs and at the bottom Fulcrum stood up while Penry stayed down. He started back up the stairs to Bandy just as Crookshank and several other COs came in from off the tier. Fulcrum turned, yelling, trying to explain to them while backing away that it was all an accident and the men on the stairs and all across the tier picked up the call then everyone was screaming and laughing. Bandy wormed his way to the edge of the stairway against the cage and the handrail and he was facing the lop and the man was crying now.

The buzzer sounded and the door at the top of the stairs slammed to. The COs below took down Fulcrum then climbed the stairs. Bandy turned his face to the cage to hide but Crook-shank grabbed him by the hair and lifted him like a fisherman would a fish and hit him full on the forehead with his baton.

He woke in the infirmary shackled to the bedrail. With his free hand he felt out the bones of his face for fractures. There was swelling and a few stitches but nothing felt broken. He could hear a radio playing classical music somewhere nearby. A black-and-white wasp worked at a corner of the lone east-facing window, vibrating against the glass then scraping at the caulk on the sill. He pushed himself up in bed and his restraint rattled on the bar. A man three bunks down pulled the sheet from his blond, frizzled head and rolled toward Bandy very slowly and looked at him with one open eye then rolled just as slowly away. The restraint was loose and he tried halfheartedly to fit it over his hand but it wasn't that loose. He didn't know what he would do if it was: stretch his arm, sleep on his stomach. A trustee came in the room, his face hidden behind a stack of folded sheets. He was short and stocky, brown skinned.

"How long I been here?" Bandy said to the man, surprised at the pain behind his eyes when he spoke.

The man put down the sheets on a table in the corner of the room then produced a clipboard from the shelf below. The pencil scratched loudly in the quiet ward. "Three four days. Doc says you got brain damage. You woke up before when we were feeding you. You don't remember?" He put down the pencil, turned, and looked at Bandy. His mouth was wide and uneven and his longish black hair made him look androgynous in the way old women sometimes are. Bandy knew him from Texas, from the coop.

"I don't remember," Bandy said.

The trustee smiled and came closer. "How's brain damage feel?"

"Not too good. There was another guy came in here with me."

"Lyman, right? Goes by Fulcrum?"

"Yeah, he dead?"

"Nah. Some stitches was all. They took him out yesterday." The trustee, Bandy couldn't remember his name, came and sat down on the bunk across from him.

"What about Penry?"

"They ambo-ed him out before they even scraped you off the floor."

Bandy asked him what else he'd heard and the man got to his feet and went to the window. "El Capitán, Crookshank, he came and got your homeboy. Tossed him right out the door. See ya bye-bye. Kicked his ass all down the hall."

Bandy slid back down into the bed and rested his arm on the rail. The trustee filled a paper cup from the water cooler by the door and brought it over.

"I know you from Texas," the man said. "My name's Trinidad. People called me Sapo then. They don't call me that no more." There was a new seriousness in his manner when he said this.

Bandy studied the man, drank down the water. "I remember."

Trinidad grinned and leaned over and plucked Bandy's chart from the foot of his bed and held it up for Bandy to see. "I read your name here or I wouldn't've guessed it was you."

"I been sick. I was in here awhile back getting some tests. You weren't here then."

"No, I just got this transfer."

"I got meds I'm supposed to take. It say that on the chart?"

Trinidad nodded. "I'll tell the doc you're up and living and see if I can find them." He stood up and nodded to Bandy then left.

Bandy looked again at the wasp in the corner. The sun was going down and the room was warm. In the failing light the walls were the color of turmeric. Later, a different trustee brought in dinner trays for the men in the infirmary. Bandy couldn't stomach the food and the trustee took it away without him touching it. He slept a deep, dreamless sleep.

The next morning Trinidad came back and brought Bandy a cup of water then dragged a chair over beside his bed and sat down.

"Hey, you remember Foot?" he said.

After thinking how he should answer for a few seconds, Bandy said that he did. He sat up and his head throbbed with the change of position. "What about him?" Foot had been called Foot because he was as big as Bigfoot. Bandy had fought him when he'd first been sent to the coop. He'd been transferred along with a couple dozen other Idaho convicts by bus in the heat of summer. Bus therapy, they called it. During the fight Bandy had cut off two of the man's fingers and after that they called him Hand instead of Foot.

"I never seen nobody fight that hard like you did," Trinidad said.

"Different times."

"You were a bad fucker, man."

"Look where it got me."

Trinidad stood up. "We all get bloody." He smiled. Bandy felt he should say something to keep the rhythm of the place. The pace of things was important. He had nothing to say. "I got mopping to do," Trinidad said.

"All right."

Bandy tried to sleep again but couldn't. He could still hear the radio off somewhere and began to wonder if it was imagined, some residual jangle in his brain from being clubbed on the head, like seeing stars but hearing them. Hospital beds, he thought. Here we are. Tracy in Lake Fork. The hospital there had been a brick building in a town with not many of those. He closed his eyes. There was so much he couldn't remember. He thought of Iona and used the well-worn memories of her to guide him through the haze of the landscape. He followed her home.

He woke to footsteps in the hall. The door opened and it was Trinidad pushing a food cart. Bandy took the tray he was given and nodded his thanks and ate. The other men stayed under their blankets and Trinidad made no effort to wake them. He retrieved his own tray from a separate shelf under the cart then sat down in the chair he'd brought earlier. They ate together and when they were finished Trinidad took Bandy's tray.

"I got to go to the can," Bandy said.

"There's no CO to break you loose so I got to roll you."

"I know how it works." Bandy sat up in bed and Trinidad locked the back upright then rolled him through the dormitory and into the bathroom. It was a large room with tall, narrow toilets mounted to the wall and handicap bars all around. Trinidad helped

Bandy over the rail and stood him on shaky legs. "I got it," he said to Trinidad, and Trinidad left him to it. Bandy sat down on the cold rim of the toilet and felt so weak and small he worried briefly that he might fall in. When he finished, he climbed back into the bed. He lay there for a moment with no air in his lungs and a cloud filling his head. "Done," he said after a minute.

Trinidad came back and looked at Bandy then looked into the toilet. "I'll bring you back when you got a shit."

"Won't be today."

"Whenever."

"They say anything about my meds?"

Trinidad steered the bed out of the bathroom. "I told the doc and he said he'd get them. It won't do any good me saying anything twice. Just pisses them off."

"They were gonna bump me."

"Out? They was gonna bump you out?"

Bandy didn't know why he was talking about this, maybe it was because the two men shared a little history, their time in the coop, or maybe it was because Trinidad had been kind to him since he'd been here. Not that, he thought, but regardless, he didn't seem to be a threat. It didn't matter; he was already talking.

"I had the legal rep start all the paperwork and my jacket from Texas came back a lot cleaner than I remembered it. They must've lost some of the files or something." Or I built myself up in my mind, Bandy thought. Mental toughness begins with destroying weakness, weak moments, weak memories. "The rep said I was looking good for maybe a spring or summer contract. I think being sick, they don't want me so bad anymore. I fucked myself with this, though." At first Bandy felt relief, to have his doubts out in the air then he felt assailed, cornered because now the trustee knew something about him, something that was true and not history or legend.

"Fulcrum fucked you," Trinidad said. "I heard all sides and all sides say you were out before Fulcrum got banging. He's holding the bag, not you."

"If I would've kept my mouth shut."

Trinidad pushed the bed next to the window. Below was the Ad-Seg rec yard, nobody was in it; it looked cold outside.

"I could get you work in the world if you got out," Trinidad said. "I got a brother keeps real busy over Montana way. Pays pretty good but there's no health plan." He smiled. "No retirement either, unless you count what we're doing here."

Bandy turned and looked at him, shook his head. "If I get out, I'm staying out."

"Maybe I'll have him get in touch with you and make sure you don't change your mind. Because things change. The world's changed. You might need the work. You been in here a long time."

"I got my kid waiting."

"That's good, really good, but sometimes they don't like you so much when you're standing in front of them in civvies. When there's no wall between you."

"My boy doesn't know me as anything but this."

"Like I said."

"He wants to see me. He's got me all set up."

"If you got it handled, you got it handled." Trinidad smiled again, not in such a friendly way this time, and left Bandy. He went and put the other men's trays on their bunks and Frizzy made a stink over it being cold. Trinidad hit him one quick punch in the eye and took his food away without letting him have any. The blond man covered his eye and started to protest but Trinidad came back and stood over the bed and the man rolled over and didn't move. Trinidad went out then and the blond man got up and stole another man's tray and took it back to his bed and ate with his back to Bandy.

The sky was blue and cloudless. The prison walls framed it all around and Bandy knew the fields were out there going on forever beyond the walls but he could only look up to the sky and down into the blacktop yard. A man was there now, stretching his back, walking, then he stopped and looked up to the sky and he and Bandy both looked up; it was only blue and because of that and because of its emptiness Bandy thought it was much harder to face than the wall.

Two days later he was judged fit to stand and returned to his cell. The door was already open when they got there and he was pushed inside and he stumbled and fell to the floor. The door racked home behind him. He picked himself up off of the floor and sat down on his bunk. His body hurt. He lay down. The furnace must still be busted, he thought. He blew out a lungful of air but couldn't see his breath. It was still cold. He kicked the scratchy wool blanket onto his legs then pulled it to his chest.

Fulcrum started coughing. Bandy waited for him to say something but he never did. Eventually the cell lights were shut down and only the lights on the catwalk remained. Hours later, near dawn, all sound on the tier ceased and the echoes stopped and Bandy finally slept.

In the morning Fulcrum stayed in his cell hiding under his blanket while everyone else went to chow. Bandy left him to it.

Trinidad found Bandy in the mess hall and sat down. "Penry's a vegetable," he said. "Brain dead, not damaged. I hear Fulcrum might not be taking the hit for it, either. It might go to you." The noise of the feeding prisoners was a steady roar in the chow hall but Trinidad kept his voice at a whisper and held his forearm over his mouth so nobody could see what he was saying.

"Why aren't I in De-Seg then?"

"Maybe they're waiting for it to play out on its own." The frog-faced man smiled, dark eyes almost childish. "I could talk to Crookshank. He'd listen to me."

"I'll take care of myself."

"It wouldn't cost you anything."

"Everything costs something."

"My favors are good favors."

Bandy stood and dumped his tray and waited by the door. He went back to his block after chow even though he was up for yard time.

Fulcrum wasn't in his cell and his cage was locked down. Bandy went to his bunk and looked at pictures of the ranch and fell asleep reading Tracy's most recent letter. He woke and thought he heard Fulcrum moving around in his cell and called out to him but there was no reply. "I'm hearing things I don't like," Bandy said. "You better talk to me. You better say something." If Fulcrum was in his cell, and Bandy was almost sure that he was, he remained silent.

The next day Bandy talked a rookie CO into giving him a pass to visit the Education Center and he set up another appointment to speak with the legal-aid rep. As he was signing the sheet the rep was on his way out the door and he told Bandy to write his name and ID number on a piece of paper and he'd look it up and see him next Tuesday. The rep was a different one than the last one he'd seen. This one was a young kid, probably still in college, with mousy hair and yellow teeth while the last had been an older black woman. Bandy thanked him and went to shake his hand but the rep just looked at it.

"The other lady already started my paperwork," Bandy said.

"I'll call her," the rep said. Then he left. Bandy sat down at an empty table and flipped through a stack of pamphlets about adult education and let himself imagine what it would be like if he got out. He thought of Trinidad's offer: nothing he hadn't done before, nothing he wanted to do again. His hour passed quickly then they told him to stand in the box by the door and when the CO came by he was led back to the tier and into his cell.

On Friday Fulcrum and Bandy and twelve others in their pod were up for showers. The shower room had a concrete floor and tile everywhere else and no dividing walls. The showerheads were spaced every three feet so the sprays intermingled and the men were forced to be close to each other but there were twice as many showerheads as men so they spaced out. Bandy went and stood next to Fulcrum. The cold room quickly filled with steam.

"Why're you dodging me?" Bandy said.

"I'm not," he said. He was lying. Bandy knew that he was lying. "Crookshank's full-timing me. I was assed-out before the stairs, before Penry."

"That's your problem."

"I owed Penry two in white."

"For what?"

"It doesn't matter. I owed him and now I owe Crookshank."

The CO watching them horse-whistled at a couple of guys at the end of the line and told them to knock off the grabass then he turned and went out to the other room where there were benches and a wall of sinks, brushed steel mirrors. Fulcrum stood on his toes and pressed his forehead into the thin spray of water then stood flat-footed and looked at Bandy. "Crookshank says if I burn you for Penry, he'll forget the two."

"That doesn't make any sense."

"Yeah, it does. I got everything set up outside. He doesn't want to lose me. But he needs somebody to fall under the tires."

Bandy watched Fulcrum's face, all the lines and components. He was Bandy's closest friend.

"I ain't kidding you, brother. He wants somebody for this and it ain't me."

Bandy shut off the water to his shower and rested his hand on the shut-off valve. "Why're you telling me this now?"

"Because unless you got a shiv in the cupboard"—he rocked his chin at Bandy's waist—"I got nothing to worry about. Right now, you're just another sickass naked motherfucker and I ain't scared a naked. We're friends, brothers, so I had to tell you straight up, but I'm not dumb enough to do it when you're bristled."

"Don't do this." A steady cold rage was building in his stomach.

"What does it matter? If they let you out, which they won't, you'll be too sick to enjoy it. Hell, you'd only be in De-Seg for eight months. Sixteen at the most. As long as you been in here, what the fuck is another sixteen months?"

Without thinking through what he was doing, Bandy snatched Fulcrum by the ear and the back of the neck and bashed his forehead into the shut-off handle as hard as he could until Fulcrum went limp. It happened very quickly then it was over. Nobody seemed to have seen it through the steam or heard it over the sound of the water and the talking. The CO was still in the other room. With clenched fists, trembling, Bandy stood over his friend and let the water spray over his shoulders. A stream of dark yellow piss ran from Fulcrum and swirled in the clear water. Bandy stepped over him and went to the doorway and called to the CO that he was done and the CO said to come out and Bandy went and picked up a towel from the cart and took his kit down from the shelf like he was going to have a shave, but he didn't know what he was going to do. He felt like he should run.

The CO watched him then went back to reading his magazine. One of the men from inside called out then several that Fulcrum was hurt. The CO looked at Bandy. He was young, slightly demented looking, the same man that Bandy had talked out of a pass to the Education Center.

"You saw him when I came out," Bandy said. "He was fine. You saw him." After a moment the CO nodded yes because he was supposed to have been watching everybody the whole time and only let the inmates move as a group.

The CO went out shaking his head and Bandy sat down on the bench with the towel over his lap and rested his hands on his knees. There was a lot of talking and yelling in the showers then more COs came in. Crookshank arrived and the smell of liquor came with him. He was a big, top-heavy man with a crooked face. He stared openly at Bandy then told him to get up and go back inside. Fulcrum wasn't moving and nobody was doing anything to help him.

"Turn that fucking water off," Crookshank said. The convicts hesitated a moment then did as they were told. Crookshank asked the young CO what had happened and the CO said Fulcrum must've slipped.

"Where was he?" Crookshank said, and pointed at Bandy, motioning to the towel around his waist.

"He was already out."

"You were watching them both?"

"No," the CO said nervously.

Bandy's legs were weak and his blood was pumping in his ears. The steam began to fade and the other men hugged themselves and covered their shriveled penises and the COs with glasses took them off and wiped the steam from them on their undershirts. Fulcrum's head rested in a small, pink pool of blood and his feet were curled together one on top of the other. He was facing Bandy. His forehead was bloody and looked dented like it was made out of cardboard. One of the convicts asked how long they had to stand there freezing their dicks off. Crookshank told the green CO to take them out and Bandy went out of the room with everyone else and didn't look back. Nobody was allowed to shave. They dressed and slipped on their shoes and picked up their kits and stood by the door. The buzzer for morning count went off and the CO told everyone to hurry the fuck up and they were walked back to the cells and the count took twice as long with them being late and everybody complaining.

Chapter 8

SACKCLOTH AND ASHES

IT WAS DARK when Crookshank and three other COs came to Bandy's cell. No one spoke. The door opened. He didn't protest. There wasn't anyone that could help him. It was always strange and slightly exciting to be out and around in the off hours. They went down the stairs and through the sally port and silently passed the UC cage and through three more gates then down two flights of stairs deep into the basement. Their footfalls echoed down a long, well-lit hallway.

They went through a door marked CURRICULUM STRATEGIES and Bandy was pushed into a chair. The door closed. There was a desk against the wall and Crookshank sat on it. The other COs stood. A plain, windowless room. They'd passed a dozen other doors identical to the one they'd come in, and Bandy wondered if the rooms were all the same, mirroring the cells above, an equatorial split. He feared he might be killed and didn't want to die below ground.

Crookshank handed Bandy a medical report with his name on it and told him that he'd tested positive for hepatitis C. Bandy had no idea what that meant.

"Doc says you're pretty far gone," Crookshank said. "Your liver. I guess you've been sick for awhile, now it's caught up with you." He tapped his temple with his index finger then pointed at Bandy.

"Trinidad told me I should be nice to you. He said you aren't the one I'm looking for, says you're up for discharge. He's right. I looked into it. Unbelievable, the state of things to let someone like you back out." He smiled.

Bandy didn't say anything. The CO from the shower was there and he wouldn't look Bandy in the eye. Stan from the UC was there as well. The third CO was familiar but Bandy had never spoken to him.

"I know it was Lyman that took Penry down. Fulcrum, whatever the fuck you call him. The charge will go to him, not you. So you know."

"Is he dead?"

"No, he's in the ICU at St. Al's sleeping off his little slip in the shower." Crookshank's relaxed manner suddenly dropped away and he stood up and punched Bandy in the sternum. The light spun in the room and Bandy gasped for air and wanted to lift his hands above his head to relax his lungs but he resisted the urge. It passed, then Crookshank hit him in the chest again but this time Bandy was ready and he breathed out before he was hit and it wasn't as bad.

"Penry died last night." Crookshank looked stiffly around the room at his subordinates, sighed, flexed his right hand. "You want it?" he said to the CO from the shower. "He dumped that assault-injury on your jacket. That'll be there for a career, Mike. You deserve something for that."

"I'm not doing shit, sir," the CO, Mike, said. "I don't even want to be here."

"It ain't his fault," Bandy said.

"Mike," Crookshank pleaded. Mike shook his head no and stepped back against the wall. "Boys? I know Penry was a bit of a douchebag, but still—he was our douchebag. He would've done it for you. With vigor, he would've done it. Just crack him a couple. We gotta at least make a showing here." While Crookshank was speaking none of the COs even looked at him. They weren't going to do it. Bandy knew he should feel relieved but he didn't. Something should be done. He didn't know what, but something.

"It's my wife's birthday today," Crookshank said. "I guess it wouldn't really seem right." He cocked back to hit Bandy again but pulled his punch and patted him on the chest instead. "Did we scare you?"

Bandy didn't see the point in lying. "Yeah," he said. He felt emptied out, as if something important had escaped, some necessary ballast. The medical report was on the floor. Crookshank muttered something about how he had to order a birthday cake and went out. Bandy was given the report and lifted from the chair and taken back to his cell. He'd told Trinidad he didn't want any favors but now he owed him; it was the way things were.

After that, time went very slowly. Bandy's health continued to decline and he was put on a special diet and no longer allowed to eat with the general population. Trustees brought his medication and meals. He rarely left his cell except for showers. He began having nightmares. Twice he woke up and Crookshank was standing outside of his cell watching him, arms crossed, smiling. Bandy closed his eyes and opened them and he was still there. He never spoke.

Christmas and New Year's came and went without celebration. Even the truly hard convicts sometimes bent under the weight of the holidays. The mood was that of a siege. There were three suicides in one week and one of them was Fulcrum. The talk on the tier was that the doctors at St. Al's had drilled a hole in Fulcrum's head to drain the blood and relieve the pressure on his brain, but the hole didn't heal right and became infected. By the time he returned to Indian Creek, he was done. He was no longer protected or strong enough to take care of himself. Bandy felt bad for his old friend, but he'd made his choice and that choice had opened his veins.

In the middle of January the U.S. started a bombing campaign against Iraq. Bandy had almost forgotten that he was in America at all, that he was an American. He had no idea where Iraq was or what the war was really about. He heard talk but that's all it was, nobody inside could know for sure. He thought maybe nobody outside knew either, but he was relieved that the U.S. was again at war because it meant that his country finally hated someone more than him.

He was transferred to the minimum-security cellblock and given a cellmate, a man named Williams, an older black man; he was soft-spoken with nervous hands. Bandy quit reading Tracy's letters and destroyed many of the photographs. Insomnia became a problem. At one point the doctor had said that a certain level of dementia was to be expected with his condition. The legal rep came and went, came and went.

He woke from the dream and Williams was sitting on his chest with both hands pressed to his forehead holding him down.

"You okay," Williams said. "Quit screaming. You okay."

Bandy pushed the old man toward the wall and squirmed from beneath him and struck him several times in the face then crawled across the floor to the corner and sat with his knees pulled to his chest.

Williams was hurt and bleeding from his nose. "Crazy person," he said. "They give me a crazy person." He screamed at Bandy like a madman and Bandy realized he was being mimicked and screamed too and it felt like he'd reentered the dream. He pressed the heels of his hands into his eyes until he saw white light. He heard piano music. He looked up at Williams again and time must've passed because he had toilet paper stuffed in his nostrils and he was back on his bunk watching Bandy.

"I never had no problem with you," he said. "Williams goes easy. I never said nothing to you, did nothing to you. Been a month of screaming and talking to yourself. Never sleeping even when you're sleeping. I don't say nothing. I figure you gone out your head." Williams nodded vigorously. "I figured right."

Bandy apologized. In his mind he saw the words. He couldn't be sure of what came out of his mouth, something. Williams nodded, seemingly placated, then: "Hell on me," he said loudly. "Morning, noon, and always at night. People say it's bad in Ad-Seg but I begged the motherfuckers to put me in there. Get away from you." Bandy went to stand and Williams jumped up and stood in a fighting crouch on his bunk. "Don't come fucking near me," he screamed. His eyes were ice blue from glaucoma and made for a strange contrast with his dark skin. He was gaunt to the point of severe malnutrition and his large infantile forehead matched the curve of his swollen stomach. Bandy put his hand to his own face and was surprised to feel a beard. He touched his scalp and wondered when they'd shaved his head. "My God," Bandy said.

"You been talking to him too, fucking wingnut." Williams screamed at him again, doing an obvious impersonation, mixing in a few jumbled words of prayer. Bandy didn't pray, didn't remember praying. He worried that there could be more unknown segments of his personality than known.

Williams sat down again. "I ain't killed anybody for twenty-seven years, but if you touch me again, you'll wake up dead. Hear me?"

"I hear you."

A week later, Williams was transferred to another cell. Then Bandy's contract went through. It just happened, like it had never been an issue at all. He was released and put on a bus to Boise. From there, he caught another bus north to Lake Fork.

A few miles outside of town he asked the driver to pull over and after a short argument he got off the bus and stood in the road, looked west. The snowbanks were melting and the hair and bones of a roadkill deer were piled up wet and matted at the pavement's edge. Blackbirds sat on the telephone wires as black and unmoving as the wire they were perched on. He walked on stiff legs down a long hill. Cars blew by him without slowing. At the bottom of the hill a road branched east and he followed that for half a mile then went north on Farm to Market toward town, away from his parents' house. He wanted to see town first. Lake Fork had always pulled him away from the ranch and still did. He walked and watched the road, transfixed by it. Where the asphalt wasn't buried in snow it was cracked and filled with dead weeds or smeared with tar, different layers and permanence, fleeting and firm.

Soon he was exhausted and stopped and stood. There were houses scattered along the road and in the fields; no cars in the driveways, no pets, some trash, debris that looked to have been blown in: tarps, axes stuck in splitting blocks, bark and kindling from the remnants of the woodpiles, children's toys as colorful as candy. With the dwindling snowpack the houses seemed to be emerging from an ice age, completely depopulated but somehow standing.

So now I'm out, he thought. He didn't trust any of it. He'd had this dream before. He looked down at his feet and at the slush puddle he was standing in. The shoes they had given him were cheap and thin and now they were soaked and cold.

Breathe, he told himself. He breathed. There were no cars in sight but he could hear them. I can't be out here. In the name of the convicted, the guilty, and the innocent I pronounce you fucked in broad daylight. You're out. You are out. He leaned back on his heels and splashed around in the puddle with his toes then stomped his feet, water went everywhere and it was pretty in the sun.

Crookshank had come to his cell personally to tell him that he was being released. He seemed pleased to pass on the information and even shook Bandy's hand. The CO on R&D came to his cell later that week. "Let's go," he said.

Bandy stood up from his bunk, terrified. "I'm not ready." The CO laughed at him and took him by the arm and led him through the doorway. They walked off the tier and nobody said a word; it was a silence that didn't exist. He saw all the mouths moving, spit flying and twisted faces.

Over the course of several hours he was processed and led through more hallways that he'd never seen or couldn't remember seeing. He was given a small gym bag with his things and two weeks' worth of his medicine in it, prescriptions for more. He was taken to the last sally port. He looked inside the bag they'd given him while he waited for the last door to open and found a bottle cap in the bottom underneath his wallet and the rest. He imagined how these things had been locked up as long as he had and traveled thousands of miles between different lockups. He wondered why someone hadn't just thrown it all out. His wallet was empty. He was given a manila envelope with a check for $364.55 in it, and a printout showing his total wages minus what he owed on the canteen books.

The wind blew over the snowbanks and cut through his clothes and chilled him. He clenched his fists and dug his nails into his palms and tried to make himself believe that he was outside. The cold was real. The air was real.

The car was a station wagon. It stopped and waited for Bandy to move. He'd wandered out into the road. He'd forgotten where he was. The station wagon switched off its engine. The driver's-side door opened. He didn't want to move. He smelled the cold metal smell of snowmelt.

"Bandy?" Iona said.

He closed his eyes and didn't open them.

"There're cars coming. You need to get out of the road." Iona took him by the elbow and he leapt back as if he'd been sprayed by a hose. He stumbled and stepped into the snowbank up to his knee. He avoided looking at her and went back to the road and stomped his foot and settled the snow deep into his shoe and considered taking it off then decided against it and turned and started walking, limping slightly toward town.

"It's all right. It's me," Iona called after him, quietly like she always had. He kept walking. This bad dream, he'd seen this before. He heard the car start behind him then two big diesel flatbed trucks drove by. One was loaded with fence posts and a massive spool of barbed wire while the other was hauling a large plastic container that Bandy thought might be a swimming pool until he read the lettering on the rail of the bed and realized it was a septic tank. The drivers of both trucks were young men, kids almost, tan with short hair, one jug-eared and both obstinate in their unwavering stares. He stopped when the station wagon pulled up beside him, but didn't turn to face her when she spoke.

"Do you want to walk in, or do you want a ride?" Iona said. "I won't tell Tracy I saw you if you don't want me to."

He felt like he was being marched up against a wall to be shot.

He turned and looked at her. It was all wrong, she was old. He'd never thought of her old. How had he thought of her? All ways but not old. "Why are you here?" His voice sounded foreign in his own ears, menacing almost.

"Should I be scared of you?"

"No," he said. "God, no."

"Get in the car then. I can't leave you out here looking like that."

He looked at the parts of himself that he could see, none of which seemed to be the parts he thought Iona was talking about.

"Just get in. It's all right. Just come on."

He walked around the back of the car. There were cans of paint and brushes and rollers in the back all laid out on a drop cloth. He climbed stiffly into the passenger seat. Iona started the car and put it in gear. He couldn't remember the last time he'd ridden in the front seat of a car. It seemed very small and bullet fast.

"You look sick," Iona said, not looking away from the road.

"I don't have AIDS."

"I didn't say that."

"It's my liver." He held the gym bag on his lap like an old woman would hold her purse. Iona glanced at it. In his mind he could hear the change hitting the dresser top, the bottle caps bouncing off and falling to the floor, his wallet, his keys, the jangle of the chain on the lamp when Iona woke up.

"What you got there?"

"Nothing."

Iona nodded. "They give you an empty bag when they let you out?" She kept both her hands on the steering wheel.

"It's not empty. It's got my wallet and stuff in it. My medicine. I have a check I need cashed."

"All right. I have to stop at Mort's and you can go to the bank."

"Who's Mort?"

"The hardware store. The bank's across the street."

"I know where the bank is."

"There're three banks in town now."

Bandy toyed with the zipper on the gym bag. "That paint's strong. The fumes."

"I'm doing a property-management thing."

"A what?" He felt deaf and his vision seemed to dim, as if his senses were retreating from the overstimulation.

"I clean summer houses that have been sitting all winter and get them ready for the owners. I do little repair stuff, but mostly painting, a lot of painting, house-sitting too." She seemed happy, or terrified, he couldn't be sure. "We were working on your parents' house while Tracy was still in the hospital, getting it ready for him when he came home. I met some people that were looking for help and they introduced me to more people. It's better here now; the town, working here. There's more money blowing around and people aren't as ignorant and mean as I remember them. Maybe it's just me. Maybe I got older. Of course I got older. We both did, but this place is changed. You'll see." She paused. "I'm talking too much."

"You sound different than I remember."

"So do you." She rolled her window down and a receipt slid across the dashboard and almost blew out Bandy's window but he snatched it out of the air and gave it to her. He was careful not to touch her hand. He was surprised his body had reacted. He looked out over the hay fields along the road, the shorn rows spiking through the melting snow, the taller stalks from the turn of the swather at the far edge of the field like dust blown into a corner.

More houses everywhere, also blown-in looking, storm delivered, random. Maybe a little fear is normal, he thought. Nothing about you is normal.

There was an unnamed lake that Bandy and his father had hiked to a few times. The winter after Neil Guntly died Bandy snowshoed to the lake by himself. When he got there he stood on the lake ice and he knew where he was but still had a hard time recognizing it. The winter had stolen it. And as they entered Lake Fork he felt the same sensation of slow discovery and wonder and loss at the buried things, the missing things. There were still landmarks to orient by: the mountains, most of the big trees still stood and some of the small ones had grown large, and of course there was the lake. But the buildings, the hotels and restaurants that crowded the shoreline confused it all. He felt lost in time. The city jail had the doors swung open and a new cedar fence had been built around it with a sign hung on the gate advertising it as a historical site, a place of interest.

"I did my first night in there," Bandy said.

"I remember."

He felt rotten and was about to apologize and explain himself—for what? Twenty years ago? He didn't even know this woman. That was a lie. He wished he didn't know her but he did. He knew her better than he'd known any woman, and that was the truth.

She pulled into the hardware store parking lot and shut off the car. He didn't want to get out. He felt something should be said, some instruction given. Iona got out and came around to his side and leaned down and looked in on him through the open window. She pointed across the street. "First Trust is right over there. I'll be fifteen or twenty minutes."

He opened the door and Iona stepped back. He got out of the car and held his bag against his stomach.

"Are you going to be all right?"

"I'll meet you back here." He felt guilty even looking at the people on the street and in the cars as they drove by. He glanced at Iona.

"It's okay," she said.

It's okay, he thought. I'm out. Out of my fucking head. He took a few steps away from the car and stood in the middle of the sidewalk then turned and looked at Iona again. "I don't know," he said. The wind blew a plastic cup down the sidewalk and it bounced off Bandy's foot and he kicked at it and it tumbled on.

"You'll be all right." Iona smiled and walked away. Bandy felt terribly exposed and alone after she'd gone. He stood and watched traffic then turned and he could see the lake between the buildings with the ice mostly melted and the clouds reflected in the black water that looked like ice, or a picture of ice, ice with no mass. He stepped into the street without looking and was almost run down by a lumber truck. His heart was pounding in his chest and he felt that he might as well be naked because it all felt like that dream, that naked dream.

The line at the bank was long and when Bandy opened his bag to get his wallet people stopped talking and turned to watch him. He awkwardly held up the envelope with his check so they could see it and they went back to looking at the teller and the clock above her. His father used to bring him to the bank with him. He'd always been proud to walk in the door with the old man. People respected him because he never gave them a reason not to. Bandy realized that for as long as he lived this would never be the case.

The teller cashed his check without asking to see any ID. The transaction was impersonal enough to seem familiar and for some reason this annoyed him. He needed to be confirmed as a free man, but he didn't say a word. The teller counted out the money and fumbled it into an envelope before handing it over. Bandy snatched it out of her hand and crammed it into his wallet, change and all, and left the bank.

Iona was waiting in the car with the engine running and the radio on. He got in. She turned off the radio.

"All done?"

"I thought people would've forgot about me."

She backed the car onto the street and joined the flow of south bound traffic. "It was in the paper that you were getting out."

"Ah fuck."

She nodded. "Anything else you need to do before I take you home?"

"Why the hell would they put that in the paper?"

"It's still a small town."

"Is it?" he said. Angry, he felt betrayed.

"People are curious."

He felt sick to his stomach. "Bunch of assholes that don't know how to forget."

"That's one way to look at it."

They drove by a new church on Lake Street then another on the highway outside of town. Bandy pointed at the sweeping rake of the roof rising from the field like the prow of a giant land-locked ship.

"They're putting them up everywhere," Iona said. "Bible churches, Mormons, Seventh Day Adventists—there's a whole revival thing going on. Don't tell me you haven't been saved."

He looked at her and she smiled but he could tell she was forcing it. "I had enough of the Jesus freaks, ya know? They run 'em pretty heavy inside."

"You want to know something weird?" she said. "I listen to them on the radio. I don't know why. Most of the time they piss me off but I still listen."

"I haven't heard them on the radio."

"It's all the same. It's stupid, I know it's stupid. I think I like them to make me mad."

"Better than buying into it."

"Not if they're right."

"They ain't right. They might not be wrong, but they ain't right."

"We can only hope."

He knew what she expected him to say so he said it. "Pray," he said. Iona smiled.

They passed the scattered businesses on the highway, the storage units and snowmobile dealerships and dropped lower into the southeastern edge of the valley onto the roads that Bandy recognized, roads that hadn't much changed. But instead of turning left off of the highway toward the ranch, she turned into a gas station and parked in the back of the lot away from the pumps. They sat in the car.

"How's this going to work?" she said.

"I don't know."

She turned and leaned against the door and studied him. "How sick are you? Are you dying?"

"I'm fine."

"You're a liar."

"Do we need to get gas or are we just sitting here?"

She started the car and backed recklessly across the lot to the pumps. "Go ahead."

He got out of the car and turned on the pump and unscrewed the cap and watched the numbers tick by and breathed in the fumes and got a head rush from it. He finished and hung up the pump. Iona was writing something in a notebook, a ledger: all business. She didn't need him, surely didn't want him.

When Bandy came in, the clerk stepped back from the counter and bumped into the cigarette display and knocked a few packs to the floor. She had binoculars in her hand and Bandy realized that she used them to read the numbers on the pump. He'd startled her; he walked slowly toward the counter and pulled out his wallet. He laid down the money he owed.

"Please, don't come in here again," the woman said. Her hair was dyed a dark red and her face was aged but pretty beneath her makeup.

"I've never been in here before."

"I know who you are. I know your son." She paused. "Ben Meeks was my brother. You paid your debt, I understand, but don't come in here and make me look at you." The woman had long red fingernails and she saw Bandy looking at them and made a fist so he couldn't. "You can get your gas somewhere else."

"I won't come back." The bells jingled on the door as he went out and the woman watched him through the front window and when he got to the car he turned to see if she was still watching and she was. He climbed inside. "This isn't how I thought it'd be."

"How'd you think it would be?"

"I thought I'd be nobody."

"Maybe you are." She turned and looked at him, really looked at him. "I'll kill you if you hurt him. Do you understand me?"

"Yes," he said. It felt like the first time he'd said the word, like the first time he'd meant it. "Why'd you give him my name?"

"Because he's yours."

"Besides that."

"There isn't any besides that."

"He could just as well be somebody else's."

"He isn't. You can tell by looking."

"I don't know," Bandy said. "I don't know."

"Why in the hell would I give him your name unless I had to?"

They pulled out of the gas station and crossed the highway and drove over the hills. They turned east at the church which had also been marked as a historical site. The graveyard was covered with snow. They went down the narrow dirt road that led to the ranch. The clouds were fat and unmoving overhead. Iona drove slowly to avoid the ruts. They drove over the ground where he'd killed the policeman. He could see the roof line of the barn in the distance. The barbed-wire fences were sagging from the weight of the winter and the small snowbanks were coated in gravel and looked like plain dirt. "You mind stopping the car?"

Iona stopped.

"Is he up and around yet?"

"He's still in his chair. He has therapy two days a week."

"You have to pay for that?"

"What do you think?"

"I don't know."

"Yeah, we have to pay for it."

"It costs a lot though?"

"We'll figure it out."

He felt like the car was moving even though they were stopped. To the north and east he saw a housing development and once he saw that he started picking out dozens of new houses tucked in the trees on the mountainside. He pointed at them and Iona said simply, quietly: "New." He wondered where these new people had come from and for what reason they chose his valley.

"There's a couple of big developers from California that have been buying the old farms. They cut them up for subdivisions. Pretty soon you'll have your own little island."

"I don't want an island."

She pointed to the fields to the north and south. "All this is either selling or sold. They're going to build a golf course, a clubhouse and a restaurant, condos, custom homes."

Bandy raised his hands from his lap a few inches then put them back down.

"Yeah, I know," she said. "A strange wind, as they say."

"You can drive now. I'm as ready as I'm gonna be." He smiled, miserable, transparently so. "You stay out here, too?"

She glanced at him and shifted in her seat. "I can leave if you want."

"That's not what I meant. The kid said you married Bill."

"He died, Bandy, almost two years ago. I thought you knew that much. And his name's Tracy, not the kid."

"You married again?"

"No. I moved down here to help Tracy. That's all. I'm not doing anything but that."

"Are you gonna stay? It sounds like you like it here. You're doing good."

"I don't know what I'm gonna do. I work every day. I come home every night. That's all."

"Go on and drive," he said. "I'm ready."

They parked in the driveway in the dancing shadows of the

willow tree and sat in the car. Bandy hadn't seen the ranch since the cabin had burned. He'd never seen it with his parents dead in the ground. He imagined his mother stooping beneath the hanging branches of the willow to greet him. His father staying in the barn until it was dark and long after that and finally coming inside and sitting down at the table surrounded in a cloud of cool air, getting the bag balm for his hands, a cup of black coffee before bed. He and Bandy used to sit at the table and talk about when Bandy would be running the place, how with a little luck, maybe another world war, he could turn a profit. It was never morbid, this speculation, and looking back this seemed strange. They'd been talking about Jack Dorner dying, but they'd also been talking about Bandy living on.

There were two pickups parked in the driveway near the house. Smoke dumped from the chimney in weak bursts. Ruined blue tarps were stretched across the west side of the barn roof and someone's old tractor was parked in the empty hay shed. All of the snow from the driveway had been pushed up into a neat, long wedge. The snow where the cabin had been was unmarked and showed no sign of ever being anything. He couldn't be sure he was even looking in the right place.

He got out and walked around the car then stopped and waited. He whistled, waited; no dog. There should be a law. He remembered the snow strewn with mud and shit and hay from fall to spring, like a bomb went off. A cow bawled inside the barn and the sound hung in the air then moved away like the shadow of a bird. He left Iona and went into the barn through the tack room but all the tack was gone from there, only a stiff and cracked bridle hung from the wall, the metal parts rusted black. The door shut behind him and it was dark. He held onto the coarse leather of the bridle with one hand

and waited for his eyes to adjust. Dad, he thought, and almost said it. He missed his mother and father and it would get worse. There was a wad of burlap sacks in the corner with a rock dropped on top of them to keep them there and for a second he took it to be a cat and he sucked his teeth at it but then his eyes righted and he saw it for what it was and smiled to himself, sucked his teeth at himself. The steer bawled again, louder this time. It brought its hooves down nervously, forcefully onto the floorboards and stretched its neck out over the gate. Bandy went to it and rubbed the knot on the top of its head and it bawled again and showed the whites of its eyes. A thin string of drool swung from its bottom lip.

"You've got lungs," Bandy said. He could hear people talking outside the barn. "I might just stay out here with you. That be all right?" The steer tried to lick his arm and he pushed it away by its jaw. Iona called to Bandy and a chill washed over him. "I guess it's time," he said.

His cheap shoes sounded wrong on the barn floorboards. Like an invalid, he shuffled through the yellow light of the tack room and stepped into the glare of the driveway. Again it took a moment for his eyes to adjust. There were three people in front of him. Two of them were easy enough to pick out from their silhouettes: Tracy in the wheelchair, Iona being a woman with long hair, but the third—his eyes were coming back, the mist of the sunlight swirling and the shadows coming together.

"Don't look so stupid. You remember me. Jesus, you were bigger at fourteen than you are now."

Bandy couldn't place the voice.

"It's Wilhelm Guntly," Wilhelm said.

Bandy walked over and shook Wilhelm's hand but the old man seemed taken aback so Bandy let go and stepped away and took

Tracy's hand instead and held it. Thinking the whole time: I'm doing everything wrong. They looked at each other. "You don't look so bad," Bandy said.

"No," Tracy said. Bandy felt thin and sick when his son looked at him. Wilhelm came up beside him and stabbed a bony finger into his ribs.

"It looks like someone put you in a dehydrator," the old man said. Bandy forced a smile. "Tooth's missing," Wilhelm said.

"Stop being an asshole goddamnit," Tracy said. "He just got here."

"Well, look at him. He'll get it worse than that. He better get used to it," Wilhelm said.

"Wilhelm knows me," Bandy said to Tracy.

"I know of you," Wilhelm said meanly. He hadn't bothered to lace up his boots when he came outside and the tongues lolled out beneath his bunched-up pants. "Why'd you come back here?" he said to Bandy.

"Because I asked him to," Tracy said.

"I'm asking him," Wilhelm said.

"Where was I supposed to go?" Bandy said.

"Someplace else, I'd say. Look at you. Goddamn look at yourself," Wilhelm said. "Typhoid Bandy, bringing home the disease."

"Wilhelm," Iona said, shaking her head and laughing a little. She took hold of Tracy's wheelchair. "Let's get inside. I need to make dinner."

"I ain't eating with it," Wilhelm said. "I can't hardly look at it."

"Then don't," Tracy said. "You old prick."

Bandy held up his hand in a calming gesture to Wilhelm, a normal gesture. "I should thank you for the letter that you and Ellen sent telling me about my mom."

"It was Ellen's idea," Wilhelm said. "We did it for your family, not for you."

Bandy looked out over the fields toward the low hills and the seamless rolling blanket of snow. It didn't feel fake but it didn't feel real either. "If I had another place to go."

"Here's changed."

"I seen all the new houses and shit."

"So why don't you go live in one a them?" Wilhelm said, and turned and went to his truck and got in. He rolled down the window and cranked his head around to look back and his eyes were wild for the turning. "You're tracking shit into this house." He brought his arm out the window and pointed. "You should've stayed gone and you know it. This ain't your home anymore. Don't you see, people don't want you here." He hesitated a moment then drove away.

Bandy nodded and out of nervousness worked his tongue in the gap where his tooth used to be. Tracy watched him along with Iona. He wanted to speak but he didn't know what he could say. "I'll leave," Bandy said.

"Nobody's leaving," Tracy said. "He doesn't know fuck-all."

"Tracy," Iona said.

"Well, he doesn't." Tracy leaned his weight into his wheelchair but the wheels were sunk in the mud. "Goddammit," he said. Iona pushed him toward the house. Bandy walked behind then as they neared the house he hurried around them and held open the mudroom door. Iona tipped the chair back at the threshold and rolled it over the single low step and into the mudroom. Bandy squeezed by them and opened the door into the kitchen. The chair left muddy tire tracks on the new linoleum. He went back to the mudroom and took off his shoes and returned in his stocking feet.

The kitchen was warm. Nothing was where he remembered except the woodstove and it had fallen out of use. The flue wasn't even connected and the stovepipe in the wall was plugged with a red bath towel, the stovetop covered with mail and newspapers. The walls of the kitchen had been repainted light blue. Bandy couldn't remember what color they used to be but blue wasn't it. The kitchen table beneath the window that looked out into the yard and the willow tree was in the same place but it was a different table and smaller with only three chairs instead of four. Open on the table was a copy of the *Lake Fork Observer* with a picture of Bandy taken outside of the county courthouse the day he was sentenced and another more recent picture that was taken before he'd gotten sick. Bandy leaned forward to read the caption and Iona flipped the paper shut. "It just said you were getting out," Iona said. "Not much else." Bandy looked at Iona then at Tracy.

"It's what got Wilhelm going," Tracy said. "He just read it then you showed up."

The kitchen was quiet. This is right where I am, he thought. The cabinet doors were gone and the plates and glasses were open for the viewing. It felt like a hunting cabin. Bandy couldn't imagine what his mother would do if she saw her house like this. Tracy smiled a thin smile and Iona watched her son and fidgeted with her hands, her fingernails.

Bandy didn't have anything to say and he was having trouble breathing so he left them and went into the living room. The carpet was gone and there was wood flooring in its place and Bandy figured it was the floor that had been under the carpet the whole time. The floors looked nice and they were slick beneath his feet. There was a maroon couch with a tear in the armrest and a blue recliner with an afghan folded over the back. Beside it, there was a new-looking woodstove on a prefab base and a plywood wood box. A television with rabbit ears sat on a coffee table against the wall. He heard the refrigerator open in the kitchen and Iona ask Tracy what he wanted for dinner but he couldn't hear what Tracy answered. He looked into the downstairs bedroom off of the living room. There was a bed and a table and some books, a dresser with clothes folded on top of it, nail bags in the corner: Tracy's room. He shut the door and turned and mounted the stairs. The upstairs had fresh paint too. He went into the room that used to be his when he was a boy and sat down on the box spring and mattress on the floor and took off his socks. Iona must be staying in his parents' room. He cleared his throat then rubbed his chilled feet one at a time and tried to recall exactly how the room had looked before but he couldn't even remember what the wallpaper had looked like or if there had been wallpaper at all. He stood up and tried to open the window but it had been painted shut. He smacked his palm against the sash and tried it again and it opened.

The failing sunlight easily climbed the eastern face of the mountains; the snow and dark rock and the trees seemed to be in a kind of heightened relief, as if the disappearing sun was pulling them west toward the valley floor. Logging scars and roads, the flash of metal rooftops. The line of sun continued to climb and the mountains darkened as their inner snow light was decanted: the death of the alpenglow. The clouds above the mountains had not moved; they seemed permanent. The light went blue and a chill came on suddenly and Bandy shut the window. He sat back down on the bed then climbed under the blankets with all of his clothes on. He knew Tracy and Iona were downstairs wondering what he was doing, but he was too tired to worry. He pulled the pillow under his head and sooner than he could've hoped he was asleep.

It was dark and silent when he woke up. He stayed perfectly still and listened to the sounds of cooking downstairs, pots and pans, a stove door banged shut. He tried to orient himself in the direction of the door. He couldn't be sure. Then a light came on in the hall and Bandy realized he had left the door open while he was sleeping and that was something in itself. Shadows swept across the hallway wall as someone came up the stairs. He sat up. The half-lit figure of Iona stood in the door.

"You're awake," she said.

"Just now."

"I made dinner if you want to eat."

"Okay." Bandy smelled food then and wondered if that was what woke him. His stomach was tight with hunger. Iona turned and left and Bandy got out of bed and pulled on his damp socks and went downstairs holding onto the handrail.

The TV was on in the living room but no one was watching it. Tracy and Iona were both in the kitchen. Bandy stood in the doorway and blinked and smiled a little. He pressed his hair flat and wished he'd taken a look in a mirror before he came down.

"Have a seat," Tracy said.

Bandy pulled up a chair across from his son. The newspaper from earlier was folded up on the windowsill under a small ceramic chicken with sugar and a spoon in it. I'm in a kitchen, he thought. He felt like he was in a TV show. Iona served Tracy and Bandy each a plate with a pork chop and steamed carrots and a baked potato then served herself and poured three glasses of milk and sat down in the middle chair facing the window. They hesitated for a moment then Tracy started in and Iona then Bandy.

The food tasted better than he could've imagined; it was almost overwhelming. As he ate he was thinking tomorrow I can get up and cook for myself. I don't care if it's a bowl of cereal. I'll get up early and no one will be here to watch me or sit with me or tell me what or where or count me or care what I do. That was something, he thought, like an alarm had sounded: wanting to be alone.

After he finished, Bandy thanked Iona again for the food. He looked at her; he stared. Again he thought, she has gotten old. I'm old. He had an urge to open the paper on the sill just so he could see his young face again. The heat of the kitchen was making him sweat through his undershirt.

"I'll do the dishes," Bandy said.

"No you won't," Iona said. "Go on in there with Tracy."

"Come on," Tracy said, and wheeled himself back from the table. "I thought Wilhelm would've called and begged forgiveness by now," he said to his mother.

"He'll call tomorrow," she said.

"He won't stay mad," Tracy said to Bandy.

"I know him," Bandy said. "Or I knew him. He'll stay mad enough."

Tracy shrugged his shoulders and said, "Maybe he will, maybe he won't," and wheeled himself into the living room. Bandy stood up and followed him.

Fulcrum used to say there were exactly three different types of people, but he never told Bandy what they were. Bandy thought now maybe he knew: free, convict, and ex-convict. That about summed it up. Once one comes in contact with the other they aren't the same. Maybe Wilhelm was right, maybe I am tracking shit into this house.

They watched a nature show about bald eagles in Alaska.

"I'm on all kinds of drugs," Tracy said later without prompting. "If you were wondering why I'm being weird."

"I didn't notice," Bandy said. The braces on Tracy's legs were splattered with mud from the driveway. "It hurts I guess, your legs."

"It's bad in the morning."

"You'll heal. It'll take time but you'll be up and at it."

Tracy looked at Bandy. "What about you? Last time I saw you, you were a beast."

"I'm all right. It's my liver."

"That's bad isn't it?"

"Could be worse. They got me on some medicine. It ain't so bad." The narrator on television was British and Bandy liked to listen to him talk.

"I'm pretty tired of being babied, ya know." Tracy yawned and sang a few notes then looked at Bandy blinking with watery eyes. "I just want to be normal again."

"You should feel lucky."

"I know. But Ma's always hovering, and Wilhelm. I don't mean to sound ungrateful."

"It's how you sound."

"I am grateful."

"You should be."

"I'm not complaining."

Bandy was irritated by the kid and thought it was a little early for that.

Tracy picked a piece of dead grass from the wheel of his chair. "It's weird, isn't it?"

"What?"

"Being out. Sitting here. I don't even know you. Ma being here, and she knows all about you. Things I'll never know." He rocked back and forth in his chair. "Maybe things I don't want to know."

He laughed a little. "If I were you, I'd be bouncing off the walls. I mean, what a mess to walk into since the last time you were home."

Bandy looked at the boy: the smiling face that wasn't strange to him even though the two of them were indisputably strangers. He could hurt me, Bandy thought. The delicateness of the threat surprised him. It was like the virus he'd contracted, too small to see, easily killed until it was in you, then it was too late.

"What was it like in there?"

Bandy wanted to hear him say it. "In where?"

"In prison," he said bluntly. "Locked up."

It didn't change anything hearing him say it. "They moved me around a lot. I was in Texas and New Mexico, two different joints in Idaho. I guess you get used to it."

"Why'd they send you to Texas?"

"Because they could."

"Is it like the movies?"

Bandy hesitated. "Things are different when you have to do them. When it's you."

Tracy nodded and laughed a little with his mouth closed. "Did you even have movies?"

"Sometimes we had TV and there's movies on TV," Bandy said, and took it like the joke it was.

Iona came out of the kitchen and switched off the light behind her and glanced at Bandy and went upstairs. The curtains were still open and the glass was fogged from the cooking. Bandy worried the blanket on the chair with his thumb and forefinger and remembered that he'd left the bag with his things in it in Iona's car and felt a strong urge to go and get it so nobody would mess with it. But nobody was going to mess with it. He took a deep breath. The eagles on TV were eating dead salmon on the banks of a wide, green river. They were covered in low tide slime and fought one another over scraps.

"They must smell like shit," Tracy said.

He felt Tracy's eyes on him then Iona came back downstairs and went into the kitchen, there and gone like nothing. Bandy wasn't sure of his footing, his mind. He spoke: "Your grandpa, my dad," he said. "When he was young, him and the other ranchers in this valley shot and trapped everything. They shot eagles." He thought about his dad shooting coyotes and hanging them on the barbed-wire fence that marked the southern edge of the rangeland. Had that happened, he wondered. Had he been there? He'd seen the black-and-white pictures of the young bounty hunters knee-deep in pelts: mountain lion, coyote, fox, bear, wolves as tall as colts. It would be easy, he thought, to get something like that mixed up in your head. He got kind of lost in trying to remember what he wasn't sure was real or not and drifted off then came back to himself and looked at Tracy.

"Was anything left when you got here?"

Tracy pointed the remote and changed the channel. The screen went blurry, black and white; it was a God's-eye view of a city with crosshairs over it, a smart bomb, exploding ghosts and white light, radio chatter. What had been there, a perfectly square rooftop, was gone, only a black splattering hole remained. They cut to a reporter bathed in night-vision green with animal-shine eyes. The camera overlooked a Middle Eastern city, Baghdad, it said across the bottom of the screen. There were artillery blasts in the background, antiaircraft streaking across the sky, the glint of a river.

"Video-game war," Tracy said, grinning. "You don't even have to get off the couch." He changed the channel back to the eagles.

Bandy didn't know what he was talking about. "Did you hear me?"

"Yeah, I heard you. It was empty, everything but the stove. Someone—I already told you this in the letters." Bandy shook his head, no. He'd torn up so many letters, so many pictures. He thought of the old man, Williams, screaming at him, imitating him. Tracy went on: "Someone came in and stripped everything." He seemed annoyed to be repeating himself. "All the plumbing and wiring, everything. Water heater, all of it. They even took the toilets. You wouldn't believe it."

"None of the little things, though, like the papers and pictures. You didn't throw that stuff out, did you?"

"The house was empty. There wasn't any personal stuff," Tracy said. "I already told you this."

Bandy didn't remember. Iona called for him to come into the kitchen and he got up without thinking and went to her. She told him she had put some of Tracy's clean clothes out if he wanted to change and there were clean towels in the bathroom if he wanted a shower. The gym bag was on the table.

"Thanks for bringing that in."

"Sure. It's not much," she said, nodding to the bag.

"No. It's light." He was staring again. "We're standing here talking. In this house of all places."

"Yes we are," she said. "Sit down for a minute." They sat. "I work every day so you're going to be alone with him a lot."

"Okay."

"That doesn't bother you?"

"Does it matter?"

"He's not as tough as he acts."

"Not many people are."

"I'm sorry for all that happened."

For a moment he didn't know what she was talking about. He couldn't believe she brought it up. She might as well have started screaming at him.

"I don't expect you to forgive me, or to even understand why I did what I did, but I'm sorry. It ended badly, as bad as it could've."

He couldn't do this; he picked up the bag from the table. "I think I'll shower before I go to bed."

"Okay," Iona said.

"Night."

"Okay."

Tracy had fallen asleep with his head on his chest. Bandy went carefully up the stairs so he didn't wake him.

The water took a long time to get hot. Once it did he stood under it and held out his narrow arms and looked at them and the room filled with steam and he turned up the hot water until there was no hot water left then he turned off the cold and got out. He dried himself and sat down on the toilet and watched the steam slowly disappear. He stood up and swiped his hand over the mirror and looked at his face and it was still him. He looked away quickly and wrapped a towel around himself and went down the hall. His feet knocked dully on the old floors, the raw bones of the house talking. Iona's door was shut and he could see the light coming from under it.

In his bedroom he shut the door and hung the towel on the doorknob. He picked up and studied a pair of his son's underwear that Iona had left out for him then pulled them on. It was a very uncomfortable thing to do, although they fit, although they were clean. He climbed under the blankets. The house was stone quiet. He switched off the lamp on the floor next to the bed. True dark.

Sleep would not come easy this time and he knew it as soon as he blinked and opened his eyes and there was no difference between the two. He began and suffered through an inventory of the reasons why he should leave and why he shouldn't be allowed to be out at all. He wondered if regret would ever relax its hold on him. It doesn't have to be that way, he told himself. Sleep and tomorrow you can be a new man, a free man.

But he didn't sleep. He turned and twisted and tried sleeping on both sides and on his back then switched his head with where his feet were then finally moved to the floor and tried there, but nothing worked. He understood that it would be difficult to sleep in the world but he thought of all places here would be the best. But he had, he remembered. He'd taken the nap earlier and now he was awake.

He got out of bed and dressed and went downstairs in his bare feet. He switched on the kitchen light and had a drink of water from the faucet. He'd forgotten what water should taste like. He took another long drink with his mouth pressed to the cold metal of the faucet until he felt his stomach begin to swell with it then he cupped his hands and washed his face. His jaw was trembling and a string of drool hung from the side of his mouth. He closed his eyes, still bent over the sink, hugging it. Old memories crowded in and shook him upright. He dried his face on a dish towel then opened the refrigerator and looked into it for a long time then closed the door without taking any food.

Quietly he began to open drawers and cupboards looking for some sign of his parents, perhaps something Tracy had missed. There was nothing, a small tin container of brass pop rivets that appeared to be old enough and worn enough to be his mother's but he didn't remember them. His stomach fairly sloshed with water. He rattled the tin a few times then put it carefully back in the drawer where he'd found it. In the pantry closet he found a sleeping bag on the shelf and with it under his arm he opened the front door and went out into the mudroom. His shoes were still there and he slipped them on his bare feet and walked into the clear, electrically cold night.

The moon was high and bright, the color of milk in a blue glass; three days from being full, it was cleaved on one side. He blinked several times at the thin halos surrounding the moon but they remained. They were an illusion: a snowball dropped in black water, ripples spreading from it. The house was dark and looked abandoned. The snow was blue on the road. The cold and the silence were woven together and stretched so tightly that there were creaking sounds in the air, nautical sounds of binding rope. He stood beneath the stars and shuddered and swayed as they turned and muddled together, nameless and named, the whole great splatter. Bandy supposed his sense of wonder was familiar to everyone that had ever looked to open sky, an experience universal and absolutely unique in its tenor and depth of isolation. The night air washed over him and he was not sad or conscious of his body and its weight: He was free.

Loudly, he crossed the driveway, crushing ice and newly frozen mud puddles and mud with its thin crust giving beneath his weight then squishing and spreading but not sucking at his shoe or deep enough to cover it. The moon was to his right and his shadow struck out obliquely from his course. The land was still, all of it, under the dented moon. He didn't like to be seen in open spaces, or seen at all. The darkness protected him and blinded what eyes; no one, no eyes. He thought maybe he'd spent too much time inside to ever live like a citizen again. A yellow, nostalgic feeling began building in his chest. His heart, the heart of the land, had gone. Pine pollen is blown from the tree in a cloud but the tree remains. The opposite of this was how Bandy felt: The tree didn't remain, not living anyway. He feared that what had mattered was on the wind and it wasn't coming back. He went on and entered the barn.

There was no light and he knew there was no light. He shut the door behind him and felt his way along the wall until he touched the stall fence. He smelled the steer first then heard it moving and breathing. Bandy sat down against the slat boards of the fence and felt in the floor as the animal came toward him then he felt its nose touch his shoulder from between the boards. He sat up and looked back at it and even in the dark he could see the liquid shimmer of its eyes, almost like blood, like Fulcrum's eye filled with blood. The boards of the fence creaked as the steer leaned against them. "Fulcrum," he said to the steer. "Al Lyman. The name I never called you. We're old friends, right? We're pals. How's being a cow? About the same, I bet. You're still locked up, shitting and eating, staring at nothing. What'd you use to say, wash and repeat? Wash and repeat, for how many years?" He talked evenly to the dumb animal like it wasn't dumb at all. He talked to it like it was his friend in shadow, a hulking dark ghost. He was back on the tier. "You know what's coming, don't you, Lyman? I know you do. You were always better at telling what would happen than I was. You were a predictor of things." He paused, thought about his dead friend. Fulcrum hadn't been smart or lucky. He was Fulcrum; it could go either way at any time. "Good old Lyman. I bet you hate it when I call you that, but I don't care anymore what you like. You're dead. You don't get to care anymore, do you? It ain't right that I still do. You ask me, the dead should never forget and the living should be let off." Bandy smiled at the dark. "No, I mean it, really, fuck you." The steer pushed its head against the fence and Bandy's arm was pinched so he took it back. The steer moved away and Bandy remembered the sleeping bag and spread it out and took off his shoes and climbed into it with matted hay and mud and dried cow shit stuck to his pants. He wriggled his way against the bottom board of the fence and leaned his back against it. "I don't know what to do, Lyman," he said. "I don't know what I'm gonna do out here." The steer returned to the fence and breathed on Bandy's shoulder then lifted its head and settled. Bandy listened to him, his great bellows driving the sleep, the dark fires, into Bandy's head. He slept.

Chapter 9

OPEN GROUND

IT WAS FULL DAYLIGHT when Iona came out to the barn and woke him. The barn door was open and Lyman was outside standing in the sun, black, shit-spattered, and steaming. The smooth fields beyond were white and rusted with dead grass.

"You have a bed inside," Iona said.

Bandy thought he could use a few more hours' sleep. His legs ached. He sat up in his sleeping bag and leaned against the wall. His breath steamed out of him and Iona turned her head and blew air like she wanted to see if it was that cold for her as well or as if she were smoking and wanted the smoke clear of her face. She was bundled in her jacket and had on a red ski cap with a ball on top and matching red gloves.

"I can't sleep in there."

She ignored him. "The war's over. It was on the news."

"What war?"

"Iraq. Desert Storm."

"Did we win?"

"Of course we won. We have Stormin Norman." She smiled.

"What a fucking meatpie."

Her smile faded and she squatted down in front of him and

spoke slowly, concisely, as if he were a child. "We can find you a different bed if that's the problem."

"It's not the bed. I don't know what it is."

"Tracy thinks you're out here because you don't like him."

"It isn't him."

Iona looked outside to the fields. "Is it me?" she said coldly.

"No, it isn't you either." He cleared his throat, rubbed his face with his hands. He couldn't explain it to her.

"You're staying in there tonight, or at least come out here after he's asleep and go back in before he gets up. He's having a hard enough time. Do you understand me?" He nodded that he did. "There's breakfast inside. I'm going to work." She studied him and he dreaded what she would say. "You're just being fucking creepy."

"Why do you care? What does it matter to you?"

"Because he's giving you a chance and you're being an asshole about it. That's why."

Bandy didn't know what to say. She was right. She turned and walked away. Her car started and the fan belt squealed and she revved the engine then let it idle for a long couple of minutes then Bandy listened to her drive away.

He went through the stall gate and out the barn door and walked with his hand shading his eyes against the sun and went to Lyman and rubbed his shoulder and pulled on his ear. "You thought you were the only one that got yelled at?" The steer leaned its neck into Bandy and nearly knocked him down. "Easy, you big fucker." He stepped around the steer and climbed the corral fence because he knew the gate would be frozen stiff and stood on the other side and leaned against it. The sky was clear. Two weeks of this and the snow would be gone. The muscles in his back were stiff and his head ached a little but otherwise he felt strong. The crisp air raked his nostrils and made his eyes water. Talk to Tracy. He kicked his heel against the fence board, not hard just bouncing it, kept bouncing it, thinking.

Out of the corner of his eye he caught a glimpse of something moving and turned and it was Tracy pulling back the curtains in the living room. Bandy stood there and looked at him then waved. Tracy waved.

The kitchen felt like a sauna. Tracy was in the bathroom, the door was shut and the sink was running. The woodbox was empty so Bandy went back outside to the woodpile on the back side of the mudroom and loaded up his arms. He dropped the wood in the box then picked up a couple pieces and fed one into the stove but the other wouldn't fit so he stood it on end on the floor. He went back into the kitchen and took off his coat and hung it on the hook. He heard the bathroom door open. "You eat yet?" Bandy said.

"No," Tracy said.

"Come in here and I'll fix you a plate. Your mom made some eggs."

Tracy wheeled himself into the kitchen and took his place at the table.

"Morning," Bandy said.

"Morning."

Bandy got up and took two plates and two forks from the dish drainer and dumped the eggs out equally on the two plates. "Toast?"

"Sure."

"Coffee?"

"Whatever you got."

Bandy opened the bread bag and put the toast in the toaster and set it. "Where'd you get that firewood?"

"Paddy Flat. Wilhelm took me to get it. It's lucky we went early, before all this."

"Good thing," Bandy said. The house felt too small and he wanted to go back outside, but he was going to show Iona that he could do this, that he could be a part of things. "You been watching the news?"

"Why?"

"Your ma says we won the war."

"It's a cease-fire. I guess that means it's over. Seems like it just started."

"I don't even know where Iraq is."

"You're not the only one."

"You're lucky, ya know," Bandy said. "You can't get drafted anymore, not with your feet like they are. You gotta be 4-F now."

He looked saddened by the news. "Did you get drafted?"

"Signed up like an idiot."

"Do you regret it?"

"Not anymore. I guess I used to."

"Why would you think I'd be happy to be 4-F?"

"I don't know. Your ma will be." Bandy could tell he'd hurt the kid's feelings but didn't much care.

"I don't want to be a cripple."

"You aren't gonna be a cripple. Forget I said anything. Listen, I've been thinking I need a job. You got any ideas?"

"You don't need a job. You just got out."

"I need to start paying my way. I got some bills."

"It's not like we're paying rent, ya know. Ma and I can feed you and we'll be even." Tracy took the cup of coffee that Bandy handed him and sipped then set it down on the table.

"I got medicine I need to pay for. I'd like to have some spending money too."

Tracy paused. "Do you have any skills?"

"Sure." Bandy laughed then stopped when he saw Tracy was serious. "I worked in the machine shop. I can weld." He leaned over and looked into the toaster because it should've come up by now, and the elements were still black. He followed the cord and it wasn't even plugged in. He plugged it in and watched the glow come up from inside.

"You can probably find something if you can weld. I know there're a couple machinists in town, fabricators. We could look them up in the phonebook."

The toast popped up and Bandy pitched the pieces onto the plates and put the plates on the table and sat down. "You need anything else?"

"Salt. Butter."

Bandy stood up again and after a short search found the butter dish and the salt and pepper on the shelf above the stove. He sat back down. "All right," he said.

Tracy took a bite of his eggs then salted them heavily and took another bite. "How's sleeping in the barn?"

Bandy finished chewing and swallowed before he spoke. "I'll sleep inside from now on."

"It doesn't matter to me."

Bandy didn't say anything. The kid was lying; it did matter to him. Bandy could see it in his face. He stabbed at his eggs and loaded them on top of his toast then put down his fork and folded the toast in half and ate it like that. Tracy watched him eat. He finished and took a long drink from his coffee then picked up his fork again and scraped his plate clean.

"Did they let you have metal forks in prison?"

Bandy didn't want to talk about that. Everything he'd said about being inside since he'd been out sounded shrill and false, like he was making it up, or worse, bragging. He put down his fork. The kid was watching him, waiting.

"Maybe a long time ago they did. Now they don't. Everything's plastic now." He lifted the salt shaker then put it back down, tapped it on the tabletop. "When I first went in they'd give you a mess kit: cup, spoon, salt shaker, and a plate. If anything went missing they wouldn't let you eat. They'd give you water and biscuits but that was all."

"I'm never going to prison. I'd rather die." He sat there with his little fake show of bravery and Bandy wanted to knock him down.

"I bet it keeps you up nights thinking about how you fell, doesn't it?"

"I try not to think about it."

"Because you think you could've saved yourself."

"Yeah."

"But you couldn't have. You know that don't you?"

Tracy leaned back in his chair and watched his father, eyes working like he was solving a puzzle. "I didn't have to go on the roof."

"Yes, you did."

"I could've gone in through the upstairs window. I would've been fine."

"It wasn't up to you then and it sure as hell isn't up to you now. Once you're going, you go."

"Are you talking about jail or me falling off the roof?"

"I'm talking about everything."

The kid scraped the last of his eggs up against his last hunk of toast and pushed them together then ate the eggs and threw the toast in his mouth right after. He chewed and swallowed. "I think you're wrong."

"Then make up your own mind. You don't have to listen to me."

"I know I don't."

Bandy smiled at the kid, sliding along the edge of his control, his performance. He needed to bring it back down, cool it off. "I started calling your steer Lyman," he said. "But if you got a name for him already, I'll call him that."

"Who's Lyman?"

"Some guy I knew."

"What was he in for?"

"It doesn't matter."

"Did he kill somebody?"

Bandy hunched a little. "You don't always have to go digging for bones. It's a bad habit. I think you'll find that a lotta shit has nothing to do with you and asking questions just pisses people off." Tracy's eyes flashed and Bandy was about to apologize then Tracy said: "The muffler shop. They always have a sign out. They'd hire you, I guess. They always got bums working in there."

"Bums." Bandy felt the blood go hot in his arms and chest and it was welcome, his anger was welcome.

Tracy shoved his plate away. "You can take my truck if you want, I don't give a shit."

"I'm not a bum."

"You're an asshole." He spun the chair around and went into the living room, then into his bedroom and slammed the door.

Bandy put on his jacket and went outside. He tried to start Tracy's truck but the battery was dead. He looked at the house for a minute then walked out the driveway feeling defeated. It had already begun to slip through his fingers.

The bright sunlight and the movement warmed him and he unzipped his jacket and walked at the edge of the road at an easy pace with his hands in his pockets. The ice in the ditch bottom was as flawless as the wing of an insect and where it climbed the stalks of dead grass it was braided looking and smooth like slag on a bead. He saw something round and blue buried in the grass and thought it might be a ball and he wanted it, he wanted to kick it down the road like he'd done as a boy. He stomped on the ice and it fell away with a skittering sound and he pushed it aside with the toe of his boot and the tall stalks flopped upright and swayed. It was an oilcan and it was empty. He threw it over the fence into the field.

He walked on until he came to the creek then he stopped and stood on the road and stared at the water. It rushed through the large double culverts beneath the road and boiled against the banks, swollen and clear gray, marked by the snake tracks of current, almost chemical looking, toxic it was so cold. He used to swim here, riding the eddy lines, drifting. There was a bridge then, not culverts. He wondered if the bridge had collapsed or if it had been replaced before. Wilhelm would know. Tracy might. The water would come up with the snowmelt and flood the fields and maybe the road. Some memory of working with his father: walking the ditches, scooping out the debris, water rocketing by muddy then clear.

He walked on and climbed the first hill, dropped into the trough of the next. His bowels went suddenly watery. He looked around him then stepped from the road into the borrow pit onto the hard snow and crouched behind a leafless willow bush and shit then stomped on the snow with his heel until he broke it then wiped with hunks of the snow crust and powder. He climbed onto the road and looked over his shoulder at the stain he'd left. He felt like an animal, like a beast pursued, skinless and running. He went back and kicked snow onto his shit and buried it completely.

When he covered the ground where he'd shot Meeks, he didn't alter his pace. A red-tailed hawk sat on a fence post. There was another culvert, dry, yawning with icicle teeth. He thought of a prison cell, everything was a comparison: It was pointless to compare but the grooves were too deeply worn.

At the church he went into the graveyard to rest before he went on. The snow was hard frozen like limestone or salt flat and populated with cities of crystalline hoarfrost that tinkled and shattered when he walked through them. In the center of the cemetery there was a lone pine thick with needles and in the dazzling light it cast a shadow on the snow like a giant black pinecone. He crossed the shadow to the northernmost corner of the cemetery to his parents' grave. All the markers were small, nothing gaudy, no obelisks or mausoleums, simple graves. He remembered some that were plain, unfinished concrete with initials scratched in the mud before it dried. The graveyard was part of the Finnish church but his family wasn't Finnish. It was the burying place of the Long Valley more than it was the church of the Finns. Bandy knew no Finns. They were all dead and gone.

There was a layer of ice on the stones like there was on everything else. He tried to chip it off with his hands but couldn't so he kicked at it awkwardly and it cracked. He pulled his jacket sleeve over his hand and knelt and wiped the stones clean and felt the engraved words and numbers blindly with his palm. A car went by on the highway; the people inside didn't see him. He stood and crossed the graveyard and stepped over the low fence and hopped the ditch, scrambled onto the highway. The asphalt felt stable and stone-deep, as if he'd stepped from ship to shore. Ahead in the sunlight the road was wet and steaming.

The man's name was Gutierrez and his brother was Angel, together they owned and managed the Muffler and Brake Shop on East Lake Street. They looked like different models of the same man, both tan and short, thick around the middle. Gutierrez was the older of the two, and he was bald with a neatly trimmed white goatee. Angel's thin white hair was combed straight back, flat to his head; his face was clean-shaven and he had a pachuco cross tattoo on his right hand between the thumb and forefinger. The photographs in the office showed families and grandchildren in Little League and bass fishing trips, car shows. They seemed to be serious men, intelligent men, and Bandy wondered why they were so ready to hire him. He hadn't lied about being in prison because it was his only work history.

"People that work for us," Gutierrez said, "either go to college or go to jail. You already went to jail. You planning on going to college?"

"No," Bandy said, smiling a little. "I think I missed that train."

Angel smiled and nodded then looked at his brother.

"It's backwards as hell, but he might be perfect," Gutierrez said to Angel.

"I'll work hard," Bandy said.

"Sure you will. Do you like fishing?" Angel said.

"I haven't done it for a long time. I don't miss it."

"Good," Angel said.

"That's real good," Gutierrez said. The two brothers smiled at each other then they all shook hands.

When Bandy got home, the house was dark except for the light in the kitchen. Iona was there, sitting at the table reading a biography of Abraham Lincoln. There was a book about John Adams in the living room and Bandy wondered if she was going through the whole lot one by one. They both watched Dan Cole's headlights through the window as he turned around and drove away.

"What were you doing with him?" Iona said.

"I walked into town. He picked me up on my way back. He's shitfaced. He wouldn't shut up about Tracy falling. Says it was his fault."

"Christ, it had nothing to do with him. He just wants attention. Why would you walk all the way into town?"

"Tracy didn't tell you?"

"Tell me what? Why? What'd you do?"

"Nothing. I got a job. The muffler place hired me. I'll need to catch a ride until I get my license sorted out, get a rig. Is that all right?"

"I guess."

"I get off at five. I can figure out some other way to get home if that's too late."

She shut her book and put it on the windowsill then rubbed at a dried ring of a coffee stain with the edge of her thumb. Her hair was piled on top of her head with two yellow pencils stuck through it holding it in place. Loose strands hung about her neck and shoulders like something underwater. She had a smudge of blue paint on her forehead. She pushed out the chair across from her with her foot and Bandy sat down.

"I don't know how long I can do this, be in this house," Iona said.

"With me?"

"Yeah, with you."

"You can't leave me and Tracy out here on our own. It won't work, crippled as he is. You better take him with you if you're going."

"You're not throwing him outta here."

"You're the one that wants to leave. I'm just stating the facts."

"I wouldn't be leaving town, Bandy. I just wouldn't be staying with you. Being in this house is too much. I can't face down my past every morning.

"You think it's easy for me?"

"I know it's not. You don't need me here to yell at you for what I think you're doing wrong. You don't need me here at all."

"Maybe I do."

"No, you don't. You need to take care of yourself."

"I don't even know what it is that you remember: this place, me. What're you scared of?"

"I remember it all. I wish I could forget."

"Then tell me what I was like. Tell me how I was because I don't remember. I don't remember being here and it being like this. It doesn't feel like anything I ever knew. I don't recognize anything."

"What did you expect? You thought you'd get out and what? Your parents would be alive? It's been twenty fucking years, Bandy."

"I didn't think you'd be here. I didn't think the house would be like this."

"You've always thought you had something coming to you, something owed."

"I paid my debt."

"And what a waste that was. You spent all that time sitting in a cell and you're the same. Why didn't you just kill yourself?"

"Watch it."

Iona sat back in her chair and looked at the darkened window.

"You can stay out here. You owe me that much," Bandy said.

"See? See what I mean? I don't owe you anything."

But in her eyes Bandy could see the debt she owed, and after a moment the hard set of her jaw relaxed, and she bowed her head. "I leave at seven thirty so be ready if you want a ride."

"Okay."

She stood up and went out of the kitchen and Bandy listened to her go up the stairs.

Chapter 10

DRAWN OUT

TRACY PULLED BACK the blanket and inspected the pink almost neon proud flesh of the surgical scars on his feet. They seemed too precise, devoid of the character that the scars on Bandy's hands and face had. The color would fade and the swelling too and then they'd be even less. He pinched the roll of fat on his stomach and sat up and wrestled himself into a shirt and a pair of sweatpants then lowered himself from the bed into his chair. He went down the hall to the bathroom and brushed his teeth and washed his face then dropped the side of his chair and pulled himself onto the toilet. After he finished, he lifted himself and put some weight on his feet and felt the pain gather there, swarm like insects under his skin. He sat absolutely still for a moment, frozen in a kind of horrible amazement at the extent of the pain. Slowly, it faded and he took several deep breaths and went to the sink and washed his hands.

Bandy was in the living room sitting in the blue chair. It looked like he'd been there all night, gaunt and pale; a hermit recently discovered, dully surprised.

"Morning," Tracy said.

"Morning."

"You don't work today?"

"No, it's Saturday. I got the day off."

"Me too." Tracy smiled and Bandy nodded. He turned his chair and went into the kitchen and took his place at the table. His mother set him a cup of coffee.

"I've been sleeping better," he said.

"That's good."

"I was about to give the barn a shot."

Iona quietly hissed her dismissal. She looked tired.

"What about you? You all right?"

"Fine," she said, smiled.

Tracy slid his hand across the table and wiped some crumbs onto the floor. "He seems better now."

"Compared to what? Yesterday? Last week?" They were whispering.

"Why don't you give him a break?"

"Why don't you?"

He ignored the question and turned and looked out the window.

"Some guy asked me out on a date yesterday."

"Who?"

"He owns the house next to where I'm working. He's from San Diego."

"What'd you tell him?"

"That I'd think about it." She glanced at the clock on the stove and got up and grabbed her purse. "I'll see you tonight." She kissed him on the forehead.

"Wait."

"What?"

"What about Bandy?"

"What about him?" She searched his eyes. "Are you kidding?"

"No. I see the way he looks at you."

"We're not talking about this. I'll see you tonight."

The house was very quiet after she left. He went back into the living room and sat by the window. Bandy was reading last week's paper and didn't look up when he came in. Out in the field the creek was swollen beyond its banks with snowmelt. A lake was forming in the lowlands. The wind made shapes on the water, ever narrowing waves lapping at the shifting seams of the grass banks. The mountains were still covered with snow but it had mostly melted in the valley. The sky was clear and a pale blue.

He picked at the armrest on his chair and tore off a small hunk of plastic and tossed it on the floor. The armrest was almost gone and there were pieces of it scattered along the baseboard. When he looked outside again, there was a robin in the yard kicking up the dead grass and eating whatever it found. He opened the window and the cool wind flooded through the room. Bandy looked up briefly then went back to his reading. There was the crack of a gunshot in the distance. The echo of it soared over the fields with the sound of thin, quickly torn fabric. Tracy looked for who was shooting but didn't see anyone.

"Did you hear that?"

Bandy looked up, nodded, looked down again. Tracy went to the window in the kitchen and looked up the hillside. There was another gunshot, another, then Tracy saw them. It was two small boys, thin, ten maybe twelve years old, carrying guns, .22s by the pop of them. They came out of the trees and walked down the hillside to the road. He watched them until they were out of sight then wheeled himself through the kitchen and into the mudroom. He fought his way into an old pair of laceless Sorels then went back to the living room.

"I'm going to go see who that is. You want to come with me?"

"No, I'm reading."

"Aren't you bored yet?"

"I worked all week. I'm tired."

"How can you not be bored? You never do anything but hang around here and go to work. Why don't you go into town and get drunk or something?"

"Why don't you?"

"Because I'm stuck here. I'm in a wheelchair. I'm not old enough to get into the bar. I got about a thousand reasons. If I were you—"

Bandy threw the newspaper onto the floor. "I fucking hate it when people say that."

"Sorry."

"Another winner."

Tracy smiled uncomfortably. He thought Bandy might be joking but he couldn't be sure. There was a mean tilt about him this morning; he sat crookedly like his bones hurt. Tracy knew well enough to give him some space. He went to leave.

"Hold on a second, we need to talk."

"Okay."

"Is there anyplace where my folks' things might've ended up? Like a secondhand store or a church basement or something?"

"I don't think so. I think it's gone. Ellen said there was some boxes and stuff but I never saw any."

"What if the cops managed to pinch whoever cleaned us out? Maybe they have everything in evidence."

"It would've been in the paper."

"We could check."

"Wilhelm would've heard about it. He would've said something." Tracy pointed at the door. "I'm gonna go see who's shooting out there. You're sure you don't want to come with me? It'll be something to do.

Bandy shook his head. "Did you even file a police report?"

Tracy paused. "Wilhelm said it wouldn't do any good. Because it's your house."

"He doesn't know that. Let's go into town and file one now."

"For what? What's missing? What isn't here that was here before?"

Bandy got up and went to the window.

"See what I mean?" Tracy said. "You can't file a stolen-property report on memories."

Bandy snapped around and came at him. "You think I don't know that?"

Tracy rocked back in his chair, afraid he was about to be hit. "No."

"Did I sound sentimental?" Bandy said. "Did it sound like I was getting weepy over some trash that got left behind or a fucking water heater?" His veins were out on his neck and his bottom lip was wet with spit. Tracy pushed himself away but Bandy grabbed his chair and stopped him. "There's more to it than that. Somebody came here and ripped this place apart."

"I fixed it."

"You didn't. You patched it. This ain't my house. It ain't yours. It's nobody's. Nobody should even be here."

Tracy couldn't speak.

"You wanna know what it was like inside?" Bandy jabbed his thumb under his son's jaw and wrenched his head back and leaned into him. "You wanna be me, or do you wanna call me a bum? Which is it? Huh? Answer me. What do you want? You wanna ask me questions all fucking day? Well, that ain't gonna happen. We're gonna get this straight right now." Bandy dug deeper for a moment and really hurt him then released him and stood back. There was a hint of remorse in his face but it could be pity or even pleasure. "My fucking family was here. Their last days, every day that I was gone. That ain't nothing. That's what's fucking missing."

Tracy cleared his throat and stretched his jaw. "You should've seen what it was like before. It wasn't livable."

"Who says it's livable now? That I can live here?"

Tracy didn't know what to say. He had to leave. He went through the kitchen and into the mudroom and rammed his chair over the threshold and dropped off the step to the muddy path. Slowly, and with great effort, he made his way out the driveway. He'd thought this whole time that Bandy was proud of him. He'd never considered that all the work he'd done was somehow wrong or inadequate, that it wouldn't be appreciated. There was nothing when he moved in, nothing worth saving. He thought they would be friends; if not like a father, Bandy would be like an older brother. His ideas about family suddenly seemed very childish.

The muscles in his arms and shoulders burned and a sharp pain began throbbing at the base of his neck then spread down his spine. The screen door slammed and he turned and saw Bandy walking after him. He pushed harder to get away; he was making sounds, moaning, he was working so hard.

The county road was covered in a packed layer of pale gravel and it was easier going than in the driveway. When he looked back, Bandy had stopped coming after him. They watched each other from across the corral. Bandy lowered his eyes then squatted down and held his head with both hands like he meant to crush it. The steer was standing broadside between them watching them both. Tracy passed the edge of the fence line and started up the road toward Wilhelm's and lost sight of his father.

He hit three hard strokes on the hand rims then coasted for a little ways. He wanted to get a hold of his mom before she came home. He needed to warn her. They wouldn't be living there anymore. He'd have to forget about his plans for the house, for him and Bandy. He could do it; he could leave anything behind. They should've never let him out. They should've executed him. Tracy was filled with a real hatred for Bandy, one that he recognized as being saved for his mother and Bill, a familial hatred that could only rise from the shoulders of love. The hate made him feel legitimate instead of bastard; it gave him a sense of purpose. Nobody can hate like family, Bill used to say, except stepfamily. Tracy smiled at that.

His momentum faded and he eased his way around the corner and started up the long hill to Wilhelm's. At his crawling pace he had time to take note of every alluvial rut and displaced stone. The passing of the fence posts became slower and slower as the hill steepened. Then he could go no further and he stopped and gripped the hand rims. His arms trembled and he was suddenly afraid. He looked up the hill and regretted it. He wasn't going to make it to the top, and he didn't know exactly how he was going to get down.

Behind him in the distance the boys were shooting again. He turned to see how far away they were, if he could see them, and as he did the chair shifted and he lost his grip. He rolled quickly backward, and when he tried to stop, his left hand slipped but his right hand held fast and he snapped around and one of the front casters banged firm into a rut and he was rolling back down the hill.

The wind chilled the sweat on his face and chest. The hand rims were warm in his palms, getting hot. The corner at the bottom of the hill was backed by a barbed-wire fence and coming up fast. He was sure he was going to crash and it was going to hurt. All over again it was going to hurt. But the front wheel stayed locked in the rut somehow then he was on the flats again, coasting easy, terrified, feeling better than he had for months. His hands were raw and his eyes watered from the wind. He pushed on even though he didn't need to and carried his speed. He looked for the hunters in the field but didn't see them. He thought he'd ask them to help him up the hill, or to go and get Wilhelm, because he couldn't go home any longer. Bandy would be there. It was his house. Tracy was thinking that Bandy should leave, not him; he'd done all the work, paid for everything. The house was more his now than it was Bandy's. Then a rock or a rut or something caught one of his front casters and he was thrown from the chair. He came down hard on his shoulder and the side of his head and his teeth slammed together and a dull note rang in all the bones of his skull.

He was on his stomach in the road and he lifted himself up onto his elbows. The wind was knocked out of him and it hurt and he was afraid. After a moment his breath came back. His head was bleeding and the blood was warm flowing down his face on his hands. The chair was in the borrow pit upside down and leaning against the fence. His legs seemed all right; he seemed okay. The blood from his head ran into his eye. He rolled onto his stomach and wiped it out as best he could then rolled onto his back. He lay still. He watched the clouds and listened to the wind. He could just hear the wind chimes at the Guntlys'.

Then there were footsteps on the road, fast then slow as they came closer. Tracy didn't turn to look to see who it was; he knew who it was. He tasted blood in his mouth and swallowed it.

Bandy stood over him.

"Get away from me."

"Are you all right?"

"How do I look? Do I look all right?"

"No. Let me help you."

"Don't touch me." He wanted to sit up but he didn't move. Bandy brought the chair from the ditch. His boots were covered with mud and cow shit from the corral. Tracy sat up. The armrest on his chair was bent and the paint was scraped away to the metal in one spot. With Bandy's help he pulled himself into his chair.

"I'm not paralyzed."

"I know you're not. Look at your head." Bandy took off his shirt and handed it to Tracy for the blood. He was thin and muscular and had scars all over his chest and stomach; some looked like they'd been put down with a ruler they were so long and straight.

"I don't want to be afraid of you." Tracy held the shirt to his head and he could smell his father.

Bandy took a hold of his chair and turned him around and pushed him toward the house. "You don't have to be. I didn't mean what I said." His voice was a little shaky. "There's something wrong with me."

Tracy twisted around and looked at Bandy and he believed him. He needed to believe him. They went down the road. The sun was warm and it was good to be out in it.

"Do you trust me?" Tracy said.

"I don't have any reason not to."

"Well, that's enough, isn't it? You don't have to like me. I know you don't like me. I can live with that."

Bandy didn't say anything and they went along. Tracy wished he would say something. When they neared the house, Lyman came out of the barn to greet them.

"Are you gonna tell your mom what I did?"

"No. I won't tell her."

"You're a good kid. You deserve better than me."

"You're what I got."

Bandy rocked the chair back and lifted him up the step and they went inside.

Iona came home in the evening and found Tracy at the kitchen table with a shaving mirror held above his head looking at the cut in his scalp. A bread bag filled with ice was melting on the table and dripping onto the floor. The scrapes on his arms were raised and meaty looking. He explained to his mother what had happened. Bandy wasn't around. Tracy didn't know where he went. He was out in the driveway a minute ago.

Iona had paint on her hands and she didn't think it very hygienic to dig around in Tracy's head wound without washing them but she did it anyway. The cut was still bleeding a little and it was deep. Iona brushed his hair away and pinched the wound shut. Tracy squirmed. "Hang on," she said, and went into the bathroom to find something to clean it with. She could hear Tracy talking but not what he was saying. There wasn't anything but rubbing alcohol and Q-tips. She grabbed a tampon from the box under the sink and carried everything back into the kitchen and put it on the table. She opened the alcohol and dipped a Q-tip inside and pressed the Q-tip into the cut on Tracy's head. He set his jaw and blew out through his nose.

"I hope it hurts like hell."

"Thanks, Ma."

She cleaned the cut even though it looked clean and pressed the tampon onto it. She grabbed Tracy's hand and put it on his head and told him to hold it there.

"We don't have a proper bandage?" He pulled the tampon away and looked at it. Iona scowled at him and he put it back.

"Do you have to be an idiot?" She picked up the melting bag of ice from the table and tossed it in the sink. She shouldn't call him an idiot. "You're sure you didn't hurt your legs." She pulled up a chair in front of him.

"I'm fine." He leaned his head down without her asking and she lifted his hand away and dabbed at the cut again then put his hand back. When he looked up she could see the dark flecks of color in his eyes. She stood and gathered the bloody Q-tips and threw them away in the garbage under the sink and wet a dish towel and wiped his arm then wiped the blood off of the table.

Bandy came in holding a small bouquet of flowers, sugar bowl and blue camas.

"Those are real pretty," Tracy said.

Bandy raised an eyebrow to the boy and went to the sink and filled a jam jar with water and put the flowers on the table. Iona thought that he still looked like an inmate. He stood straight yet kind of slouching like a boxer, as if some invisible fingers pinched at his clothing and held him there. His muscles, although withered, still stood out against his shirt where they had been knitted most firmly, on his neck and at his shoulders and chest. His eyes were still clear and bright for anyone to see, to shy from. He'd brought flowers. The preciousness of the act made Iona a little weak.

"I'm gonna go feed Lyman," Bandy said, and looked at Tracy. Tracy smiled and went back to the table and rested his elbows on it. Bandy went outside. Iona turned on the oven. She didn't know what she was going to cook, or why she felt compelled to cook at all. They didn't deserve it. They deserved each other.

"What's with you two?" she said.

"Nothing."

"Something's up. Did he have anything to do with you getting hurt?"

"No. I just fell out of my chair. He wasn't even around."

"Why wasn't he?"

"I don't know. He was here reading the paper."

"Then he came and found you? He helped you?"

"Why's that so hard to believe?"

"I don't know," Iona said. "I just don't believe it."

"Then don't."

"Don't gang up on me."

He laughed. "Nobody's ganging up on anybody."

"I need you on my side."

There was a look of recognition in Tracy's face.

"We have to stick together."

"We will," he said.

She almost trusted him, but he didn't understand what was at stake. They were all they had. He might not understand for years. She touched his cheek and went upstairs to the bathroom and undressed and turned on the water and waited for it to warm on her hand then climbed in and snapped the curtain shut. She set the water as hot as she could bear, hotter, and leaned into it. There might be some hamburger thawed in the fridge but they might've eaten it already, she couldn't remember. The look on Tracy's face. "I'm all right," he'd said. He knows how he hurts me and he doesn't care. He doesn't know the half of it. And Bandy brought flowers. He brought me flowers. Or did he just bring them for the house? Did it matter? What kind of man does that? She'd told the guy from San Diego that she couldn't go out with him. She didn't know why. He was nice enough, and not too old. He had a lot of money. It made no sense that she'd turned him down. It made no sense that somebody like him would ask her out in the first place. For a moment she'd considered canceling the contract she had with the people next door so she wouldn't have to see him again.

But she was done with all that, letting men turn her like canyons bend a river. Really, they could fuck off and die because she was doing great and didn't need any of them.

She turned off the water and stood and dripped then twisted her hair and wrung it out. The paint was still on her hands. She'd forgotten to wash her hair too, hadn't even touched the bar of soap. The bathroom was full of steam and she didn't know how long she'd been in there already but she turned on the shower again and didn't worry about the temperature being right and washed her hair and scrubbed the splotches of paint from her hands.

When she was done, she shut off the water and stood still and listened, heard a door shut. She got out of the shower and dried off and put on her robe and stepped into the hallway. The light was on in Bandy's room. She stood in the doorway. He was digging around in his dresser with his back facing the door. She asked if he wanted dinner.

He turned, not surprised. "Tracy said he wasn't hungry."

"I asked if you were."

"I could eat."

She felt a chill in the hallway and pulled her robe tight around her. Bandy shut the dresser drawer and came toward her. Iona thought she knew what he was going to say but when he spoke she was mistaken.

"I'll figure something out for getting back and forth to work. I know it's a hassle, you driving me, being seen with me. I'm a freak show."

"Don't say that."

"Sometimes people come by the shop just to look at me."

"No, they don't."

"They do. I'm like a monkey. Gute and Angel are threatening to sell peanuts."

Iona smiled. Here was something she recognized, a man she remembered. He used to make her laugh until her stomach hurt. There was a dim memory of him impersonating Richard Nixon while he two-stepped her around the cabin. That was before he enlisted. They'd been so happy; she couldn't remember them having a fight until he came back, but of course they had.

"I'm proud of you," she said.

"I haven't done anything."

"You haven't done anything wrong. For you that's pretty good."

He smiled, looked at the floor, an old confidence rising. "Tracy must've got the accident-prone part from you, huh?"

It was sexual, bringing up their son; it referenced them sharing a bed. She wasn't going to wade into that water, they were alone out here and she didn't know what might happen. She thought she did, that she could control it, but she knew what it was to feel her control slip away. "How about spaghetti?"

"If you want."

"I'll get dressed."

"Hey."

She waited.

"Never mind." He smiled and Iona smiled back at his broken smile and his worn-out face.

"Make sure Tracy doesn't fall asleep before I get done with dinner. I'll be down in a minute."

"Okay."

She left him standing in the middle of his bedroom with his hands at his sides. She smiled walking down the hall and while she brushed her hair and dressed.

Chapter 11

HOUSES ON THE HILL

TRACY SAT AT THE kitchen table and stared into the steaming black hole of his coffee. The radio was on and tuned to the local station. The Saturday lunch at the old folks' home would be chicken fried steak, green beans, and Jell-O. Dinner would be fried chicken, vegetable medley, and tater tots. The weather was supposed to continue to warm up and reach a high of sixty-eight. Iona was gone to work. Bandy had left the house early and was probably out in the fields walking somewhere. There was a new pair of crutches leaning against the wall beneath the coatrack. They'd been there a couple days already. Tracy wheeled his chair across the kitchen and used the crutches to lift himself up and stood and picked up the wall phone and called Wilhelm. Ellen answered and they talked for awhile in the awkward way they always did on the phone then she passed it off to Wilhelm and Tracy asked him if he could borrow a .22.

"You saw those two kids from over the hill."

"Yeah, I saw them."

"Uh-huh. What the hell have you been doing with yourself? I haven't seen you since I don't know when."

"You know when. When Bandy showed up."

"I've been thinking about that."

"Don't hurt yourself."

"I won't. Maybe I should apologize."

"Tell him, not me."

"Maybe I will."

"I'll be up in a minute," Tracy said.

"I'll be here."

He hung up the phone and opened the door and slowly made his way across the driveway to the shed where Wilhelm's tractor had been parked all winter. It was dark in the shed and there was an oily layer of dust covering everything. Spiderwebs broke on his hands when he reached down to prime the engine. It took ten or fifteen minutes and he had to climb down twice to scrape the corrosion off a plug wire with his pocketknife and spray starter fluid in the intake, but it was running, filling the shed with black smoke. Tracy reached down and pulled his crutches up onto the seat next to him and backed the tractor out of the shed. He motored along and scanned the fields looking for Bandy but he wasn't there. Dark mounds of earth showed where he'd been working along the irrigation ditches.

Wilhelm was standing in the driveway with his coat collar flipped up around his ears and an old ski cap perched on the top of his head. "You're not leaving this piece a shit here are you?" he said over the clatter and roar of the motor.

"It's yours, ain't it?" Tracy set the brake and turned the key off. The absence of sound was so complete that for a moment it felt a little strange for Tracy to breathe.

Wilhelm squinted at him. "What the hell'd you do?" The scrapes on Tracy's arms were starting to heal but the skin was pink and raw looking around the scabs. He leaned forward so Wilhelm could see the cut on his scalp.

"I fell out of my chair."

"And? Were you getting towed behind a car? Look at your goddamn arms."

"I was coming up to see you and I got halfway up the hill and
couldn't make it so I turned around and ended up augering in."

"Maybe I shouldn't give you a gun."

"Did I miss breakfast?"

"I told Ellen you were coming so she's making another round.
Come on inside."

Ellen did a little hop when she saw how scraped up he was.
Wilhelm told her what had happened and she scowled and told
them both to go sit at the table.

"You're in trouble now," Wilhelm said. He pulled up a chair
next to Tracy. The .22 was leaned up against the wall beside the
table. Wilhelm picked it up and handed it over. Tracy held the gun
and looked at it. He felt that he should do something with it so he
found the safety and flipped it on then off then on again. He was
uncomfortable holding the thing so he handed it back.

"How's your mom?" Wilhelm said. He put the gun down on
the table.

"Fine. Working a lot."

"The criminal?"

"Don't call him that."

"Sorry, the ex-criminal."

"He's working like a dog."

"We saw him out in the field. Looks like a man that don't want
to go home."

"He's still getting used to us."

"You hear about Dan?"

"No, what?"

"Sandy gave him the boot, and he got run off that job you and him were working on before he got the last check. He's living in his storage unit, running around with that cute little waitress from the Huckleberry, Georgie."

"You're kidding."

"He's digging a hole and apparently climbing in." They sat there, then: "I hear Bandy's with Gutierrez?"

"Yeah. The muffler man."

"Gute ain't bad. Angel, I don't know him very well. I hear he's hell on bass. I got a scope somewhere for that thing if you want it."

"That's all right. I'm not planning on actually hitting anything."

"Better leave it here then," he said. Tracy gave him a look then Ellen came with a plate and set it in front of him and snatched the rifle from the table. "Not where we eat," she said, and leaned it up in the corner by the front door.

"See? She's mad at you. One piece of bacon. She probably dropped it too."

Tracy took a bite and chewed and smiled at Wilhelm.

"Or she stole it out from the cat's dish."

Tracy paused then kept eating.

Ellen came and sat down with them. "How's your mother?"

"I already drilled him."

"Well I haven't. How is she? How's Bandy?"

"They're fine," Tracy said. "Working a lot."

"Are you stir-crazy yet?" Ellen said.

"Sitting around the house all day, watching soap operas," Wilhelm said, his eyes swimming a little.

"That's why I came up here."

Ellen reached over and patted his arm. "What if you got hurt and had to go back to the hospital? You can't do that. It'd kill your mother."

"She's not the only one," Tracy said. They sat and the whole house, it seemed the whole world, was still, not uncomfortably so.

"I bet hospitals and hell smell exactly the same," Wilhelm said quietly. He looked at Tracy and smiled. "But you're young, you got your whole life to heal. Now if you were old, like Ellen, then you'd be in trouble."

Ellen swatted at Wilhelm's face, missed, slapped him in the shoulder. "At least I bear up to it. You'd complain to Saint Peter about the long line and the bright lights."

Tracy finished his food and Ellen took his plate and he thanked her. "You want to come out shooting with me?" he said to Wilhelm.

Wilhelm itched his nostril and gave Tracy a sideways look. "If we drive we'll have to shoot from the road, and that's illegal."

"That bothers you?"

"No, it makes me want to go even worse."

"I'd rather walk."

Wilhelm didn't say anything, nodded. "It'll be hard to carry that rifle and work the crutches." He stood up stiffly and stretched his back. "I got a sling somewhere. Hang on a minute."

Tracy waited and watched Ellen clean up in the kitchen then Wilhelm came back and tossed him an old greasy canvas sling. "We're walking then," Wilhelm said.

They met the two boys on the road coming toward them. They were dirty and scared looking and their cheap sneakers were coated with mud and grass seeds.

"Poachers," Wilhelm said, and grabbed one of the boys firmly by the shoulder. "You know what we do to poachers?"

"Let him go," the younger one said.

"It's okay," Tracy said.

"Don't shoot me, ya little demon. I'm only sassing," Wilhelm said. He let the older boy go and slapped him on the back of the head like they were buddies. "What're your names?"

"Olin," he said. "And that's Jake."

"Orlin?"

"Olin, like the skis."

"Like the skis?" Wilhelm said. "Your dad's that ski racer, isn't he? Regan Piatt? I've heard of you boys. Future Olympians. Their dad, he made a run for it, I'll tell you what. Did you ever see Regan Piatt ski on the TV?" he asked Tracy.

"No. I met him before, though. I met these two before."

"Did you get any squirrels?" Jake asked.

"Nah," Tracy said. "The guns are just for looks. We're headed home." The two boys turned and looked at the house in the distance.

"Is it okay that we hunt here?" Olin said.

"You been out here for weeks already," Wilhelm said.

"Nobody said anything to us," Jake said.

"It doesn't bother me," Tracy said. "Quit being a bully," he said to Wilhelm. Wilhelm acted like his feelings were hurt. The boys smiled.

"Stop by on your way home and I'll introduce you to Lyman," Tracy said.

"Who's Lyman?" Olin said.

"The cow," Tracy said. "Lyman the cow."

"Is he mean?" Jake said. "He stinks like hell."

"He's ferocious," Wilhelm said.

"We'll stop by," Olin said.

"Good. See you around." Tracy slung his rifle over his shoulder.

"I'll carry that if you want," Wilhelm said.

"I got it. I brought the damn thing."

"See ya," Olin said, Jake said.

"Piatts," said Wilhelm, growling at them.

They watched the boys go down the road for awhile then started out again. Tracy was tired and his armpits hurt from the crutches.

"What'd you mean just for looks?" Wilhelm said. "Why're we out here lugging these things around if you aren't going to shoot?"

"I might shoot. I don't know. I was hoping we'd see Bandy."

"So you could shoot him, or so you'd be armed when you did?" Wilhelm laughed.

"To see if he wanted to go with us."

Wilhelm slowed then stopped. Tracy kept going and even sped up a little. The old man caught up a few seconds later, slightly winded. "Regan Piatt and his cousin, Bixby, they get their names in the paper every month or so."

"For what?"

"They're thieves, they're always in trouble." The old man laughed a little. "You and those boys could be related, the jailbird family."

"Bandy wasn't a thief."

"No, he wasn't. He's a murderer."

"That's right. He is."

When they got inside the house Tracy sat down and put his feet up on one of the kitchen chairs. He was exhausted. Wilhelm opened the fridge and took out a plate covered in tin foil. "Can I eat this?"

"You haven't even looked to see what it is."

Wilhelm looked. "What is it?"

"I don't know, leftovers. Get me a fork, one a those beers, too."

"The breakfast of ex-champions." Wilhelm smiled.

"It's afternoon."

"Fair game then."

They ate off the same plate.

"How come you think Bandy couldn't have changed?" Tracy said later.

"Oh, I'm sure he's changed, but into what."

"He's not that bad." Tracy put down his fork, looked at Wilhelm. "Ellen told me once that I reminded her of your son, Neil. Were him and Bandy alike when they were young?"

Wilhelm paused. "Not really. Maybe a little. I guess all friends are alike in some ways, that's why they're friends. Bandy wasn't ever like you are now, if that's what you're getting at. You aren't him. I can see the resemblance to Neil, though. You got his heart. Me and Ellen have talked about it."

"I don't know what that means."

"It means you don't want to be like Bandy. You'd never fit in that skin."

"It can't be easy to be locked up for that long then to get let out just like that. It's practically time travel."

"You can't apologize for him. It's a closed circuit between fathers and sons—it only flows one way." Wilhelm sat up in his chair and pointed out the window. "Your brothers are here and they got company." All the tenderness had gone out of his voice. The two boys were at the corral fence with Bandy, pointing at Lyman.

Tracy picked up his crutches and stood. He wanted to get some distance between him and Wilhelm. They were talking like they weren't friends, weren't equals, and it made him uncomfortable.

The boys waved when they saw Tracy come outside. Bandy nodded. Tracy turned to shut the door but Wilhelm was in the way. The old man put his hand on Tracy's shoulder and shut the door for him.

"I'm headed home," he said. "I'll grab my rifle later. You can keep the other one here for you to use." He set his tack out the driveway without acknowledging Bandy or the boys. He seemed to be in a hurry. Tracy thought he was wrong; there was no closed circuit, not between anyone. The lingering pressure of the hand on his shoulder was proof of that.

Chapter 12

A DOG THAT FETCHES ROCKS

BANDY AND IONA HAD dinner alone, some venison that Wilhelm had given Tracy and a bowl of sautéed morels that Bandy had gathered on one of his walks. Iona had her hair pulled back and was wearing eyeliner. She looked good and Bandy watched her. They hadn't planned on being alone. Tracy was at Wilhelm's watching a football game with the two boys from over the hill, Olin and Jake. Bandy felt a certain lightness about the evening, an airiness. He felt relaxed. Iona seemed happy. They stabbed at the mushrooms with their forks, a thin slice of the venison. Iona was looking at him. He didn't look away. It was something that had been happening more and more. He didn't try to smile or fidget.

"Still," Iona said.

"What?"

"You still scare me."

"Bullshit."

Iona's expression didn't change. She touched her nose then her cheek. "What's it like when you look at me? Is it like you're looking in a mirror?"

"I quit looking in mirrors."

Iona shook her head. "No, you didn't. You're always fixing your hair."

"That's for work. Angel makes me do it so I don't scare the civilians."

"You probably have a girlfriend."

"Right. That's it."

She hesitated. "Ever since you came back, I can't look in the mirror without seeing both of us, where we were, where we are. It's like everything that happened didn't actually happen or it's about to start all over. Either way, it scares me. Does that make any sense?"

"What about Tracy? Where's he fit in?"

"He's outside of all this. He's got a chance."

"But if you're doing fine and I'm doing fine."

"I don't want to let him down."

"You can't avoid that. It's what people do."

"Maybe that's the difference between the two of us. I won't let him down. I won't let it happen again. Mostly, I don't want to do any of it twice. That's why you scare me. Not because I think you're going to hurt me."

He reached across the table and tried to take her hand but she pulled away.

"Don't do that."

"What were you just saying?"

"I don't know. I didn't mean it like that."

"We're here, living right here. It ain't the past." They sat quietly for awhile then she stood up and took their plates to the sink. She turned and faced Bandy but looked at the floor. "You've been alone for too long. You can't be alone for that long and not have it mess you up."

"How long have you been alone?"

She looked at him. "Not as long as you."

"It ain't a contest."

"I don't want you to be alone, but there's no mystery to it, we're both monsters."

"We don't have to be." He stood up.

"We're both ruined. We have been for years, both of us."

"I remember what we were like when we were happy."

"I don't. I told you. I remember the wrong things. I remember the bad things. Maybe that's how we were."

"Is it because I'm sick?"

"No, it's not because you're sick."

Bandy tried to take her hand again.

"Don't do that. Let's keep it like this. Just the way it is." She turned away and went out and he listened to her climb the stairs. A chill washed over him. He stood in the kitchen for awhile then he did the dishes, slamming them around, almost breaking them. When he finished he heard the shower running upstairs. He went into the living room and waited like a nervous boy for her to come down but he heard her door shut and her footsteps directly above him and the familiar creak of her bed. He didn't know what he'd been hoping for, but whatever it was it wasn't happening.

He went back into the kitchen and opened a beer and sat down at the table and skimmed last Sunday's paper and waited for Tracy to get home. He didn't want to be alone. The refrigerator motor sounded sick when it came on. Bandy walked over and put his ear against the side of the fridge; it didn't sound good. He didn't know how to fix it or anyone that could and he wished he wouldn't have noticed it at all. He switched on the radio on the counter and it was already tuned to the college station out of Boise so he left it. He listened to some people talk and the message was that people were basically good. It gave Bandy a headache. He switched it off. Then he heard a car outside and Wilhelm came in with Tracy behind him clicking along on his crutches. The old man went for the fridge and opened it and looked in. Tracy nodded to Bandy and went through the kitchen and directly to bed.

"What'd you do to him?" Bandy said. He and Wilhelm hadn't spoken since the first day he was back. Bandy no longer felt he needed to bend his knees to him. It was up to Wilhelm how he wanted to play it.

"I didn't do nothing to him. He said he's tired. You mind?" Wilhelm said, holding up a beer.

"I don't need them all."

"Want one?"

"All right."

Wilhelm sat down at the table and Bandy asked him how the game was. "Boring. I slept through the last half. I'll be up all night. The Piatt boys liked it. I don't think they get much entertainment at their house."

"You take them home?"

"Just now." A grin spread across his face. "They're living up in that A-frame that Bill McKinley threw together. You ever go up there?"

The question banged on the steel tank of Bandy's bad mood. "Why would I?"

"Dunno."

"Did you tell Tracy?"

"What's the point? Bill's dead. It's just a house now. I can't believe it's still standing. Roof looks like a sheet hanging on the line." He scooped the air with his open hand. "Hell, if I told him it was Bill's, he might go and fix it up."

"Maybe he would."

"Yeah, maybe." Wilhelm sat for a few seconds looking at Bandy then leaned forward in his seat. "You remember when your dad got that bad sliver?"

Bandy had to think about it but he remembered. It was an accident at the mill, an unlucky moment when a half-round log had bound and kicked back and splintered. A chunk of Doug fir the shape and general size of a splitting wedge stabbed into his father's upper thigh. He remembered a night visit to a hospital and bloody clothes. "What about it?"

"You ever think how much that must've hurt?"

"No."

"Or Tracy's feet, his ankles?"

"What're you getting at?"

"I don't know. Seeing Tracy get hurt, I've been thinking about pain lately." He forced a smile. "Mostly how I don't want any."

"Well, you're pretty tough to be around—it's painful for me." Bandy started to laugh then had a coughing fit. When he'd finished he looked up and Wilhelm was giving him a hard look.

"I've been thinking I've been lucky."

"Maybe you have been."

"It ain't gonna last."

"Why're you talking to me about this? I thought you were too good to talk to me at all."

"I've been meaning to come by, but it ain't that easy, is it?"

"If you say so."

"It's damned hard having you around." There was a waver of emotion in the old man's voice. He cleared his throat. "You give Ellen the whoogillies. She's scared to death of you."

"I give everyone the whoogillies."

"Not everyone. Not Tracy."

Bandy was strangely flattered. "I'm not leaving."

"Past that."

"That's right, past that."

Wilhelm shook his head, sipped his beer. "Dan Cole told me awhile back that when men like me get old, we window-dress our lives, whitewash all of it to make ourselves feel better."

"Men like you."

"That's what he said."

"Everybody does that. It's a survival thing. They talked about it in the joint. Repressed memories."

"You believe that?"

"It doesn't matter what I believe." Bandy flared his nostrils at the old man. "Dan Cole's a bit of a cunt."

Wilhelm smiled broadly. "Tracy says you're adapting."

"I guess."

"You're doing all right?"

"I'd complain but who'd listen?"

Wilhelm lifted his beer can and looked at the label like he didn't know what it was or how it had ended up in his hand. He took a long drink then set it down. "Did you know the week before you showed up was the week when Neil died?"

"Yeah."

"You did?"

"He was my friend, wasn't he?"

"Well goddammit, he was my son and every so often I need to go look at the picture on the mantel to keep his face fresh in my mind. It was a long time ago." He paused and picked at something in his teeth with his thumbnail. "I got no reason to hold what happened against you. I got comfortable blaming you, especially after you weren't around anymore, after what you did. It was easier for me to blame you than to blame myself. Dan was right about that much: I beat it to fit, to get the weight off a me I put it on you. But I'm the one that bought that car for him. I'm the one that taught him how to drive. You were just riding shotgun. It wasn't your fault. You were a kid."

"I'll tell you something, there was me when I was little, running around the ranch, being a nuisance. Then Neil died. Then the army. Then what happened on the road. After that it's dead air, a big gray block that doesn't count. And now—well, now it's now, ain't it?" Wilhelm nodded. "So what's that, four things minus lockup and the present?"

"What about Tracy?"

"Five."

"What about—"

"Six." Bandy held up his hand. "I'm drawing the line at six. But you've lived your whole life, got married, had kids, grandkids. I got six. I won't forget about Neil."

"Made me feel bad."

"I didn't mean to."

"I had it coming." They sipped their beers and watched each other. Then: "How's Gute and Angel? They paying you the big money?"

"Sure they are."

"About six bucks an hour, ain't it?"

"Beggars and choosers."

"Take a long time to get on your feet on six bucks an hour."

"Who's off their feet?"

"You and Iona. Tracy. I know you got bills."

"Yeah, we'll be all right. Angel was talking about selling me and Iona a pickup. Do it in payments."

"And you'll drive her car?"

"It's falling apart." The refrigerator switched on and Bandy looked at it sidelong. "I think we'll trade it or sell it in the paper. Tracy's gonna want his truck back on the road soon. We can't afford to keep three rigs going."

"I bet you'd miss your little rides in the morning if you had your own rig."

"You don't know how to let off, do you?"

Wilhelm shrugged his shoulders, yawned. It began to rain and the drops slapped against the window. "Spring's goddamn sprung."

"Are you gonna leave or do I need to throw you out?"

"I'm going, I'm going." He felt Bandy's beer can then his own. "Something wrong with your fridge? Your beer's a little warm."

"It's making a noise."

"I could probably fix it."

"I'll do it."

"You'll break it worse."

"Get outta here."

"Fine. Night."

"Night."

After Wilhelm left Bandy shoved the fridge sideways so he could look at the back. He didn't know where to start. He should've accepted the old man's offer. It might be good to spend some time with him, talk about the old days, about family. The motor kicked on again and Bandy ripped the plug out of the wall and it was silent. He stood there in a thin pool of gray water and inspected the plug then crammed it back in the outlet and the motor came back on louder than before. He went to the front of the fridge and threw his shoulder into it and slammed it back where it belonged then went upstairs to bed.

The only sound was the rain drumming on the roof metal and dripping from the eaves. He got out of bed and walked down the hall to Iona's room. There was light coming from under the door. He knocked twice and walked in. She was sitting up against the headboard reading. She didn't look surprised. He stood in his boxer shorts and a T-shirt and went to speak but she told him to be quiet and pulled back the covers. "Shut the door," she said.

Her hair was still damp from the shower. He buried his hand in it at the nape of her neck and felt its cool thick weight. She slid from beneath him and stretched and switched off the lamp and pulled her nightgown over her head. Bandy could see her body in the dim light. He'd missed so many years with her and now they were like this. They were both these new-old people. She felt very dear to him and the feeling of loss faded as he held on to her. His hands were shaking and she held them and breathed on them. "Do you have anything, you know?" she said. "I can't risk getting pregnant again."

"No."

She climbed out of bed and pulled on her robe and Bandy listened to her go downstairs. After a few seconds the front door opened. He sat up and listened and heard a car door open and close then she came back inside and up the stairs. She took off her robe and she was wet from the rain and she got back in bed and handed Bandy the condom.

"You keep these in your car?"

"No, I stole it out of Tracy's glove box," she said. Then: "Why's Wilhelm still here?"

"He isn't. He went home."

"There's a pickup parked at the end of the driveway."

"Nah."

"There is. I saw it. The dome light was on then it switched off."

He went to get out of bed to go to the window but Iona pushed him down. "It's just Wilhelm messing with something in the shed." He opened the wrapper and Iona kissed him then helped him put it on. They were very careful to be quiet because of Tracy downstairs. Their restraint made what could have been violent tender. After, they lay in the dark in the quiet of the room and faced each other. Bandy felt something should be said. They held each other's hands for a long time then Iona suddenly loosened her grip and let go.

"Hey," he said.

"Don't."

He reached for her and she pushed back his hands. She took a deep breath.

"It's fine," he said. His calloused hands scraped on the sheet.

"You need to go. You can't be here in the morning."

Bandy hesitated, not sure if she meant in her bed or in the house. He got up and looked at her, but couldn't see her in the dark. He went back to his own room and lay down. Confused as to what he'd done wrong, he couldn't sleep.

The next morning they had coffee together alone in the kitchen. Everything had changed. Iona wouldn't look at him. The flowers he'd picked had wilted slightly in their jar. When he finally spoke to her she told him to be quiet and just wait a minute. Tracy slept in or stayed in his room because he'd heard them, they couldn't be sure. Continuing the routine, Iona drove Bandy to work.

They sat in silence in front of the muffler shop and watched Gutierrez through the front window where he sat at his desk reading the paper.

"I'll see you tonight," Bandy said.

"Okay."

"Are you all right?"

"Fine."

"What'd I do wrong?"

"Nothing. Get out. I need to go."

"What'd I do?"

"Nothing. It was a mistake."

"No it wasn't."

"It can't work."

"Why not?"

"I told you, it's us. How we are. It's just us."

"I don't understand."

"You should. It's right in front of you. I can't believe how stupid I am. I can't do this. I can't. Go on, get out. I don't want to be late."

He got out of the car and thanked her for the ride like he always did but today it sounded ridiculous. She sped off without letting him close the door and it flapped open and she had to stop before she turned onto the highway and lean over and pull it shut. He watched her drive away then walked in the side door of the shop and waved to Gutierrez through the window and went to the back room with the footlockers and spare parts stacked up like dinosaur bones and pulled on his stiff and greasy coveralls.

He'd been pitied and he was ashamed. Lack of will was the cause, had always been; it disguised itself as criminal, as misanthrope, but it was obedience, cowardice. He understood why he was flawed but was helpless to change it: Rivers refused dams, wilderness refused roads. In the end you give up. You realize nothing can be avoided and nothing is.

At lunch he sat on the curb along the side of the building and ate an apple he'd found on the workbench. He had a gallon jug of water and his knuckles were bloody from a slipped wrench. He could smell Angel's cigar smoke drifting over from inside. A pickup with Boise plates pulled up in front of Bandy and a guy got out.

"You Angel's cousin?" Bandy said, thinking that if this was the truck that Angel was talking about selling them, it was way too nice for them to afford.

The man looked behind him then back at Bandy. He wore chinos and a black sweatshirt, Red Wing work boots. He had dark eyes and hair, and was lean like a fighter. "No," he said.

Bandy took another bite of his apple, chewed, studied the man, something about him was familiar. "I'm at lunch. The office is in the front if you need work done."

"Are you Dorner?" the man said. He had convict ink creeping out the bottom of his sleeves and up from his collar.

"Who're you?"

"Trinidad told me about you."

"Trinidad?"

"You know him from the coop, from Texas, Indian Creek. People used to call him Sapo?"

"What did that fucking spic tell you about me?"

The man grinned at Bandy. "He said you might want to help him out, like you two had an agreement."

"There was no agreement."

"That lady that dropped off, she your old lady?"

Bandy stood up.

"Take it easy, homeboy." He smiled. "Your old lady looked pissed off. She looked hot."

"I didn't ask Trinidad for anything."

"He's gonna pay you for your time. It'll only be a couple days."

Angel came around the corner and looked at Bandy and the stranger, pointed at his watch.

"I'm coming," Bandy said to Angel.

"Yeah?" Angel said.

"Yeah. Go on."

Angel hesitated then went back inside.

"Come back here at four thirty," Bandy said to the stranger, and threw his apple core in the garbage can on the sidewalk and went back to work. It couldn't hurt to hear him out, maybe make some quick money, see some country. He needed to do something: to act to avoid being acted upon. And there was his debt to Trinidad; he couldn't ignore that.

He left the garage half an hour early and met Victor, he said his name was, in the parking lot. He got in the truck, pointed forward. Victor nodded and started the pickup and they drove through town.

"What kind of money is he talking?"

"Three thousand for you."

"For what?"

Victor didn't say anything.

"I'm out. I can't buy that for three grand."

"But you need money. Mufflers?" Victor said. "You need more money than from mufflers. Your old lady needs more than muffler money."

"Shut the fuck up about her. Five or I'm not going."

"Okay."

"Shit. Okay."

Victor turned around in a gas station parking lot and a woman that had brought in her Volvo earlier that day to have a new muffler put on saw Bandy and smiled. Bandy waved. He felt rotten.

"When do we leave?"

"Tomorrow. I'll pick you up here at seven." Victor stopped in front of the shop and Bandy got out of the truck and Victor pulled away. The shop doors were still open and Angel and Gutierrez were sitting on the workbench playing cards.

"He's back," Angel said.

"I'm back."

"It's the weekend. I brought beer." He pointed to a cooler on the floor.

Bandy grabbed a beer and hoisted himself onto the workbench. "I need to take Monday off. Maybe Tuesday." He opened the beer and took a long drink then another.

"Who's the cholo?" Angel said.

"A friend of a guy I know."

"He looks like a hard guy," Angel said mockingly.

Gutierrez discarded then Angel. Gutierrez took a card. "Fuck," he said. He looked at Bandy. "How are you gonna buy that pickup if you take so much time off?"

"Who's doing who a favor here?"

"You need a truck. We need our cousin to quit borrowing money," Angel said.

Iona pulled into the parking lot. "Can I take the days or not?" Bandy said.

"If you come back in a better mood," Angel said.

"Go ahead," Gutierrez said. "We'll see you Wednesday or so."

"Thanks." Bandy turned to leave.

"Hey, remember," Angel called after him. "College or jail."

"Yeah, I remember."

That night at dinner and afterward Bandy couldn't figure out how to tell Iona that he was leaving. The thought crossed his mind that he might not be coming back. He sat on the couch next to Tracy. It was a dead room and the TV babbled in it. Tracy was doing his ankle exercises and sweating from the effort. Iona was reading, had been reading since she got home. Bandy was the only one looking at the TV and he wasn't really watching it. That went on then Iona went to bed then Tracy.

Late in the night Bandy decided what he would say to Iona. He went to her room but she didn't answer when he knocked and when he tried to go in she'd put a chair or something in front of the door because it didn't have a lock. He stood and looked at the door. He didn't hear her moving around inside so he went back to his bedroom.

He couldn't sleep; there was no use in trying. He went back to Iona's room and forced the door open enough to push the chair out of the way. Iona switched on the light while he was struggling with the door.

"Get out of here," she said softly.

"I'm leaving tomorrow."

"I don't care what you do tomorrow. I want you out of my room now. Get out. God, I was sleeping." Then: "Where are you gonna go?" She was still not fully awake; she smiled lazily and stretched and yawned. "I mean, really. Where can you go? You don't have anyplace but here."

"I have to leave town for a few days. I need to talk to you. We need to talk."

"Not now." Iona turned onto her side. "Jesus, you're hopeless. Get out. You probably already woke up Tracy."

The light switched on in the hallway and Bandy heard Tracy hobbling up the stairs on his crutches. From below he called to his mother and asked if she was all right.

"See?" Iona said to Bandy. "I'm fine, Trace," she yelled.

"Jesus fucking Christ." Bandy went back to his room and slammed the door. He listened to Iona and Tracy's murmuring voices then heard Tracy come down the hall. Bandy sat on the edge of his bed in the dark and didn't move. After a minute or so Tracy left and went back downstairs.

In the morning he went to Tracy's room before it was light and told him he'd see him in a few days. Tracy looked confused and Bandy left the room without waiting for him to say anything and went into the kitchen. Iona was at the table reading a magazine, chewing on a plastic pen cap.

"I need a ride to town."

"It's Saturday."

"I still need a ride."

"You're seriously leaving?"

Bandy picked up Iona's purse and dug through it and took her keys. "I told you, I don't have a choice."

"Of course you do."

"Not this time."

"The only person in this house that doesn't have a choice is Tracy." Iona tried to take the keys from Bandy but he didn't let her. "Slow down. Christ, just stay here. I didn't mean for what happened to happen, Bandy. I really didn't, but we can work this out."

"I thought you were dead. Everything that happened to me happened because of that. Do you know what that means?"

Iona's lips parted slightly and her eyes narrowed. "You can't blame me." Her face worked slowly, painfully into a smile, near tears. "Were you sad? Did you miss me? Is that what you're trying to say? Because you sure as hell didn't seem sad when you were sleeping around on me or getting thrown in jail and making me bail you out over and over again. You didn't seem sad at all. It was the happiest I ever saw you."

He couldn't speak.

"You can't blame me," she said. "I won't fucking have it."

Tracy was in the doorway leaning on his crutches wearing only his boxer shorts, a map of his bedsheets pressed into his cheek and chest.

"I'm sorry," Bandy said to Tracy.

"Go if you're going," Iona said.

"I'll leave the car at the shop," Bandy said to Iona. "See ya," he said to Tracy, and looked at his legs, his bare and scarred feet. "Couple days," Bandy said, and walked out the door.

He parked along the side of the shop and waited in the purple-and-gray light of the morning for Victor. He hadn't brought anything with him outside of a pair of gloves and his stocking hat. He didn't bring any of his medicine or vitamins. He didn't want to seem weak and he could miss a few days; it wouldn't kill him. Victor showed up on time and Bandy put Iona's keys under her seat and climbed into Victor's truck. The heater was roaring and Bandy took off his hat and tossed it on the dashboard.

"Morning," Victor said.

"Yep."

They drove through town and passed the beat-up trucks belonging to the early birds eating at the Huckleberry. Wilhelm's truck was there but Bandy didn't see him in the yellow light of the windows. They jostled over the cut-up road. The lake was glass and the city park downtown was empty and looked forsaken.

Bandy didn't want to do this but this was what he was doing. His anger was like a pebble in his fist. Ponderosa pines towered over the road and blocked the sky; they were like columns, guards urging him on, as if the gates were closing behind him.

On the highway Victor opened the glove box and handed Bandy a map of Idaho and Montana. The pages had been torn out of an atlas and taped together.

"Where?" Bandy said.

Victor leaned over and studied the map as he drove. He traced his finger north across Idaho then east into Montana. "Butte," Victor said.

"The hell is in Butte?"

"Trinidad's brother, big bad Berto." He made a clucking sound with his tongue.

Bandy waited for him to say more but he didn't. He figured he'd find out soon enough and there wasn't any need to dwell on it one minute longer than he had to. Victor switched on the radio to the oldies station and they drove. The day was nice for driving. Bandy felt his anger fade, and a strong feeling of despair replaced it.

They crossed the county line and went down the Goose Creek grade. It was already full summer in the valley below: creek shattered, willow wended, a good valley. They drove through ten or fifteen miles of cattle country then passed a sign for another new golf course. There were townhouses and condos partially hidden in the pines on the hillsides and they struck Bandy as being somehow predatory. He still didn't understand where all these people came from. It was like they were refugees, people set upon by some unknown force who had saved nothing from their past lives but their bank accounts, or maybe it was their bank accounts that had driven them from their homes and into the mountains. He remembered his father telling him stories of the Okies being turned away at the California border during the Dust Bowl and it struck him as some kind of polar shift. The wealthy were invading and it wasn't out of necessity; they weren't driven by famine or depression. They did it at their leisure. What right did they have? As much as anyone, was the answer he came up with. They had to do something after all, everybody did. You're either running from or running toward, usually both, always both.

At the valley's edge the road narrowed and they joined the Little Salmon and Bandy thought, now I'm too far away to walk home.

"Is that kid your old lady's or yours?" Victor said.

Bandy remembered that Iona had seen a truck in the driveway. He'd been followed home too. Victor knew where he lived, where Iona and Tracy lived. "He's our kid."

"What happened to him?"

"Stay away from him. Stay away from my house."

"I was just making conversation I got a buddy got his legs blown off in the Marines, training accident."

"He fell off a roof. He'll walk again."

"Sure, he will. Hey, you like living in that town?"

"We aren't talking anymore."

"No?" Victor said, but after that he was silent. Bandy glanced at him and he was smiling.

The road stayed with the river and the water dumped over a series of modest drops and the pools below were dark and moss cradled. Spears of shadow from the trees began incrementally then the canyon walls climbed higher and the shadow became complete. The river boiled against the rocks and a foul-looking yellow foam was dammed up in the slack water and on the backs of fallen logs. Trees and brush along the banks were strung with dead grass and grocery bags, tires, flood debris.

The canyon eventually opened up and the trees retreated. The hills were steep and wrinkled with subsidence and game trails and covered in thick green grass. Black cows were scattered about grazing high above the river; some would inevitably fall and become four-legged rafts. The drainages dividing the hills were clogged with small trees and buckbrush. The Main Salmon swallowed up the Little Salmon in one great bend and pushed on stronger for it.

Victor pulled into a service station. The bathroom was broken so Bandy pissed behind the dumpster while the gas pumped. Victor went inside and paid. Bandy wasn't about to pitch for gas. They drove on and the day got warmer. The gray, rusted rock of the canyon tore through the smooth fabric of the hills, estuaries of grass.

"Trinidad said you killed a cop." Victor hadn't spoken for some time.

Bandy didn't feel that he should have to explain himself. He glanced at Victor but didn't say anything.

"You were in the coop?"

"Yeah."

"I'm just like you. I owe him for some shit. That's why I'm here."

"What kind of shit?"

"The kind you end up owing people for."

"I'm not his fucking pal. We were in the same lockups a couple a times, that's it. We shared a roof."

"He didn't talk about his brother?"

"It was a long time ago. I don't remember anything that anybody said."

Victor smiled. "Yeah, Berto, he's my albatross. You know what that means, albatross?"

Bandy didn't care what it meant and he didn't feel like talking so he didn't. The road opened up and they dropped into the lush farm country of the Camas Prairie. The sky was blown over with thin, torn clouds.

The last time he'd been this way he'd been with Iona. They'd stopped in town and had breakfast and a few drinks. From there they'd driven north, windows down, stripped to the waist in the midday heat, drinking beer from the cooler in the backseat. Her bare legs beside him, brown and smooth. She had a scar on her knee like someone had stabbed her with a Phillips-head screwdriver.

In Fern she told him to wait and went into her father's house. Bandy leaned against the car and kicked his boot heel in the dirt. The house was gray and silvered as a snag with the nails popped on the siding like someone had whaled on the back side and driven them that way. Springtime, the ground was wet a few inches down then dry and gray below. The dirt was better in Lake Fork. The curtains parted and Iona's father pressed his hands to the glass and looked out. Bandy held up his hand to wave but the man banged on the glass with a bony fist and turned and disappeared in the blur. Bandy listened to Iona and her father yell indecipherably at each other. Then a girl, Iona's sister, Faith, came out and told Bandy to go and that Iona didn't want him to stay anyway, but if he could, would he mind giving her a ride to Lewiston? Bandy nudged her aside and walked into the house without knocking.

"You coming or staying?" he said. The floor was wood and sticky with something and Bandy lifted his feet several times to test the extent of it. There was nobody in the room. The yelling continued from the back of the house then it stopped and Iona came and told him again to goddammit wait outside. She said her father loved her very much and he didn't want to see her disappear. She was drunk and so was Bandy and he thought she was being a little dramatic. He remembered thinking disappear is exactly what I'm going for. Goddamn disappear me. He went back outside. The sun was bright.

Faith had taken the beer from the backseat of his car and wandered out to the highway. She sat on the cooler drinking, trying to thumb a ride. Bandy lifted her by her arm and got a beer then set her back down. Before he got back to his car, a truck stopped with three men in the cab and one got out and helped Faith put the cooler in the back and they passed beer into the cab and Faith climbed onto their laps and she was gone.

Iona came outside carrying a large green suitcase. A suitcase she later told Bandy had been her mother's, one of the only things she'd left behind. It seemed to Bandy then, and even more now, that it would've been the first thing she needed to leave. He imagined Iona lugging her suitcase down the driveway and pitching it over the fence and climbing after it. Maybe Bill had picked her up. He told himself to stop thinking about it. He couldn't, though. He couldn't decide if he should've never gone to her room like he did or if he should've gone much sooner.

At Grangeville they turned east. Several small towns came and went, logging towns judging by the makeshift mills and the yard debris. Poor people, busted trucks, motorcross bikes and snowmobiles that looked like they'd been dragged behind a truck or thrown from a cliff: hard, beautiful places with sawdust and gravel in their cuffs. They followed the Clearwater then the Lochsa, its amber water like thin, new oil in the sun. The canyon was winding and slow going. Then they left the river and began to gain elevation. A cow moose was licking a pile of road salt at the county plow station and as they passed it lifted its knurled head and looked around. Bandy glanced at Victor to see if he'd noticed and was glad it was only for him.

The mountains had been logged and burned or burned then logged; gray, narrow trees like matchsticks or pine needles stabbed into sand castle walls. A railroad model in its sparseness; logging roads as straight as saw kerfs. They continued to climb and from elevation Bandy could look out over the extent of it. New trees were growing too. In parts it had not burned or been logged because it was too steep and boulder-strewn with buckbrush everywhere. He knew exactly how these mountains would look in twenty or thirty years because this is how everything around Lake Fork used to be and would most likely be again. The real question was what had it looked like in the beginning.

At the summit there remained squat gray snowbanks cross-sectioned by the plow and the blower where you could read the history of the winter in the layers like the rings of a tree. Victor pointed up onto the hillside and stopped the truck. "Deers."

"It's just deer, asshole. Even if it's a bunch of them. Deer."

Victor cocked his head; he seemed to be appraising Bandy's face, his tone. "Deer," he said. The snow was firm and the deer were small and they traversed the hillside and disappeared into the trees without breaking stride or slipping. Victor got out of the truck then Bandy. There wasn't any traffic and the wind blew cold and fast over the snow and whipped the men's clothes tight to their skin. Bandy pissed and his stream of urine was shattered as the wind pressed on his back and swirled around him and gusted on. He felt sick already, his guts knotted. He wished he'd brought his medicine, but thought it was probably his head that was hurting him now, not his body.

They climbed back into the truck and drove on and passed a road sign half-buried in the snow that marked the official site of the Montana border. The sun burned directly overhead; it was nice to no longer be looking into it.

Missoula was clogged with road construction and detours and when they came out the other side Bandy was behind the wheel with a six-pack of beer on the seat beside him. Victor slept with his head against the passenger window, but he woke up before long and opened the glove box and handed Bandy a newspaper clipping. The article said that a local bar owner in Butte had killed a man in self-defense. The dead man had a criminal record and it was a violation of his parole to carry a firearm, or to even be in the bar where he was shot. The police weren't releasing any names until the case was closed. No charges were pending. There was an article about some kids killed in a car wreck and a new theater, too. He gave the paper back to Victor.

Victor pointed to the article. "Trinidad's brother, Berto."

"The dead one?"

Victor smiled. Bandy didn't like his smile. He slowed down a little, no longer feeling compelled to hurry. I'm in the wrong place, he thought, kept thinking. I'm doing the wrong thing. It wasn't a conflicted feeling; it was the feeling. Victor stayed awake but he didn't say anything else after he put the newspaper clipping back in the glove box.

"Are we gonna kill him?" Bandy said later.

Victor didn't answer.

"The guy. The bar owner."

"Not tonight."

"You got a gun?"

"No." He smiled. "I'm on parole."

"Well, there you have it." Bandy turned and gave Victor a rotten smile.

Victor rolled down his window a crack and the cool air swept through the cab. The radio reception had gone again. It was a great flat nothing, an endless field of grass. Bandy pulled over to piss again near where Highway 1 drops down to Philipsburg and Anaconda. The wind smelled of rain, and what Bandy first took for clouds up ahead he realized were in fact low hills preceding distant peaks, tall and jagged. He wanted to go home.

A short time later they passed a sign announcing the distance to Butte. "We're almost there," Bandy said. Victor's eyes were closed, but he wasn't sleeping. "Shit," he said quietly.

They came into Butte. Our Lady of the Rockies looked down on the shambled town, her great toxic pit and brick buildings and ruined streets. Bandy pointed to the statue like a doll on a dresser but Victor's eyes stayed closed. "Wake up," Bandy said. Victor opened his eyes and leaned into the windshield and waved off the statue as something he'd seen before.

They zigzagged through town. The potholes and railroad tracks beat hell out of Victor's truck. Butte reminded Bandy of Lake Fork in the old days, just after the mill had closed when it was crumbling into a kind of righteous, hard-earned squalor, when it used to have a personality. The people of Butte had gone through one hundred years of digging—half boom, half bust—only to become this: a town of wrecked bones and poisoned blood. They'd run it all the way to the ground. Lake Fork seemed whorish in comparison. Bandy entertained the idea that Butte would've welcomed him home, maybe with a parade.

They got back on the freeway to find a motel and found one and stayed in a shared room with two beds. In the morning when Bandy woke up, Victor was gone. The room was hot and the air was dry and raw in his nose. A dun-colored light shone in through the curtains. He hoisted himself out of bed and parted the curtains and saw the truck was gone. He sat down and massaged the bones in his hands and waited.

It was afternoon when Victor returned. He dropped two bags of take-out food on the bed.

"Eat," he said.

Bandy opened the bags and ate while Victor flipped through channels on the television.

"You talk to Trinidad?" Bandy said.

"No," Victor said without looking away from the TV.

"You're out sightseeing while I'm sitting around here."

"I was doing work."

"I don't fucking like it. I'm feeling fucking hunted." He wadded the empty food bag and threw it at the trash and missed and went into the bathroom and slammed the door. He sat down on the edge of the tub. I should call her, he thought. See if she might come and get me. Victor had either switched off the television or turned down the volume because it was suddenly quiet. Bandy listened for him but couldn't hear anything but the cars outside. He leaned forward on the tub and quietly locked the bathroom door. The food he'd eaten felt like it was alive and squirming in his stomach. Again he wished he'd brought his medicine. It wasn't good to miss any days, the doctor had told him that much. It was a cycle, a regimen, and when it was disrupted he had to start all over. He turned on the hot water and chased a spider down the drain and a dead fly then plugged the drain. The water filled the tub but he didn't undress. He just sat there and looked at it.

There was a rap on the door. "Dorner," Victor said.

He'd been in there for a long time and the water had gone tepid and looked slightly yellow. "What?"

"Okay."

When he came out Victor was sitting at the small table in the corner studying the newspaper. He didn't look up when Bandy sat down on the bed. After a few minutes Victor slid the paper to the far side of the table and wiped his hand across the tabletop and checked his fingers for dust. Still facing the wall: "I know people here," Victor said.

Bandy didn't care; he looked at Victor with a look that said he didn't care.

"Why'd you bring me then?"

"Trinidad told me to."

"Why?"

"He told me to." Victor blew air out his nose. He stood up. "I'm going to stay with the people I know. He didn't say I had to stay with you."

"I'm gonna be stuck here."

"It won't be long."

Victor left, and as soon as Bandy was alone he felt as if he was being watched. Hours passed and he stayed seated on the edge of the bed and didn't move and he could feel the weight of someone's eyes on him. Night fell and he was relieved. He stood and paced the room. He thought of Iona and being in her bed. He imagined Tracy in his chair watching TV with no one around.

Iona somewhere, maybe with someone. He put on his shoes and pulled on his coat and walked out into the parking lot. There was nowhere for him to go. The freeway roared.

Down the access road there was a sign for a truck stop and that was as good as it was going to get if he didn't want to walk back to Butte. He sat in a booth in the restaurant and drank coffee until he realized they sold beer. He kept the old, limping waitress running for more until he was drunk. Sometime after midnight he paid her and left her a ten-dollar tip and went back to the room feeling generous. The door to the room was open, which was fortunate because he hadn't brought a key. He stood swaying in the doorway for a minute then switched on the light and realized he hadn't left the door open at all but that Victor had been by and he'd brought more food. Bandy kicked the door shut and threw the bag of food against the wall.

He sat down on the edge of the bed and after much confusion with the instructions on how to dial long distance he punched in the only phone number he knew. It rang for a long time then Bandy hung up and stared at the phone. He picked it up and dialed the number again.

"Hello." She picked up on the second ring. She'd been sleeping.

"It's me." He could hear her moving around, pulling a chair back from the table in the kitchen.

"You just called."

"Yeah."

"I almost got it."

"Sorry it's so late."

"Are you all right?"

"Fine."

"Where are you?"

"Butte. I'm in Butte, Montana, in some motel."

"Are you alone?"

"Yes, I'm alone. I'm drunk."

"It happens."

He slid the receiver down his cheek and almost dropped it. "I'm sorry." Iona didn't say anything. "But you left me."

"I had good reason to leave."

"You left me and off you went and you raised the kid. Tracy. The good kid. I don't know why his name's Tracy and I don't care. It's a good name. For a good kid a good name. I don't know about those blue eyes, I don't care. I'm an awful sonofabitch and you know it. Fucking lonesome."

"Why don't you come home?"

"I'm losing my mind."

"Come home."

"I can't. Not yet. I'm gonna make some money, good money. And there's these people, this asshole, I know him from before and I owe him. I didn't want anything but I still owe him. I didn't want to leave." He slammed his fist down on the table and felt the vibration all the way up his arm. "I wanted to stay."

"Come home. We'll manage."

"No, we won't. I'll make some money and come home then we'll manage. When I say we'll manage we'll manage. I don't need you feeling sorry for me."

"Please, come home."

"Shush," Bandy said. "I'm sorry. I shouldn't have said that. Go and sleep. I'm getting us going so I can stay. You and me. You know what I mean? You do." He hung up the phone before she could say anything and stared at it, looked around the room. "You do," he said to the wall. He didn't want to be there; he wanted to be with Iona. He switched off the light and pulled a blanket from the bed and a pillow and took off his clothes and lay down on the floor. He could see under the bed and there was nothing there.

Victor didn't return the following day and Bandy stayed in bed except to go to the bathroom. He couldn't sleep that night because of his hangover and his general poor health. He stayed up watching television and slept through the next day and woke up in the evening when Victor came in and told Bandy to get dressed. They drove away from town and up into the hills. Victor parked the truck at the bottom of a long, steep driveway and he and Bandy got out.

"His house," Victor said.

"How're we doing this?" Bandy said. He needed time. He needed for it to be explained.

"Come on."

Bandy followed Victor up the hill. Victor pulled a pair of gloves from his pocket and Bandy caught a glimpse of the knife in his belt. He'd left his gloves in the truck so he ran back and got them. Victor didn't wait for him and he was winded and his head throbbed by the time he caught back up. The driveway widened and they came to a large log house. A motion-sensitive light above the garage switched on and scared him. A dog barked. Victor didn't hesitate and walked right through the unlocked front door. Bandy followed him with his hands at his sides and his heart pounding.

The ceilings were high and everything was made of logs even the furniture and the handrails. It smelled like new carpet. They walked across the new carpet and Bandy looked over his shoulder for footprints left by him and Victor but there were none. It was a new house, Bandy realized. The whole thing was new. The living room was big and bright and open but there was nobody in it. A television set was on and the barking dog sounded far away. Victor turned up the volume a little on the TV and took the portable phone off its stand and shoved it under the couch cushion.

Upstairs they went from room to room stealthily until they found the man. He was hanging a mirror on the wall in the master bedroom. He had a hammer in his hand. He was thick-shouldered with thin black hair and a belly he was trying to hide with a high waistband. He didn't look surprised to see them. Victor pulled the knife from his belt then went quickly to one side of the room and Bandy went to the other and they closed in on the man with raised hands like they were cornering an animal.

"Hey there," the man said.

They backed him against the wall and as soon as his shoulder touched it he lifted the hammer. He didn't ask who they were or why. He swung the hammer claw first at Bandy and missed then he swung it at Victor and tore a gash on his forearm and when Victor leapt back Bandy caught the man's arm before he could swing again and they wrestled for the hammer then he felt the man flex everything and writhe and Bandy held the man while Victor continued to stab him then suddenly he worried that Victor might just stab him too so he pitched the man down and stepped away. Bandy now held the hammer. The light in the room surged then dimmed. His body flooded with adrenaline and he began to shiver. Victor held his knife, bloody to the wrist. For a few moments they looked at one another then Victor held out his hands and looked at them, the gouge on his arm. He knelt down and wiped the blood off on the man's shirt and put his knife away. He motioned Bandy over and they lifted the man, still alive, onto the bed and rolled him up in the blankets. Bandy felt suddenly sick and ran into the bathroom and threw up. He finished and looked in the mirror at his watering eyes. His stomach cramped and knotted again and he undid his pants and sat down on the toilet and passed a black, watery stool.

When he came out of the bathroom Victor had a bucket filled with soap and water and he was scrubbing at the few spots of blood on the gray carpet. The bed was remade with different blankets. Victor had a piece of his own shirt tied around the cut on his arm. Bandy picked up the throw rug from the foot of the bed and tossed it on top of the stains that Victor was scrubbing.

"Let's go," Bandy said.

Victor stood and picked up the man's hammer from the nightstand where Bandy had left it and looked at the throw rug and nodded then went and finished hanging the mirror. Bandy was shivering, mouth breathing. "Christ," he said. "What's the goddamn point?" Victor acted like he didn't hear him and when he was done he tossed the hammer on the bed.

They lifted the man and took him downstairs and set him by the front door. He was no longer moving. Victor went down the hill and brought up the pickup and they loaded him into the back and covered him with a tarp. The two men looked at each other over the truck bed. Bandy felt like he was drooling and wiped his chin but his hand came away dry. Victor shook his head and they got in the truck and drove down the driveway. Before they'd reached the bottom a car turned toward them off of the main road. Victor flipped on the high beams and drove fast at the car and it pulled far off the shoulder and into the ditch. A woman was driving and there was a young boy in the passenger seat. Victor kept driving and ran the stop sign at the main road and drove fast away from town and further into the hills.

"Who was that?" Bandy said. Victor didn't say anything. "Was that his family?"

"There's no family."

"There was a kid."

"It wasn't his."

They followed the road east, headlights tracking, gloom at the edges, trees twisted and stricken. Bandy put his shaking hands into his armpits and hugged himself. He thought he could sleep if he were on a couch or a bed, the couch at the ranch, the bed. He thought of Iona and Tracy, sleep and loneliness and prison. He was going to be locked up again.

They climbed a long hill and Victor had to shift into second gear then at the top of the hill he swung the truck through a narrow gate overgrown with brush and drove fast on the dirt road like he knew where he was going. He skidded around two switchbacks and sped up a steep hill then they were on a high ridge. Bandy could see the glow of the lights from Butte over a lower ridge ahead of them. Across the darkness was the statue of the Virgin Mary that watched over the town, tall and bone white and on nearly equal elevation. Victor stopped the truck at a cliff edge and switched off the motor. He left the lights on. There were two shovels leaning against a crooked tree.

They began digging the grave. Bandy faced the statue as he worked. He would be paid for this; he would pay. Despair rang in him like a bell. They stopped and Victor dragged the man out of the truck and kicked him into the grave, not two feet deep then went back to his truck and came back with a Polaroid camera.

"Show me the face."

Bandy pulled back the blankets and stepped away and Victor

took the picture and came and stood next to Bandy and they watched the picture come up from the darkness. Bandy gagged on his own spit and bent at the waist and dry heaved. Victor stepped back.

"What's wrong with you?" Victor said.

"I'm sick."

"You're a fucking pussy."

Bandy stood up and pushed Victor in the chest. Victor smiled and put the camera down on the tailgate. Bandy couldn't fight him, couldn't fight him and win. He'd end up in the grave too. "We're almost done here," Bandy said. Victor laughed quietly and nodded. They backfilled the grave then picked up dozens of stones and stacked them on top of the dirt, then gathered dead branches and tossed them around to hide the hump in the earth. When they'd finished, Victor walked to the edge of the bluff and hurled the shovels into the night, spinning and gone, silently.

They drove without speaking back to the motel room and Victor dropped Bandy off and left without saying anything. Bandy went inside and sat down on the bed and stared at the motel room door and thought he'd never sleep again and for that night and the next he didn't.

Chapter 13

LAND OF NO USE

IT WAS TRACY that was up first. He made coffee then called Wilhelm and woke him and asked if he'd been sleeping then hung up, smiled to himself. He sat down and the joke faded and he started to feel lonely, like the house was an outpost in an ended world. There was something about the predawn darkness compared to late night, a harsher version of the same thing.

Iona came downstairs and poured herself a cup of coffee. She looked nice, simply dressed, jeans and a flattering silken blouse. Lately she'd been taking more care with her appearance and for some reason this bothered Tracy. He still wasn't sure why Bandy had left, but he knew his mother had something to do with it.

Wilhelm came in without knocking. He had a wild look about him, his chin tucked down and one eye bulging slightly, his hair doing all it could to be disorderly in an inch and a half. He wore an ill-fitting dress shirt and what he called his funeral slacks. Tracy wore the same jeans he wore five days a week and a T-shirt from the lumberyard picnic. They had coffee and Wilhelm looked at a map of Boise and wrote down some street names. They left their coffee cups in the sink and climbed into Wilhelm's truck and made the two-hour drive down the hill.

They found the store easy enough but it wasn't open for another hour, so they wandered the outskirts, Garden City, the sprawl: It all felt done in. They went to a donut shop and had donuts and drank coffee and watched the clock. At nine thirty they returned.

It was a large showroom, like a furniture store, but it was filled with wheelchairs and portable toilets, braces; long rows of shelving stocked with unmarked boxes lined the walls. Tracy sat down and the clerk came and took off his shoes and measured his feet. Iona told him what the doctor had told her and he said it was no problem. He'd get them fixed up in no time. Wilhelm wandered off for awhile then came from the back of the store with a bulky leather boot in each hand; they had steel reinforcements on the sides and buckles similar to ski boots to lock them down. He passed the boots to Tracy.

"What about these?" Tracy said to the clerk, holding up one of the boots. The clerk gave Wilhelm a questioning look then told Tracy that that pair along with all the others heaped in the back had been included in a donation from the mental hospital in Orofino. The clerk said that they were on their way to the landfill. He was a slight, white-haired man that seemed too young for white hair; elfin, he seemed appropriate for his station. Tracy didn't like him, though there was no good reason for it; he'd never been a bully. He told the clerk he'd take them in a size eleven.

"I can't sell you those," the clerk said. "They're not designed to do what you need."

"What are they designed to do?" Iona said flatly.

"I'm not sure. They're antiques. For all I know they could've been used to keep people from running away. Polio maybe, I don't know."

Wilhelm squatted in front of Tracy's chair and held the boot up next to his foot. "I think I picked right," he said to Tracy.

After a short struggle Tracy and Wilhelm managed to get both boots on. He stood and tried to walk but couldn't. They were heavy and as stiff as wooden boxes, as comfortable; foot coffins. He sat back down in his chair and took a deep breath and told the clerk he'd take them. The clerk said again that it wasn't his place to sell garbage. Tracy and Wilhelm argued with the man and after a few minutes Tracy stood up, angry now, feeding on the pain in his feet. He thought he might hit him. Iona stepped between them and opened her purse and put two twenty-dollar bills on the chair next to the clerk then stopped and produced one more and put it with the other two and walked outside. All three men watched her leave.

Wilhelm passed Tracy his crutches then gathered up the shoes that he'd worn in and they followed Iona outside. The heat of the day hit Tracy in the face and kind of knocked him out of gear and he stopped for a moment and watched the clerk through the display window as he slumped in a wheelchair. He was surprised he didn't go for the money. Wilhelm put his hand on Tracy's back and helped him to the pickup then took his crutches and tossed them into the bed. Tracy watched the clerk make his way through the store and flip the open sign around to closed and sit back down in a different wheelchair. Wilhelm helped Tracy into the cab and Iona climbed in silently after him.

A hot wind blew in through Wilhelm's open window. "Is there something wrong with me that I get mad when someone won't take my money?"

"It wasn't your money, Wilhelm," Iona said.

"You didn't have to pay him," Tracy said.

"Why did we come down here?" Her voice was clipped and loud.

Tracy leaned away from her, disgusted by her. "I don't know. I don't need fucking corrective shoes."

"Good, because you didn't get them."

"He was a turd."

"Who cares? He didn't wake up this morning to put up with you."

"The fucking little weasel," Tracy said.

Wilhelm drove. Tracy tried to focus on the traffic and the bustle of the city instead of the pounding in his feet or the guilt, and the way the presence of his mother seemed to amplify it. He smelled hamburgers then he smelled cut grass. They crossed the Boise River and the water was brown and trees were tipped into it from the banks like animals drinking. There were pale-skinned inner tubers with beer coolers trailing on ropes like flood victims walking their dead pets. They passed a mall with darkened windows, a car dealership, another, and another. A kid was riding a wheelie on his BMX bike as he went down the sidewalk. They all turned and watched him glide over the curb cuts, hardly pedaling, floating. His face was much older than Tracy had expected; he was a grown man.

They slipped from Boise back into Garden City without a noticeable difference; a sign announced the boundary. As they continued the businesses began to peter out and the trees thinned and degraded into dirt lots and RV dealerships, tract-home communities with gates and overwatered lawns, mansions surrounded by junkyards. Tracy had sweated through his shirt. He wouldn't look at his mother; he felt her anger smoldering beside him. He turned and looked at Wilhelm and the old man winked at him and Tracy found something in that and turned to Iona. "That scummy little shit woke up this morning a fool and ended up making forty dollars off of another fool so for him I bet it was a better than average day."

"Sixty dollars, you ungrateful little asshole," Iona said quietly. They turned onto Highway 55 toward Lake Fork. They didn't speak after that, not for nearly an hour. The country greened up with the elevation gain and there were farms and rolling hills with expansive vistas. They stayed in the far right lane on the steep hills. Wilhelm kept a nervous eye to his mirrors and wiped his dripping nose on his sleeve. His head looked infected from the heat and he kept huffing little breaths and swiping his sleeve across his forehead to keep the sweat from his eyes. They pulled over at the one-gas-station town of Banks to use the bathroom and get a drink of water. Tracy managed to make it to the urinal with only one crutch.

When he came out, Iona was facing away watching the inflatable boats go by on the river. Banks was a loading and unloading point for river trips where river guides, tan and lean and stricken with hangovers and morning marijuana, distractedly watched over their clientele as they milled about swaddled in life jackets, snapping pictures with disposable cameras. Tracy watched his mom from behind. It wasn't just that she'd lost weight; she'd always been fat and skinny all in the same month. It was something else. She held herself differently now. She didn't cross her arms over her chest all the time or cover her mouth when she smiled. She stood there with her hands in her back pockets and for the first time that Tracy could remember she looked comfortable in her own skin, not like it was holding her too tight or somehow binding on her shoulders.

She turned at the sound of Tracy staggering in the gravel. She was crying. She wiped her eyes. It was a physical pain Tracy felt in his chest. Something from when he was a child, he'd made her cry then. For what he couldn't remember, didn't want to remember. What was it that Bill used to say: trust neither limping dog nor crying woman. Limping son, crying mother. Iona looked away to the river and wiped her eyes on the back of her hand. A log truck barreled by on the highway and Tracy turned and watched it pass.

"I was embarrassed for you," she said. "I was ashamed to be with you."

"I said I was sorry."

"No, you didn't. You said I was a fool."

"Well, you shouldn't have paid him."

"I never raised you to treat other people like that. I don't care who they are."

Some of the people standing along the bank beside them had turned and they were watching Tracy and Iona instead of the boats. Tracy looked back at them with sad curiosity. He felt set upon.

"What do you want from me?" Iona asked.

"Nothing. I want nothing."

"Let's get in the truck," Wilhelm said. "We can talk this out on the road."

Tracy threw his crutch into the bed and stood. It felt as if the boots had been engineered to push against the most poorly used parts of his feet. He opened the door of the pickup and pulled himself in and sat down. Iona waited for him to get situated then climbed in after him. Wilhelm pulled the truck back onto the highway.

"We both know how you raised me," Tracy said.

"I did the best I could," Iona said.

"You raised me to be less than everyone else, to be small, like I don't have a right to be anywhere. Then I get Bandy to come here and I got somebody for once that's not busy kissing everybody's ass all the time, babysitting rich people's houses, somebody instead of you and goddamn Bill the butcher."

"Don't call him that." Iona laughed and hiccupped with laughter. Tracy suddenly felt his age. He felt young and weak and he knew that the more he talked the more he showed it. "You think Bandy's not afraid of anyone? He's scared of you. He's scared of me and Wilhelm. Ellen, even." She turned and faced Tracy, looked him in the eye. "Your big tough ex-con father, he ran away. He left. I'm still here. Don't forget it." She turned away from him. "I swear if you weren't my son I'd smack the shit out of you."

Tracy shut his mouth and leaned back in the seat and looked at Wilhelm. There was a vein in the old man's temple like a divining rod; he leaned over and smiled at Tracy then looked at Iona. "It's been a long day," he said. He drove cautiously through the canyon. He pointed to the steep hillsides that had been hidden in the darkness on the way down that morning and told them how a few years before there had been a forest fire along this stretch of road started by an RV towing a car with a flat tire. The fire had burned until the snow fell and thousands of acres of forest were lost. But since then the ground vegetation had returned and it was gaining ground on the black and raw trunks of the ponderosas, the burnt stones and scorched cliff faces.

"In the spring it rained like hell," Wilhelm said. "There were landslides. The river was mostly mud and trees. There weren't any plants left to hold the dirt to the hillsides. Some people lost their houses. Not many, though. There aren't many houses around here to lose. Forests are supposed to burn anyway, they're built to burn. Seedpods get opened by the heat, understory gets thinned. It's supposed to happen. Hell, trees wouldn't be made outta wood if they weren't made to burn."

Then he told them about another time years ago when a train loaded down with lumber had derailed and lost its cargo into the river. "It was all boards, all the way across, just boards," he said. Men came with gaff hooks and rope and fished the planks from the slackwater. Whole families formed human chains and sent the lumber back up the bank to the road to waiting pickup trucks and flatbed trailers. The news crews came and filmed the people then the police came and chased everyone off and stood guard through the night. The lumber washed downstream into the big water and the big rapids where it was snapped and chewed up and arrived in Banks in splinters. Wilhelm's story, like most of his stories, took a long time to tell and by the end they were turning onto the road by the Finn church.

The earthmovers were still going out in the fields, scraping the pasturelands and grading them smooth into fairways and greens. Wilhelm wouldn't look even when Iona pointed to the workmen building a cart bridge over the canal. Dust clouds hovered and yellowed the afternoon. They were working a half mile from the church, but to Tracy it seemed unholy for them to be doing what they were doing so close. He'd been right: There were more coming, and there always would be. Until it all fell apart. He thought people were like bugs. If Bandy didn't come back, maybe he would sell some land, maybe all of it. What was the difference? Might as well get it over with. What was ownership if nobody cared?

They descended the last hill to the ranch and crossed the creek. The Piatt boys were out in the field with their rifles like small sentries and they raised their arms and waved when the truck passed by. Iona and Wilhelm waved back, but Tracy just stared. They pulled into the driveway and got out and Tracy stood and waited for someone to help him get his crutches from the truck bed, but his mother and Wilhelm must have assumed that because he was on his feet he could do it himself because they left him alone in the driveway. He pulled himself up the side of the bed and stretched but he couldn't reach the crutches without climbing all the way in or going around. He let himself down and realized it didn't matter about the crutches because he was standing anyway. And for once, he thought, I'm on my feet and I'm not going to die from the pain. He looked at his boots and smiled a little and turned and began to make his way toward the house.

Iona came out then and stopped and watched. Wilhelm lifted his arms above his head and whistled. "Look at her go," he said.

"Fuck you, Wilhelm," Tracy said.

"Maybe you should take it easy," Iona said.

"If I take it any easier I might as well set my ass back in the chair. Make way. I'm coming in."

"I'm going home," Wilhelm said, and went and opened the tailgate and got Tracy's crutches and brought them to Iona while Tracy teetered toward the front door.

"Don't kill him," the old man said.

"I won't." Iona gave Wilhelm a hug and followed Tracy inside.

The house was cool from all the windows and doors being closed all day. Tracy sat down at the kitchen table. Iona watched him.

"What?" he said.

"Nothing." The light was gray and dingy in the kitchen. Tracy reached behind him and flipped on the light above the table.

"I'll make dinner later but I need a shower first," Iona said.

"Okay."

She left and Tracy stayed at the table and waited and listened for the sound of the water coming on before he set to the task of taking off the boots. He undid the buckles first then unlaced them and just as he was thinking he'd never get them off without help, his heel popped free and there was his foot, sweat-soaked and ripe. The other boot came off faster. He leaned down and gently rubbed his feet and pulled off his socks and ran his thumb over the scars, dull pain like pebbles under the skin. It seemed to be something that had happened to someone else, some story you heard of a guy that fell. The poor bastard. I heard he was drunk. He wasn't supposed to walk again. Nobody had ever said that to him and he felt like a jerk for wishing they had, just so he could beat the odds. He needed something to give it meaning.

Iona came downstairs in her robe, her hair tied up in a towel. "You got them off," she said. "Are you all right?"

Tracy nodded. "Fine." The Piatts' .22s popped someplace out in the fields. "I don't know how there can be anything left to shoot with those two around. They go after it like it's a job."

"Bandy used to shoot squirrels." She sat down. "He said cows could break their legs in the holes."

"I bet that's never happened."

"What?"

"Cows doing that, stepping in a hole like that. They spend their whole lives with their mouths pressed against the dirt and they're gonna break their leg in some ground-squirrel hole they didn't see?"

"He said that's why he did it."

Tracy felt weak and watery in the eyes. "You think he's coming back?"

His mother lowered her head and the towel shifted and she pushed it back but it was unraveling anyway so she took it off and folded it and put it on the table. She smoothed her hair back with her hands and her robe opened at the neck and Tracy saw the smooth cleft of her breasts and looked away. "I hope so," she said.

Lyman was lowing in the corral. "I should go check on him." He pulled on his regular shoes and used the crutches to go outside.

The sun was setting and there were dozens of small chalk-blue butterflies in the driveway. Tracy chased them off like pigeons and they swarmed around him then disappeared. When he entered the barn Lyman turned sideways and looked at him. He was drooling and when he opened his mouth and lowed his eyes looked like they might pop out of his head. Tracy leaned his crutches against the fence and pitched half a bale of alfalfa into the corral even though there was plenty in there already. He sat down on a five-gallon bucket and watched the steer until the barn went dark then went out.

He leaned on his crutches in the driveway and watched his mother through the kitchen window. She wasn't the fool. There was nothing wrong with her. She was his mother, and for some reason this struck him as being strange. He didn't feel connected to anything and the idea of being someone's son didn't match up with the loose wires of emotion he was feeling. He watched her and realized he was proud of her. She'd been ashamed of him and this hurt him deeply. He thought of the river of mud and trees, the river of boards, that Wilhelm had told them about. Accidents happen and afterwards it's just a matter of salvage. Maybe all the time it's a matter of getting what you can while you can, haul the lumber up the bank, save what you can from the fire. Let it go. And where's Bandy? Why did he leave? Maybe it was inevitable, a mistake from the beginning. But Bandy was his father. The scared and miserable man his mother had described took shape in his mind. It still didn't seem real, this family of his. The older he got, the more he felt like he'd been dropped off here among strangers.

He stood there for a long time and the moon cleared the mountains and lightened the vein of the road cutting over the hills. There were no clouds and the sky was deep and filled with swirls of stars like sand caught in an ocean wave. His mother was setting the table. He took a deep breath and went inside and sat down in his chair.

"It's not very good," she said of the dinner.

"I'm sure it's fine, Ma." They were together in the old house and they were safe, nothing could touch them.

Chapter 14

COLD WATER, TALL MOUNTAINS

THE MORNING AFTER THE killing Victor came back to the motel and told Bandy they shouldn't be seen together. The woman and the child in the driveway had seen them, seen the truck, and they couldn't risk keeping it. Victor went to trade it for another. He said it would take an hour, maybe two, but the afternoon came and went and night soaked the dusk and Bandy knew he wasn't coming back. He counted how much money he had on him and it wasn't enough to buy a bus ticket. He called the bus station to make sure; it wasn't enough. The sign on the door said CHECKOUT TEN A.M. He left the lights out and hoped it wasn't the kind of place with full-time housekeepers.

That night he sat in the dark, cars passed and headlights seeped in the curtains and stalked the hidden corners. There was a deep numbness in him that was almost satisfying but wasn't. The night went on and slowly the feeling of being hunted returned. The distance between Butte and Lake Fork seemed too great, but in the morning he would go. He imagined what he might say to Iona and Tracy to explain his absence. He would tell them the truth and see where it went from there. A feeling of resignation came over him and it was not unlike the first moment of stepping into a prison cell.

In the early hours he parted the curtains expecting to see the police but the parking lot was empty and the sirens were fading away in the distance. He opened the door and looked down the sidewalk. He and the maid saw each other and Bandy went back inside and dressed. He left the room key on the table and hesitated for a moment before he let the door close. Everything was still and quiet in the slate light except for a flag high on a pole already being tugged by the wind. The shadows on the mountains were like the shadows on crumpled newspaper. The rumble of the trucks on the interstate was constant and hardly registered with Bandy at all. He pulled on his stocking hat and his gloves and went west. The sun came up and his shadow stretched out in front of him, and he chased it down one step at a time.

The sun climbed higher and the wind stopped. He began to sweat. He took off his gloves and stuffed them in his back pocket. On the other side of town he scampered up an embankment and hopped the guardrail onto the freeway onramp and stuck out his thumb. After a few minutes he took off his hat. The jagged shadow of his wild hair stood above his head. He figured it would be better to sweat a little than to look like a crazy person so he put it back on. Nobody stopped for what seemed like hours then a fat man in a brand-new pickup stopped and told him to get in the back. He slept in the open air and eventually the wind chilled him beyond the warmth of the sun and he began to shiver. He was let out fifty miles east of Missoula. There was litter on the freeway, a torn trash bag, a plastic Coke bottle full of piss, wrappers of all kinds. Bandy watched the pickup keep going and disappear.

He walked until he warmed up then stopped and put out his thumb. Not much later a man in a rusted-out VW bug stopped and let Bandy in. The man said his name was Quentin. He was a small, bearded man with a thick way of talking like he needed to clear the phlegm from his throat. They shook hands awkwardly in the limited space. Bandy lied and told Quentin his name was Victor. Quentin said he was coming from Bozeman on his way to Payette, Idaho, for a wedding.

"I'll tell you," Quentin said. "Right or wrong?"

"Right or wrong, what?"

"I'm telling you, even though I can tell you already know. There're answers to be found on the interstate."

"Sure."

"I mean it. How long you been at it?"

"Since this morning."

"Right. All fucking day. I'm not afraid of killers and rapists. I always stop when I see somebody thumbing. It could be me. You could be me. Somebody picks you up—there's your answer. There's you with me."

Bandy felt like a clown riding in the little car. Quentin kept digging his thumb into the edge of his eye until it was red and watering. Bandy suspected that it was cocaine that he was on but it could be speed.

"Where'd you hitch from?"

"Butte."

"I heard some geese plopped down in the mine pit there, in that fucking battery acid they left behind, they were dead in less than a minute. Biggest open-pit mine in the world, you know that?"

"No."

"I bet they got a bigger one by now somewhere. They got machinery big as a house, bigger. Chasing the elusive— " He made a quacking sound into his fist. "Minerals, the periodic tablature. Little-by-God rocks."

"They build America." Bandy had read it on the side of a semi trailer.

Quentin laughed loudly. "What were you doing in Butte?" He said it *butt*.

"Visiting friends." He crossed his arms and leaned against the window and closed his eyes. He'd had enough.

"Tired?"

"Yeah, long couple a days."

"You hitch into town or were you traveling?"

"My truck broke down yesterday."

"Negative," Quentin said. "The interstate giveth and the interstate taketh away. May the interstate help us all."

"Fuck the interstate," Bandy said under his breath.

"Better check that tongue before you unleash the Furies. Trust me, this road has a soul that you don't want to trample on. All roads flow together, interstates and highways, dirt tracks and trails. Without roads this country we're in would be about as inviting to modern man as the Bering Sea. Pavement shows that people care enough to go and come back."

Bandy closed his eyes. "I wish they would go. I don't care much if they come back."

"They is us, friend. We are, in the most absolute way—it."

"Maybe you're it—an it. I'm just tired."

"You sick or something?"

"No, I said I was tired. I didn't say I was sick."

"You look sick."

"This is how I look."

"Don't get fussy. I didn't mean anything." Quentin reached behind the seat and came back with a squeeze jug of vodka and handed it over. "It's supposed to be a wedding present but go on and crack the seal. It's the cocktail hour."

Bandy opened the bottle and took a drink then passed it to Quentin. They had another round then Bandy leaned against the door and tried to sleep but after a few minutes Quentin smacked him in the shoulder and offered him another. They started up a hill, the car didn't sound good. Quentin downshifted to first gear and they crawled along on the shoulder while semis howled past with their horns blowing.

"There's something wrong with your car."

"Throttle linkage. I'll get it when we summit."

They didn't make it to the top before the car died. The two men got out and Quentin unhinged the rear hood and shoved it into the backseat and had Bandy drive while he perched on the rear bumper and manipulated the throttle directly. Bandy thought of slamming on the brakes to see if he could shake him and take his car but he figured it would probably break down soon enough without Quentin there to fix it so he just drove. At the top of the grade Quentin got back behind the wheel and they set off coasting quietly down the other side.

"We're going to have to do that all over again, bud," Quentin said. "We got mountains. We got mountains every which way we go."

The day went on and by the time they started over Lolo Pass the vodka bottle was half empty. Bandy was driving and Quentin was perched on the back bumper working the throttle and yelling against the wind. Bandy hadn't eaten all day and the liquor had him slowed. He drove carefully. The trees were deep green and bushy and the asphalt night black and Bandy thought as long as he kept one from the other, he'd be all right.

When they reached the summit he thought Quentin would re-
lease the cable and get back in the car, but he didn't. Even when
he pushed in the clutch and the engine wound out, Quentin kept
it pinned. He banged on the back window. "What the hell are you
doing?" he said. "Keep her going." Then he howled at the wind
some more and yarded on the cable even harder. After awhile the
grade lessened and they entered the canyon.

He tried downshifting for the curves but Quentin kept the
throttle wide open. The brakes were soft and they got worse until
the pedal went to the floor and didn't come back up. He switched
off the engine and they coasted. He pulled the emergency brake
but nothing happened.

"Start the fucking car, man," Quentin yelled.

"There aren't any brakes."

"What?"

Quentin looked at him stupidly through the back windshield.
Bandy turned and yelled again. "There aren't any fucking brakes,
asshole," he said, and when he turned back around they were air-
borne and headed into the river.

It was quiet and the river came up to meet them. Bandy felt
strongly that he wanted to get out of the car and he had the door
partially open when they hit. The water rushed in cold enough to
stun. He made an inhuman sound at the icy water and moved as
quickly as he could but it wasn't very fast. He made it out of the car
and hung onto the open door and looked around and gauged the
distance to either shore then let go and swam toward the road. He
watched his hands swing down and cup the water and pull with no
small amazement. Quentin was suddenly beside him splashing, his
eyes white, a mad grimace on his face. It was as if they were racing
one another for the shore and Bandy wanted nothing more than to

win. Quentin was moaning and spluttering for air. Bandy thought of drowning him and knew in his gut that he could. He swam away.

He crossed into the fast water and the shore came out to meet him and Bandy swam and kicked but couldn't shake the hold of the current and the shore drew back again. He treaded water. Quentin was twenty feet away doing the same thing. They bobbed along dumbly. Bandy's feet bounced off submerged boulders and he tried to stand but he slipped and dunked his head and the cold water froze his palate and gave him a headache. The car was still afloat up ahead but it was in a different, faster current. It followed the tongue of the river into a wave train and rose and fell then rose high in the air on one last wave then dropped into a hole and disappeared. The wheels came up, then the roof, wheels.

Bandy looked at Quentin. "Swim," he said. The roar of the rapids became louder. Twenty feet to his right he could see the eddy line between the current and the slackwater. He swam stiff-jointed and ineffectively like a wind-up toy and Quentin followed him. He kicked a rock and realized he was skimming by quickly in the fast, shallow water toward the rapids below. He let his legs sink and squatted down and kicked off of the river bottom and flung himself forward, flailing, desperate; and after a few sad lunges he broke into the deep water of the eddy and went limp and let the circuitous current bring him around to the shore. He crawled onto the rocks. He sat up in amazement at the pain in his whole body. Quentin floated by in the eddy with only his head above water. Help, his mouth said. Help.

Bandy crawled on his hands and knees back into the water and this time it felt warm, warmer than the wind. He waded out and caught Quentin by the shirt and dragged him into the shallows and onto the shore. There were no clouds in the sky but the waning sunlight was thin and without heat. Bandy must've bounced his head off of the steering wheel or something because he was bleeding from a cut on his forehead.

"We're gonna freeze out here."

"I can't feel anything."

"Stand up."

Quentin staggered to his feet. "My fucking teeth hurt I'm so cold."

"Walk. We need to get back to the road." Like marionettes they walked, bedraggled and clumsy up through the jumble of boulders and a cathedral stand of ponderosas to the road and the warm black asphalt. Prone, they waited for a ride.

There were no cars and it was quiet except for the wind and the distant, Bandy thought, hateful sound of the river. He touched his head where he'd been bleeding and his hand came away pink not the black-red like it had been earlier.

"You ever done that before?" Quentin said.

"What, wreck a car? Yeah, I've done that."

"Into a river?"

"No."

"Me, neither," Quentin said. "It ain't bad until you hit."

Bandy's stomach lurched and he rolled over onto his side and vomited river water and liquor. He could taste the river's sediment. Quentin sat up then stood and moved away as the thin liquid flowed toward him. Bandy tried to get to his hands and knees but he was too weak.

"You really wrecked the shit out of my rig," Quentin said.

Bandy heaved and reeled out a hot stream of bile. Through the pounding in his ears he heard an approaching car. Quentin caught him by the armpits and hoisted him to his feet. The two men leaned against each other shivering then Quentin walked Bandy to the edge of the road and sat him down. He tried to focus on the cliff wall on the opposite side of the river but his eyes weren't working right. The rocks seemed too formless and faraway to register. He knew he was going to pass out. A truck had stopped and Quentin was talking to the driver. Bandy tried to stand up to make sure he went with them but only managed to pitch sideways into the dirt and roll into some bushes and hours later that's where he woke up.

He was freezing and it wasn't like before; before he'd been cold. Now he was freezing. His muscles were so tight and knotted it felt as if they might snap bone if he didn't relax. He had to move. The river was the only sound. He looked up and down the canyon and there were no lights. With great effort he stood and made his way back to the pavement and stamped his feet but they felt like they'd been cut off at the knee for the dead-bone knock they gave in his joints. He sat down and took his boots and socks off. The stars seemed as low as clouds. It took several minutes but he tied his boot-laces together and hung them on his neck and wrung out his socks. He started walking west: wet footprints in the starlight and on to blotches of wet to nothing. He watched the treetops and the stars and the starlit river. He avoided the dark of the asphalt, the shadows of the northern ditchbank; the depthless maw of the forest.

A car has to come by sometime, he thought. Then like he'd made it happen, headlights appeared and he stepped to the roadside and held out his thumb. A semi blew past then two more in quick succession. None of them even slowed down and soon he was back in step on the double yellow line, marching barefoot in the night.

The sounds of the river echoed off the canyon walls and it seemed as if he were in a giant culvert, underground worker. He watched the water, the wavecrests and current lines lit with starlight, then the half moon cleared the mountains then the trees and it wasn't much later when Bandy saw Quentin's VW slammed up on the rocks with a tree jacked onto the roof holding it there.

He waded through the brush down to the river and crawled carefully out onto the car and looked in the broken windows and found his hat filled with fool's gold and gravel on the floorboard and the engine cover and nothing else. He jockeyed his way out onto the log then dropped down to the rocks. He slipped into the water and barked his shin but it was shallow so he grabbed onto the front bumper and pulled himself up and opened the trunk. He dug around and pulled out a small duffel bag filled with wet clothes and a plastic sack with disposable razors and soap. He chucked the bag up onto the rocks and kept digging through the trunk. At the back he found a garbage bag with dry clothes inside. They were dirty and stiff and smelled strongly of sweat, of Quentin. He threw the bag beside the duffel and climbed up after it and stripped down. While he stood naked and chilled on the rocks a stream of seven cars in row went by. He stared after the glow of their taillights then put on dry pants and a shirt. The socks he found were crusty and mismatched but he pulled them on anyway and clucked his tongue at the joy they gave him. He felt just out of the shower and warm. He emptied the duffel on the rocks and shoved the garbage bag of dry clothes inside along with the razor and the soap then slung the bag over his shoulder and climbed back up to the road. He started out again. The road welcomed him and was always there.

Chapter 15

NIGHT

TRACY GOT UP when it was still dark and ate a half dozen ibuprofens and chewed a Vicodin then went into the kitchen and cooked breakfast. He had footers to pour and he was doing it by hand because the concrete truck couldn't fit down the driveway. Iona was still sleeping. He finished his breakfast and washed his dishes then sat down again at the table to tape his ankles. They were swollen and tender but the tape held them in place and made him more confident when walking over uneven ground.

He'd started working for his mother the week before, helping her paint and clean up. He tried to think of it as doing her a favor but he knew what it was. He'd never seen her work a job where she was on her own, making all of the decisions, and it occurred to him on that first day that she'd spent the majority of her life doing what she didn't want to do. Realizing this, Tracy felt small but also root strong. He saw something in his mother and wondered why, out of all the people he'd looked to for guidance, he'd envied, why he'd dismissed her a hundred times, and why it had been so easy.

As they made their rounds together Tracy noticed that some of the houses she took care of were in disrepair, decks twisted or broken by snowpack, roofs damaged by ice dams. He mentioned that they should go into business together, almost joking but not. He could do remodels and whatever new construction there was and she could continue to caretake. Who knows, they might even need to hire some employees. She smiled and nodded and said that sounded like a good idea. She'd make some calls when they got home. Tracy didn't even have a license or insurance. He didn't care. He'd take care of that later.

He parked at the top of the driveway and unloaded his tools. His headlights were pointed off into the trees but he could see all the way down to the house by the glow. The lumberyard had delivered the pallet of ready-mix last night after he'd left and they'd put it in the wrong spot. He walked the fifty yards or so from where he had the mixer set up and the holes dug to the pallets then started packing them bag by bag downhill.

By noon he had all the rebar tied and two footers done. He kept the mixer going and didn't stop to eat. It didn't matter if he ate. Nothing mattered except finishing the pour. He needed to stay on schedule or the owners might think of him as a cheat and a liar and tell their friends to hire someone else. A bad reputation made for a quick death. Dan Cole had taught him that, and a lot more. He'd taught him as much what not to do as he had about framing.

Late in the afternoon he finally finished and rolled up. He sprayed out the mixer and cleaned his tools then drank a stomachful of water from the hose and drove into town to get some food. He thought he'd earned a meal out.

Wilhelm liked the Huckleberry so he went there. He'd been a couple of times before but only for breakfast. The bells on the door startled him slightly when he opened it and he was careful shutting it behind him even though it was busy and nobody paid him any attention. He sat at the lunch counter and put his hands in front of him. They were hard looking and stained and he liked them. There was an old man beside him eating chicken-fried steak and on the other side three middle-aged women, reeking generally of perfume, having soup and sandwiches.

The dark-haired waitress brought him a red plastic cup of water with crushed ice and a menu. She smiled at him and he suddenly had to yawn but when he went to do it, it wasn't a yawn at all but he faked it as best he could then told her he'd have coffee to start. She kept watching him; her eyes were light green and rimmed in a heavy scrawl of eyeliner, lashes stuck together with mascara. She bit her lower lip.

"Are you who I think you are?" she said.

"I doubt it."

"You used to work with Danny Cole. You're Tracy Dorner."

The old man and the women turned to look at Tracy when they heard his name. Tracy was used to this and he ignored them.

"I'm Georgie," the waitress said. They shook hands; hers soft and narrow in his. "So you're up and walking?"

"Yeah."

"It's a miracle." She let go of his hand. "Hang on, I'll be right back." She left to take care of her tables and some of the men in the restaurant proper leaned into the aisle to watch her when she was walking away, pursed their lips and exhaled, shook their heads. She returned to the coffeemaker and poured his coffee and brought it to him. She put her elbows on the counter and he could see the lace edge of her bra. "Danny always talked about you. I thought we would've met by now."

"How is Danny?"

"I haven't seen him, and I don't want to." She smiled, not innocently. "We broke up." She settled her eyes on Tracy and he felt as if the air had been drawn from his lungs. He wanted to touch her.

He desperately wanted to feel her skin, her hair. It felt good to know something as surely as that after the long uncertain winter. He ordered the same thing as the old man beside him and stayed and drank coffee after he was done eating. He watched Georgie wipe down the tables and fill the sugar and syrup jars. When he went to leave he saw she'd written her phone number on the bill.

On Saturday she drove out to the Dorner house and picked him up. His truck had died again. Iona was working late or he could've borrowed her car. He left the kitchen light on for her. As Georgie pulled out of the driveway, he looked back at the house and felt loathsome toward it: It was just a house, not a future, not a home in any sense that he wanted it to be. His attachment had begun to fade as soon as Bandy left and now he was annealed, a cold chisel. He didn't care if he ever came back here again.

"We're going to a party later," Georgie said. "But first you have to buy me dinner."

Tracy stretched his legs out and reclined the seat a little. The car was a newer Pontiac and he wondered how she could afford it. "No," he said.

"What do you mean, no? You can't buy me dinner?"

"You can buy me dinner."

"Really? I drive out here and pick you up and I pay?"

"That's right."

Georgie looked at him and smiled. "You don't look like a jerk."

"I'm fucking serious."

"I bet you are."

The place was crowded and Tracy recognized some of the people from the lumberyard and they nodded to each other. Georgie ordered them a pitcher of beer and the waitress didn't card him.

The food took a long time to arrive and was bad when it did so they drank more to make up for it and by the time they left Tracy was fairly drunk. Georgie kissed him before they got in the car. They drove down to the river. Tracy followed her to the water's edge. The moon was half full and low in the sky but it was bright enough to light their faces. She slipped out of her dress and tossed it onto a willow bush then took off her underwear. Tracy undressed and followed her into the water. They swam and the water was smooth on his skin and when Georgie touched him it felt like she was made of water too. He thought about their age while they were kissing. He thought about how she'd always be older than him, a few miles ahead at all times. She would die before him. He didn't like the idea of that, standing over a grave, alone. They stood in the slow current of the river and everything was light and slick and effortless, the sand gave beneath their feet. Death was nowhere near them. The water was like wind.

Some time later they dressed and lay down in the grass and watched the small clouds hunt the night sky. Tracy felt sober and grounded. He felt like he'd exchanged some rotten version of himself for a new one. Georgie was strangely silent and Tracy worried that he'd done something wrong. When they were ready to leave, she asked him to drive. She told him where to go and when they got closer she told him that the party was at Regan Piatt's house and asked if he knew him.

He told her about hunting with Wilhelm and Olin and Jake. He felt bad going to the boys' house because he knew they didn't have it good with their old man. He didn't want to be part of the problem, but that's where they were going.

There were fifteen or twenty people in the yard standing around a bonfire. When they entered the firelight people quit talking and stared. Regan was sitting on an old toilet in the yard with an open case of beer at his feet. Other people were sitting on a tipped-over refrigerator and on tamarack rounds. Regan stood up and came over. He shook Tracy's hand and told him welcome to the chalet. He tried to kiss Georgie on the cheek but she pushed him back. Tracy wanted to leave but they were handed a couple of beers. They stood and drank and people started talking again.

"Where're your boys?" Tracy asked.

"Upstairs sleeping," Regan said. His eyes couldn't focus and he was swaying a little. Tracy thought he would ask how he knew Olin and Jake but he didn't. Later, he was introduced to Regan's cousin, Bixby. He was a big man with a wild beard and a greasy baseball cap, hands big and calloused. Georgie let Bixby kiss her on the cheek. Somebody flipped the cassette in the boombox on the porch then there was music. Tracy drank his first beer fast and kept at it. He was nervous. He helped Regan carry wood for the fire, piss pine twisted and black and full of knots. There was tamarack in the yard, too, a half dozen cords or so, beautiful buckskin rounds. He and Regan talked for awhile about how difficult it was to find good firewood anymore. Tracy kept tripping over the junk in the yard when he went to piss at the treeline.

Later, they went inside the house and he met more people, handshakes and names forgotten. He was passed a bottle and he drank deeply, somebody whistled. Georgie sat down on the couch with a couple of her girlfriends and Tracy crept up the ladder to see Olin and Jake. It was too dark and he couldn't find his way across the loft. He bumped into the low roof and felt bad that he'd probably woken them so he stumbled back to the ladder and sat down and leaned over and watched the people below without them knowing.

Dan Cole was on the couch with Georgie. He was crowding her. She was leaning away. Tracy stayed where he was and watched until they started yelling at each other and Dan balled his fist into the back of Georgie's dress and tried to drag her to her feet.

He went down the ladder and jumped the last few rungs and landed bad and fell into a table. He got up and went for Dan but Bixby had him by the armpits and the big man threw him outside and he fell down. Dan jumped on top of him before he could get up. He didn't try to hit him. He was drunk and smiling; it seemed he thought Tracy might be joking or that he was glad to see him. Tracy rolled him over and stuck a knee in his stomach and hit him with continuous right hands until Bixby pulled him off and threw him into the driveway.

He sat up with his back against a parked car. Georgie was there and she sat down beside him. Dan was moaning and his legs were squirming and stirring up dust.

"I could do that all day." Tracy's hand hurt and looked misshapen. He had the taste of a broken tooth in his mouth.

"We should go." Georgie's eyes seemed conspiratorial and loving. Regan came over and offered Tracy a hand up and he took it. He was acting overly concerned and Tracy thought he was an idiot and wanted to hit him too. "Dan's my friend," Regan said. "I don't know you except from tonight, so you go first. Understand? I know why you did it, but you go home first."

Tracy nodded. The toilet in the yard, the refrigerator, the copper pipe. He understood. "Where'd you get all this stuff?"

"I said you should go."

"And I said where'd you get all this shit?"

Regan didn't answer; he looked at the ground. Behind him Bixby hoisted Dan to his feet and tossed him into a lawn chair. He looked at Tracy with a profound look of embarrassment, disappointment; one eye was already swollen shut and his nose and mouth were bleeding. Tracy was thinking maybe he'd hit Regan then go for Bixby and anyone else that wanted a fight when Georgie took him by the arm and hauled him away and got him in the car. He was relieved and ashamed at being relieved. She took him back to her house. She had to wake him to get him inside.

In the morning she took him home. Iona's car wasn't there. They kissed then got out of the car and stood in the sun. The Pontiac didn't seem so new anymore. The wind blew through the willow tree and seedpods went flying, slowly drifting away. Lyman bawled inside the barn and they both turned at the sound. The barn door opened and Olin and Jake came out, each carrying their rifles.

"How's Lyman?" Tracy said to the boys.

"Big," said Olin.

The boys came forward hesitantly.

"Did you eat yet? I was about to make breakfast." Tracy said.

They shook their heads no.

"Well, come on then," he said.

At the front door Olin took the gun away from his brother and checked both safeties and put them on the bench in the mudroom then they went inside.

"Sit," Tracy said. The boys sat at the kitchen table and watched Tracy. "I got it," he said to Georgie when she tried to help. She sat down across from the boys and smiled. Tracy greased a skillet and put it on the stove to warm then made coffee.

"Scrambled?" Tracy said.

"Sure," Olin said. Jake nodded yes.

"I'm just having coffee," Georgie said. The coffeemaker hissed and popped as some spilled water boiled off beneath the pot.

"I woke you up last night, didn't I?" Tracy said to the boys.

"Yeah," Olin said. "I heard you come up the ladder then I watched from the window. I watched you fight."

"Me too," Jake said.

"No, you didn't," Olin said.

"I heard it though."

Tracy nodded and opened the fridge and took out the carton of eggs and cracked the ones left in the container into a metal bowl then threw the cardboard container into the trash. He whipped the eggs with a fork then poured them into the skillet and shook black pepper on them.

Olin looked at his brother and Jake shrugged his shoulders.

"You never came over to our house before?" Jake said to Tracy.

"No," Tracy said.

"You have," Jake said to Georgie. "You came with Dan. You were at my birthday."

Georgie nodded.

"Do you know where your dad got all that stuff in the yard, the pipe and wire?" Tracy said.

"No," Olin said.

"Where's he work?"

"Him and Bixby work together. They work all over. Sometimes they run a water truck for the Forest Service but there aren't any fires this year. Not yet."

"That son of a bitch," Tracy said.

"Baby," Georgie said.

"We've been in your house before," Olin said. "When nobody lived here. It was empty. We didn't know it was yours." He looked at his brother. "Tell him, Jake."

"Why?"

"We talked about this. Tell or I'll tell him and it'll be worse."

Jake looked down at the table. "I broke your window. I threw a rock through it." He looked up. "My dad already whipped me so you don't need to."

Tracy looked at Georgie then back at the boy. "I'm not whipping anybody. It's all right. I'm not mad at you."

A car pulled up in the driveway. Iona came inside and looked at Tracy first then set her eyes on Georgie. "Dan caught me getting gas in town," she said. Tracy grunted that he'd heard her. Georgie looked at Tracy. Iona tugged on Jake's hair and smiled at Olin. "What're you two up to today?" she said.

"Going hunting," Jake said.

"We were at their place last night," Tracy said. "Me and Dan woke them up."

"You're burning those eggs," Iona said.

"Maybe I should give them a ride home," Georgie said.

Tracy scraped the eggs from the bottom of the pan and turned down the burner. He glanced over his shoulder at Georgie and told her maybe that was a good idea.

"We walked here," Olin said.

"Let them eat first," Iona said to Georgie. "They probably heard the worst of it last night." She looked questioningly at Olin.

"It wasn't bad," Olin said.

Iona opened the cupboard and brought down plates and opened the drawer and picked out forks and put everything on the table in a heap and let Georgie set the table. Tracy grated cheese to put on top of the eggs then put bread in the toaster.

Georgie said she only wanted coffee and Iona served her a plateful of food anyway. After everyone was served and room was made at the table, they sat down. Georgie picked at her food. Iona put down her fork. "Dan told me his side of it," she said. "His face is mangled. He had to get stitches. He could sue us."

"That isn't gonna happen."

"How can you be so sure?"

"Dan's a fuck-up. All the people that were at the party are fuck-ups."

"Watch your mouth," Iona said, nodding at the boys.

"I'm not talking about them."

Both Olin and Jake were watching Iona intently. She smiled at them then spoke at Tracy. "Maybe you haven't noticed but we don't have many friends in this town. They could put you in jail just to keep up the family tradition."

"I didn't know he was going to be there. It's not like I went looking to fight him."

"What about you?" Iona said to Georgie.

"I didn't know. I hadn't seen him in awhile. We broke up."

"Dan said you did it on purpose, to rub his face in it."

"No." Georgie pushed her fork around her plate.

Iona looked at Tracy and made him want to squirm.

"I could've done a lot more damage than I did," he said.

"Oh, I bet." Iona pointed at his swollen and bruised hand. She hadn't touched her food. Tracy took anxious, measured bites. It hurt to hold his fork. Olin ate quickly and as soon as Jake was done he stood up and thanked Tracy for breakfast. He picked up his plate and his brother's plate and took them to the sink. "Come on," he said to his brother. Jake stood up and Iona slapped him on the butt and Jake jumped and laughed a squealing laugh.

Olin opened the door to the mudroom and Tracy stood up. "You sure you don't want a ride?"

"We can walk," Olin said. "Say thank you, Jake."

"Thank you Jake," Jake said in a deep voice. Iona laughed but Georgie looked like she might cry. Tracy smiled thinly.

"See ya," Olin said. "We're sorry about your window. Sorry about what happened at our house."

"It's not your fault." Tracy put his hands on the boy's shoulders. "Wilhelm and me have been talking about taking you two elk hunting in the fall, how's that sound?"

Jake smiled and nodded but Olin looked worried.

"You don't have to go if you don't want to. We could go fishing instead."

"I'll ask our dad when we get home." Olin ducked from Tracy's grip and Jake followed him out.

After the boys were gone the meal inside stopped. They all sat in silence. Tracy felt worse about the boys than he did about hitting Dan. They'd always remember him fighting in their driveway no matter what he did or what he told them. The fight didn't end last night with him and Dan going home. It stayed there with Olin and Jake.

Iona got up first and put her plate in the sink. Tracy and Georgie stayed where they were. The kitchen was getting warm from the sun and there were flies.

"I'm going back to work," Iona said. "I'll see you tonight."

"Okay," Tracy said.

Iona left. Georgie cleared the table and filled the sink to soak the dishes.

"Guess it's just me and you," Tracy said.

"I guess so."

"You don't need to wash those now."

"I don't mind."

"Come here."

Georgie came over and sat on Tracy's lap and they kissed. She rubbed her wet hands in his hair and looked into his eyes. "You got anything to drink?" she said. There wasn't anything in the house so they left the dishes and drove back to town.

Chapter 16

IN KIND

IT WAS SIX WEEKS before Bandy made it back to Lake Fork. He was ragged and dark and his eyes had gone crusty; his lips were cracked and would bleed if he opened his mouth to speak. He'd worked for awhile on a road crew holding a slow and stop sign then spent the two weeks after that sleeping in an abandoned hayshed and fishing the Clearwater with a drugstore spinning rod.

When the road crew money ran out he bummed for food outside of a gas station. He ended up buying whiskey for some high school kids and they paid him with a bottle of his own. On his way back to the hayshed two local cops caught him pissing on the side of the road. A week later he was let out of jail and continued on his way. The going was slow and often humiliating. He thought of never returning, doing everyone a favor. His thoughts always returned to Iona, Tracy too.

In a gas station bathroom he saw how jaundiced and thin he'd gotten; it no longer surprised him. If he dropped dead, that might surprise him but not much else. He cleaned up as best he could and went back to the road to hitch a ride. A low feeling came over him when he put his thumb out. He'd walked nearly the whole way but he didn't want to walk in.

A man in a pickup truck stopped but when he saw Bandy up

close he made him ride in the back with a blue heeler named Cisco. The dog snapped at him and Bandy kicked at it but missed. The driver hollered at his dog to be nice and soon it was sitting close to Bandy and licking his hand. Bandy fell asleep and the dog leaned up against him and kept him warm.

He was dropped off downtown and in people's faces he could see how bad he looked. He didn't waste any time getting away from them. The bustle, small as it was, left him feeling exposed and unmistakably criminal. If he had the strength to run away, to lope through the town like a beast pursued, he would have. With his eyes scanning only the eight or ten feet directly in front of him, he walked as quickly as he could manage.

The muffler shop was closed so it must be Sunday. He looked around him. It didn't feel like Sunday. The door of the shop was locked and there was a note from the UPS man stuck to the glass. There were still cars in the garage being worked on and tools scattered around. Bandy figured that Angel and Gutierrez probably went fishing, and not having anybody to watch the place, had locked it up. He wondered if he'd still have a job. He knocked on the window a couple of times just to make sure Angel wasn't sleeping on the couch behind the desk where he couldn't see him then he wandered back out to the highway and kept walking. He wondered if Victor had dropped off his money yet, if he ever would. He doubted it. He walked on and passed the Huckleberry and hoped to see Wilhelm's truck but it wasn't there.

It was Tracy that stopped. He drove by at first then pulled to the side of the road and backed up. Olin and Jake were with him and they scooted all the way over against Tracy to make room. Bandy threw his bag in the back and got in. The boys smiled nervously and Bandy nodded back at them.

"You've been gone awhile."

"I know." Bandy could smell how bad he smelled and was embarrassed. He thought of asking Tracy to pull over so he could climb in back but he couldn't bring himself to speak. He glanced at his son and saw that the boys were staring at his hands: the leathery, yellow skin and long nails and the black dirt beneath them. He balled them into fists and stuffed them between his thighs like a child might do.

"You called that one time," Tracy said, "and it sounded like you were coming back any day. We've been expecting you. We've been worried."

"I got hung up." His voice was raspy. Tracy handed him his thermos. Bandy unscrewed the cap and smelled coffee and sipped, but it was cold water and only held the odor of coffee. He drank and the water spilled down his chin. He couldn't remember tasting water so good.

Tracy told Olin and Jake that they'd go shooting with Wilhelm later. He was going to drop them off at home. The boys didn't protest.

"I want to show you something," Tracy said to Bandy.

He turned off the highway and drove through a new subdivision on the valley floor then higher into the hills. The road steepened and he downshifted and rattled around a few washboard corners. Up ahead there was a closed metal gate that marked the end of the road, and just before it Tracy turned off into the Piatts' driveway.

Bandy remembered what Wilhelm had said about the Piatts living in Bill McKinley's old place. The boys said goodbye and went inside. Bandy got back in the truck and shut the door.

"You recognize any of this stuff?" Tracy motioned to the junk scattered everywhere, like a storm hit a flea market. The unpainted siding on the addition and on the shed was still bright and hadn't begun to gray but the house was silver and streaked by rusty nail heads.

"This house used to be Bill McKinley's," Bandy said.

Tracy laughed a little. "I think that's your copper pipe and toilet over by the tree."

There was a long silence. Bandy was too tired to take this in. "Let's go home."

Tracy pulled out of the driveway and drove down the hill, grindingly slow all the way back to the ranch. Bandy watched out the window and marked the height of the grass to the fence posts. A hot wind blew in the cab: the peak of summer. The water was low in the creek and there was algae blooming in the slack water. They pulled into the driveway.

"Should we call the cops?" Tracy said.

"No, don't do that."

"We need to do something."

"No, we don't. We don't need to do anything."

They got out of the truck. Tracy walked in front of him; he had a slight limp. He was trying hard not to limp.

The house was dirty. The mail was piled up on the table and ringed with coffee-cup stains. Tracy filled a glass of water at the sink and looked at his father then went into the living room and sat down on the couch. Bandy went upstairs and found some clean clothes and took a shower and was surprised how clear the water ran off his body; he thought it would be brown with filth. Tracy was sitting at the kitchen table when he came downstairs. A housefly bopped against the window glass then circled the table, the stove, then back to the window.

"When's your mom getting back?"

"How should I know?"

Bandy sat down at the table across from Tracy.

"You said you'd be gone a few days. Ma thought you were gone for good."

"What'd you think?"

Tracy tucked his chin into his chest and leaned back in his chair, lifted his arm. "I don't know. I thought maybe you got sent back to jail."

Bandy leaned forward and put his elbows on the table. "I told her I'd come back."

Tracy slowly blew out the air in his lungs then nodded his head. He stood up and walked toward the door.

"That's it, huh?" Bandy said.

"I gotta go."

"Where?"

"I gotta meet Georgie at work."

"Dan's Georgie?"

"No, not Dan's Georgie. I can't believe you sitting there. You got some balls. This goddamn house." The color came into Tracy's face. "What's the point if you can't even be bothered to stick around?"

"I made a mistake. I'm sorry."

"You wouldn't have to apologize to me so much if you didn't do stupid shit all the time." Bandy smiled; it was good to be home. After a moment, Tracy smiled too. "You know Georgie's half his age? It'd be like me dating a ten-year-old."

"It's not the same."

Tracy looked out the window. "Ma hates her."

"I doubt that," Bandy said. "Why would she?"

"I don't know, because she likes to go out. She's older. I don't know. Name something."

"Cradle robber."

"Don't say that." Tracy smiled a little.

"She'd probably say the same thing."

"Maybe. I gotta go. She's waiting on me."

"Are you coming back tonight?"

"I don't know. I'll see ya sometime." He walked out the door.

Iona came home while he was doing the dishes. He turned and smiled at her and went back to washing. She shut the door and watched his back and waited for him to speak. She was tired from work and wanted to lie down. She sat down at the table. His skin looked like it had been transplanted onto him from a cadaver. She had a strong urge to kick him.

"So what's your excuse?" she said.

"I don't have one."

"You didn't want to come back, is what I think. God, you look awful."

"I'm not trying to fool anybody. This horse is dead." Bandy pulled the drain on the sink and waited for all the food scraps to catch in it then took it out and rapped it on the inside of the trash can and put it back in the drain. "I talked to Tracy."

"The little shit." Iona pulled her hair into a ponytail and slid a rubber band from her wrist over her hand and hitched it around her hair, shook her head and smoothed her hair with both hands. She smiled a little and banged her fist gently several times on the table. She looked at Bandy. "What are you doing here? Seriously, I want to know before this gets started again."

Bandy sat down at the table and winked at Iona. "Before what gets started?"

"Don't be an ass."

"I wanted to come home. It just took me longer than I thought it would."

"Is this home then?"

"I don't have anywhere else. I don't want to be anywhere else."

Iona laid her head down on the table. She wondered if she did it long enough if maybe Bandy would be gone when she looked up. She didn't have the energy to deal with him right now. She'd almost fallen asleep at the wheel on the way home. She sat up, remembering. "I have groceries in the car." Bandy helped her bring them in and they put them away together.

Tracy didn't come home in the evening. Bandy fried a couple of pork chops and thawed some frozen peas while Iona sat at the table. He'd shaved earlier and she could see the tan lines on his face and neck. He couldn't leave the bare skin alone and he rubbed his jaw like he was afflicted. When the food was done, he took down plates from the cupboard and set the table. He served the food then sat down across from Iona.

They ate and Bandy told her about Tracy picking him up on the highway and taking the Piatt boys home to their house, to the house that used to be Bill's. Iona looked at Bandy and it felt like she was on a runner and every time she got anywhere the rope snapped tight and she'd look back and there would be the cabin burning and there would be Bill and there would be Bandy. She told him about the fight Tracy had with Dan. Bandy nodded but didn't say anything. He didn't look happy about it; he looked like he understood. They finished eating in silence and Bandy gathered the dishes and took them to the sink then sat back down and sipped on his iced tea looking contented.

"Are you going to tell me what happened?" Iona said.

"I got lost."

"Well, now you're found."

He hesitated then told her about Fulcrum and Penry, Trinidad, Victor and Butte, the journey home. She watched him as he spoke. She couldn't see him as anything but a threat. He could take away everything she'd worked for, everything she loved. She sat for a long time and it hurt, her whole body hurt. She ached as Bandy pulled himself away from her. He was gone, dead and buried twenty years ago. There had only been flashes, shadows in the trees.

"You didn't need anything. Tracy and I were here for you."

"You're still here."

"No, I'm not. Not anymore. I'm leaving. I've put up with enough."

"I got nothing." He reached for her.

"Don't give me that shit. Don't touch me."

"It's always been about me and you. It's always been us. We'll never have it easy like normal people. We'll never be like them, but it doesn't mean we can't be together. There's other ways to be happy if you can manage to get clear of the guilt."

"Don't talk to me about guilt. You know shit about guilt. You've been blind to it your whole life. You've got it all fucked up with self-pity and they aren't the same thing. Guilt you carry until it crushes you, self-pity you spray like piss on everybody you love. Sound familiar?" She bit the inside of her lower lip until she tasted blood.

"I'm not moralizing what I've done but I'm home now and I mean to stay. I'll do anything, but I need you here with me."

"I'll be gone tomorrow and I'm telling Tracy what happened. I won't let you fuck him up with this."

"I was gonna tell him but I wanted to tell you first."

"Don't come near me or Tracy. I mean it. You," she pointed at him, "you owe me that much." She went upstairs and sat down on her bed and cried.

Later she watched from her window as Bandy stuffed the duffel bag and the clothes he'd worn since he'd been gone in the burn barrel in the driveway. He soaked it all with gas and threw in a match. The flames leapt into the air and Bandy stumbled back with his arm over his face then lowered it and watched. Iona was done crying. She wished he'd climb in the barrel too. She'd gotten her hopes up and she was old enough, wise enough to know better. The flames burned down and Bandy walked out the driveway into the night. She listened for him to return but never heard anything. In the morning she was packed and gone before daybreak. There were a dozen houses that she was watching where she could stay. She'd even been offered a few permanent caretaker jobs. Now she could take one.

Bandy went into her room and her clothes were gone, her things from the bathroom were gone. He dressed and went to the barn and grabbed a shovel and went into the fields. His hands were shaking. He held onto the shovel so his hands would be still. For days then weeks he walked the ditches and dug out blockages in the few places where there was still enough water to make a difference. The sun burned down on him until he felt like he'd turn to ash and blow away.

He was alone and he lived in squalor, unwashed. He poached grouse with Wilhelm's .22 and ate them. The Guntlys or somebody dropped off groceries sometimes when he was away. It wasn't Iona; he could tell by the brand names. He slept in the barn and rarely went into the house at all.

When Tracy finally came to see him, he seemed a little shocked by the state of his father. They stood in the driveway a good distance apart and talked. He'd moved in with Georgie. He wasn't upset, but he couldn't stay at the ranch any longer. His mom wouldn't let him.

"How are you getting around?" Tracy said.

"I been staying home. Not much to get around to here."

"You can use my truck for awhile if you need it. Georgie could drop me off at work or I could ride with Ma."

"It's okay. I've been getting by." Bandy looked at his son. "Have you been paying my power bill?"

"Yeah."

"Let them turn it off."

"I'll keep paying it. I don't mind. You can't be out here in the dark with no refrigerator. The well pump's electric anyway. You wouldn't have water. A pot to piss in."

Bandy shifted his weight and the small stones in the driveway ground together under his boots. "I didn't know what to do around you, how to act. I needed to do something."

Tracy looked around the ranch, settled his eyes on the roof of the house. "You weren't trying to go back to prison were you?"

"I didn't kill him. Did she tell you that? I didn't kill anybody."

"It probably doesn't even matter. You were there. Crossing state lines. Who knows what else. Jesus, it's bad." Tracy had a kind of exultant look on his face and Bandy felt even more ashamed because he could tell in some small way that his son was actually proud of him, of what he'd done.

"I shouldn't have told her."

"Maybe not."

Bandy could sense that Tracy was getting ready to leave and he didn't want him to. "What about Lyman?"

Tracy walked over to the corral and banged on the fence until Lyman came out of the barn. Bandy followed him. The steer stood ten feet away and lowered his head like he was going to charge. "God, he's big." Tracy leaned and spat. The gesture struck Bandy as unnatural. Tracy's eyes flashed at his father then went back at the steer. "He'd keep you fed through the winter."

"He'd keep us all fed."

"I remember when I could almost pick him up." Tracy smiled. "You sure you don't want to use my rig?"

"I'll be all right. Guntlys are always going by, I can flag them down if I need something."

They shook hands for a moment then Bandy pulled him in and hugged him. "I didn't mean to ruin all this," he said into Tracy's ear. Tracy let him go and they stepped apart.

"I was moving into Georgie's anyway. I don't care what you did." He paused. "Ma was on your side, though. She took a lotta shit off a people for living with you. People at her work, people at the store, they all talk too fucking much. She hated it. Me and you had it easy out here by ourselves."

"Wilhelm was right, I should've never came back."

"No, you just shouldn't a left," Tracy said. "Give me a call if you need anything. Georgie's number is written on the wall by the phone."

"Okay."

The next morning Bandy showered and shaved and left the house early. He walked to the church and caught a ride into town with the Schwann's man. Angel was standing at the front door of the shop like he'd been waiting for him.

"You want to know something weird?" Angel said.

"What?"

"A guy used to work here that looked just like you."

"That so."

"Maybe a little uglier."

"What'd you say?"

"Gute's the one you need to ask."

"Where is he?"

"Fishing."

Bandy smiled, held up his hands.

"You sold it to me, man."

"You want me to talk to him or are you?"

"Go and cut the mounting bolts off that Oldsmobile on the lift and get a new header on it before he gets back this afternoon and he'll probably give you a raise."

Gutierrez showed up in the afternoon and acted surprised to see him. Bandy asked him about their cousin's pickup and Angel said it was still for sale and the next day Bandy was given the keys. They agreed to a hundred dollars a week out of his check to pay it off.

After that he drove around a lot. Once he went to the brewpub but people seemed to be staring at him so he left without finishing his beer. He couldn't drink it anyway; he was too sick. The Pitcher was boarded up and it was probably a good thing. Mostly he drove around the lake and into the mountains. He was always looking out for Iona but he never saw her.

As the weeks and months passed he began to think more about the Piatt boys' father gutting his house. He decided he'd go and see him. He wasn't sure what he was going to do when he met him. He thought about Bill and Iona living in that house together while he was in prison. It seemed like the last place he should go. He thought maybe it would be.

He parked on the road and walked up. It was early afternoon and the light was warm in the trees. There was nobody home. He walked around and looked over the debris scattered across the property. He couldn't be sure anything there had come from his parents' house. Tracy was right, none of these things held any meaning. They never had. What had been missing didn't have a shape.

He found his father's army footlocker under a drop cloth in the shed. He touched the name stenciled on the lid. The lock had been broken and the hasp was bent. Inside there were photographs and papers. He squatted down then pulled up a five-gallon paint bucket and sat. In the photographs he saw himself as a child, and his mother and father as young people standing at the gates of the mill on the lake. In the bottom of the chest he found newspaper articles about Neil Guntly's accident and the murder on the road.

A truck pulled up in the driveway and Bandy got to his feet. He picked up a shovel from behind the door and went out. It was two men, and they were alone. The boys weren't with them. Bandy went toward them with the shovel resting on his shoulder. He didn't speak. Regan and Bixby looked at one another then Bixby turned to go back to his pickup. There was a rifle on the window rack. Bandy ran and caught him at the door and hit him over the head with the shovel then again in the back once he was on the ground. Regan ran inside. Bandy took a deep breath, and on weak and shaking legs followed him.

They fought in the kitchen and broke dishes and spilled a pot of kidney beans onto the floor and slid around in them. Regan had a kitchen knife and there was no room to swing the shovel. Bandy slipped and fell against the counter and the shovel shattered the window above the sink. Regan came forward hesitantly and like he was playing tag stabbed the knife into Bandy's side just below the ribs. Bandy let go of the shovel and covered his wound.

Regan held the bloody knife like an exposed wire. "You can't come in my house," he said. "The law says I can kill you if you come in my house."

Bandy wasn't going to argue. They were the same men. They weren't different. They were low, damaged men, outliers: trespassers in this land of a million fences. Regan walked him outside still holding the knife. Bixby was sitting on the ground and Regan went to him and helped him stand. Bandy returned to the shed and picked up the footlocker. He went stiffly down the driveway with it and Regan and Bixby watched him go and made no move to stop him. Regan dropped the knife and looked at his hand.

When Bandy got home there was an envelope sitting on the mudroom bench. He put the footlocker inside on the table then went back out and opened it and saw the money. He stepped into the driveway and wadded it up and pitched it into the field as far as he could. He looked around for some other sign of Victor being there but there wasn't one. He went inside and sat down at the table and again went over the photographs. The light faded. The blood soaked into his pants and ran down his leg. He sat at the table staring at the cast iron woodstove. Around midnight it began to snow and it didn't stop.

Chapter 17

THE LAST WINTER

THE CABIN HAD BEEN BUILT on the lakeshore in the early fifties. It looked like an outbuilding for the new mansions, still referred to as cabins, on either side of it. Iona knew the big houses were there but she couldn't see them through the trees, and since she was also paid to watch those places she knew that no one was there. She was alone. Looking out across the vastness of the lake it certainly felt that way. The snow fell on the black water and the black water swallowed it.

The deck was covered and screened. A steep, rickety stairway led down from it to a narrow granite bluff where there was a picnic table under a twisted pine growing out of a crack in the rocks. Below that, there was another set of stairs that led to a narrow cove where in the summer the owners of the cabin kept a rowboat. The Powerses were Iona's first and favorite clients and they'd offered the cabin to her for the whole winter, maybe for the summer as well since they were getting too old to make the trip up from Boise anymore. The snow was a few inches deep on the rocks and stray flakes blew in under the porch door and matted the screens.

She remembered enjoying the first snow but she couldn't today. Ellen had been calling every few hours, worried about Wilhelm and Tracy and the Piatt boys. They were elk hunting in the mountains southeast of town. They should've come home when the snow started last night. The storm would be worse at elevation. She thought maybe one of them had shot something and they were packing it out. Maybe something had happened; it was possible.

Despite herself she was more worried about Bandy. What was he going to do out there alone all winter? How was he going to live? She didn't have to stay in the house with him but she didn't have to abandon him either. Maybe she owed him and maybe that impulse was completely wrong.

She decided to take him some food then remembered they'd burned through all the firewood last winter and he had no way of getting more. She went inside and called the man she got her clients' firewood from and ordered three cords and gave him directions to the ranch. Being so late in the season, it would cost her. She could afford it. She'd still take him some food and check on him. The wood was enough. No, she'd check on him. If the police hadn't taken him away yet. It would've been in the paper or on the news. Idiot. I told him. I told him I'd kill him if he did anything to hurt Tracy. But he hurt himself more. He hurt her. Tracy was fine; he was proud of his father. Iona could see it in his face and it made her blood thick to think about it. Nobody had even noticed what she'd done, where she stood now compared to where she'd been. But they couldn't know. Her secrets were hers. She finished her tea in a gulp because it was cold and brought the cup inside and washed it.

She called Ellen and asked if she needed anything from town because she was coming out.

"I wouldn't mind a visit," Ellen said.

"I'm going to check on Bandy."

"I passed him yesterday on the road."

"How'd he look?"

"The same. He didn't wave."

"You're sure you don't need anything?"

"I'm fine."

"Okay."

The Powerses kept a pickup in the carport. Iona had been using it, they told her to use it. If she didn't get her car out of the driveway soon, it would probably stay there all winter unless the plow driver towed it out for her. She disconnected the truck from the battery tender and the block heater and started it. She let it warm up then put it in four-wheel drive and went carefully up the steep driveway to the paved road.

She stopped at the store and bought groceries and a couple of the small, overpriced bundles of firewood meant for the tourists and drove out to the ranch. There were no tire tracks in the snow on the county road. Iona saw smoke coming from the house from some distance off.

There were the remnants of a bonfire burning alongside one of the sheds and footprints in the snow between the fire and the barn, none going to the house. Iona switched off the truck and got out. The fire had burned down from its large radius to a small center of coals.

Bandy was inside the barn bundled in a sleeping bag and the blanket from the couch. Lyman was tied to the post against the wall. He'd shit all over the place and he slipped in it when he tried to come toward Iona and the rope snapped tight. Wilhelm's .22 was leaned up in the stud bay behind Bandy and there was a chain hoist and a hunting knife on the workbench along with a whetstone and a bow saw. Bandy's head was down and he didn't lift it when Iona spoke. She went to him and touched his face and it was cold. She slapped him gently and he opened his eyes.

"How long've you been out here?" she said.

"I don't know."

"Get up. You'll freeze to death. You probably already have. Get up."

She lifted and Bandy stood. He felt like nothing, like a dead tree feels like nothing, not worth carrying. She walked him out of the barn and into the house. It was filthy and cold and dark. She sat him down in the living room next to the cold woodstove then went back out to the truck and brought in the wood she'd bought and built a fire. She found more blankets and bundled him up and told him to take off his boots but he ignored her and just sat there. The fire caught and Iona fed it and waited then fed it again. She closed the door and opened the damper then went back out to the truck to get the groceries.

The snow was beginning to drift up against the sides of the tires and against the stone foundation of the barn. The mountains were lost in the storm. Tracy was out there. She wanted to see him, for him to be there with her. She wanted them all to be together again and thought maybe she'd stay here with Bandy for awhile. She could ask Tracy to come back too. He could bring Georgie if he wanted. The house was big enough. Winter was coming and they should be together. There was still the potential for family, for normality. What if Tracy and Georgie had kids and she became a grandmother? With grandchildren came a promise of redemption.

She walked back to the house carrying the box of groceries. As she crossed the threshold the dream drained away. She wouldn't return; there was nothing here for her. She opened a can of soup and dumped it in a pan to warm then went into the living room to check on Bandy again. He had moved to the chair and his eyes were closed.

"Hey," Iona said. "Wake up. How long were you out there? Did you spend the night like that?"

Bandy opened his eyes and shook his head. "I couldn't do it. I couldn't shoot him."

"Why would you want to?"

He looked at her. "Because that's what you do. That's what they're for, what this place is for."

Iona remembered something she'd read of Thomas Jefferson, something he'd written about the land being for the living, for the survivors. It had to do with stewardship, taking care of a place, because if you were to ruin or pillage the land, then it would belong to the dead. It would go unclaimed because no one could use it. She thought maybe Bandy belonged to the dead now. He was on the other side of the line.

"I'm glad you came back, Iona."

She squatted down at his feet and took his frozen hands in hers and massaged them. "That's the first time you've said my name since you got out."

"No, it ain't, is it?" He smiled, his missing eyetooth: a broken predator, old wolf.

"I was worried you'd be like this."

"I'm fine. It'll work out. It always does."

She smelled the soup scorching and went into the kitchen. She poured some into a bowl and dropped a spoon into it and took it back to him. He held the bowl close to his face and let the steam heat his skin. He blew on the soup then picked up the spoon but didn't eat, kept blowing. He was slow to blink. He looked up at her.

"There's some money in the field." He nodded toward the front of the house. "Ten feet or so south of the fence. I can't throw very far."

"What're you talking about?"

"You should go find it before it gets buried. The mice'll use it for nests." He smiled.

"I don't know what you're talking about."

"It's my cut from Montana. I got paid. You can have it. I don't want it. Waste of time. I might as well a been picking up cans on the highway."

Iona heard a car with tire chains pull into the driveway but didn't open the curtains to see who it was. Ellen knocked and came inside and called, yoo-hoo. Iona intercepted her and sat her down in the kitchen and put the kettle on the stove for tea. Jack Dorner's footlocker was on the table. She hadn't noticed it before because of the mess. She opened it and she and Ellen looked through the photographs and newspaper clippings. It was a family history that included her and the Guntlys, came to a fine point with Tracy. The teakettle whistled and Iona poured tea for them both.

"Is he all right? Is Bandy all right?" Ellen said.

"No, he's not."

"The storm's getting worse."

Iona sat down at the table. "He should be in the hospital."

"Would he go if we took him?"

"I doubt it."

"We could call the volunteer fire department. They'd bring the ambulance and come and get him."

"He wouldn't want that."

"We could call the police."

"What good would that do?"

"I know what he did. Tracy told Wilhelm."

"It doesn't matter. He's had enough."

The old woman tapped the side of the locker with her finger-nail. "Where'd he find this?"

"I don't know, Ellen. I don't care."

Ellen turned and looked out the window at the storm. "Even last year I wouldn't have worried about Wilhelm being out in this. But he's too old now. He needs to stay home."

"Tracy will take care of him. They'll be okay. Don't worry."

"They have to come back by tonight, though, don't they?"

"Not if they haven't shot anything they won't." Iona stood and called to Bandy and asked if he wanted more soup. There was no answer. She went into the living room and he had his head down again and the soup bowl was tipped over in his lap and dripping down his leg. She went to him and lifted his head and his eyes were open. He was gone. He looked horrible. She had a sharp urge to cry out but she set her jaw and it passed. She took the soup bowl from his lap and put it on the floor. She used the blanket to clean him up. She hated herself for being relieved.

Ellen came up behind her and with a palsied hand reached out and pushed his eyes shut. Iona got to her feet and the two women stood back and looked at him. "He could've lived his whole life in this house," Iona said.

"He looks like his father," Ellen said. "Jack died here, too. I don't know in what room but I know it was here. Maude was in the nursing home. She passed well after Jack.

"I never talked to him, to Bandy. I brought him food after you and Tracy left, but I couldn't talk to him. I'd leave it when I knew he wasn't here. I wanted him to be well but I couldn't face him. I'm not as brave as you."

Iona took the old woman by the arm and turned her and walked her back toward the kitchen. "Would you mind leaving me here with him for a little while?"

"Oh honey, no, you come with me and we'll call the funeral home from my house. They'll take care of everything so you don't have to worry. You don't need to be here alone."

"I'll be up in awhile." Iona opened the door and walked Ellen out into the storm and put her in her car and waited until she drove away. She grabbed the second bundle of firewood and took it inside and threw it down next to the stove and watched the snow melt from it and pool on the floor.

She went and touched Bandy again to make sure or just to touch him again. She kissed his forehead and went to the stove and opened the door and picked up the poker and shucked the coals and burning logs from it onto the floor in front of Bandy and piled them together and got them burning then stacked the other wood on top of them. She stayed until the wood floor was burning and the smoke got too thick to bear. She grabbed the footlocker from the table on her way out.

From the truck she watched the flames fill the windows and eat the curtains then spread upstairs. She had the strange thought that she should've undressed him and cleaned him but it was too late. The fire wasn't going out. Bandy was gone. His time had been notched onto fence posts and block walls.

She wondered if Tracy would rebuild or if he'd sell the land. She wanted him to keep it and to try again. It wasn't the land that was bad, and it wasn't the house either. But she had to burn it, for Bandy, a final gesture. She hoped Tracy built a smaller house, a cabin. She imagined what it would look like, and what she pictured was her and Bandy's old Stibnite shack. She saw herself burning it down again and again, burning everything again. The snowflakes died against the flames.

She started the truck and drove up the hill to the Guntlys'. She told Ellen what she'd done, and what she'd done twenty years ago. She'd never told anybody. It'd been so long she couldn't be sure how, or even why. After she told her secret, her strength faded and she felt fragile, but finally unthreatened. Ellen hugged her and Iona wrapped her arms around the old woman's shoulders and cried. They stayed that way for quite some time then the two women walked to the front of the house and stood at the picture window. They watched the orange light and smoke in the distance heat the belly of the storm, and waited for their hunters to return.

EPILOGUE

THERE WAS A GUNSHOT in the storm and it was close. They crouched together and looked out from the shelter of the trees. The snow fell straight down. Wilhelm's rifle was laid ready across his lap with a sandwich bag rubber-banded over the barrel. It was difficult to tell what time of day it was or how long they'd been there. The two boys stood and started out toward the sound but the old man told them to wait. There was another shot then it was silent. Olin wiped the snow dust from his jacket and his brother watched him then did the same. When they followed the old man out from the pines the snow was well above their boots.

They found Tracy kneeling alongside the bull he'd shot. There wasn't any blood on the snow yet. He could've been sleeping. They could've been statues. He didn't turn when Wilhelm spoke. The boys came forward and Jake went to touch the animal and Tracy snatched him by the arm. "Don't," he said.

The boy looked scared.

"Tracy," Wilhelm said.

"I'm all right. Just give me a minute." He pulled Jake to him and put his arm around his shoulder.

"You did fine for yourself, didn't you? Look at him." Wilhelm took Tracy's rifle from him and went and stashed it along with his own in a dry spot under a tree. When he returned Tracy and Jake had gotten to their feet. Olin was squatted down looking into the animal's face, tongue hanging.

"You can touch him now," Tracy said to Jake.

"There'll be plenty of time for that," Wilhelm said. "Get out your knife. We got this storm to worry about."

The rich smell of the animal came up through the snowflakes and it was the smell of springtime. Slowly, Tracy undid his jacket and took his knife from his belt.

"I'll walk you through it," the old man said.

"Give me a minute."

"You're a little rattled right now. It's okay. But we need to get to work. We aren't more than a half mile from camp but this snow's gonna make it seem like a lot longer."

The cut was long and crooked, but Tracy did what he was told. Wilhelm stepped in and helped when it was needed. Steaming blood went over their hands and into the snow. The boys squatted next to each other, shivering. The snow was soon trampled and bloodied. Tracy tugged on the hide while Wilhelm worked his knife along the seam. The first two quarters came off and were laid out on squares of burlap. They spent the next half hour getting the animal flipped over onto its other side and skinned. It was a messy, impersonal business that was easy to get lost in. He dug around trying to cut the shoulder joint free and wished for one thing and it was a sharper knife. Wilhelm cut out the backstrap and put one into a plastic bag he had in his coat and stuffed the other in his pack along with the heart and the liver. It was nearly dark when all the meat was finally laid out and lashed into the burlap. It wasn't fair to make the boys and Wilhelm do much work so Tracy took three trips to their one.

He made his final haul back to camp alone in total darkness dragging the giant elk head along by the antlers like a busted wheelbarrow. He struggled with every step and foundered in the snow. His hands were frozen inside his gloves and his feet were numb. Stupid, hick-ass, macho bullshit, he thought. I'd rather be in bed with Georgie. Then he remembered where he'd been last year during the first snow. It wasn't so bad, being out in it. Walking out in it. He leaned forward and quickened his step. The snow came down and it was good to be cold and breathing and working for something, something that to him seemed older than time.

While he was gone Wilhelm and the boys had wrapped all of the elk meat in a tarp and run it up a tree with a rope tied off to the ball hitch of the pickup. There was light coming from inside the tent. With the last of his strength Tracy lifted the head into the bed of the truck. The rack was higher than the top of the cab.

Inside the tent he took off his coat and steamed. He was soaked with sweat and the blood pounded in his face. Wilhelm was sitting on his cot with slumped shoulders, his head hanging down, grinning. The boys were on the foam pad and sleeping bags that was their bed, working on taking off their boots.

"Are we having a fire tonight?" Tracy said.

"What we should do is break down and get going before we get snowed in."

The boys stopped what they were doing and looked up at Wilhelm. The old man smiled back at them then blinked making fun of the boys staring. "I'll cook if you get the fire going," he said to Tracy.

"All right." To the boys: "You can take off your boots. I'll get the wood. Get some dry socks on then you can help Wilhelm get dinner together. That sound okay?"

They nodded.

"What're you grinning about?" Tracy said to Wilhelm.

"That's a big damn elk you shot."

"Yep."

"Where're you gonna hang the rack? If you put it in the living room, you won't have anywhere to sit."

"Maybe I'll hang it on the barn."

"Bandy's gonna be impressed."

"Why? I didn't do anything. I saw it and pulled the trigger. Kinda tough to be proud of that."

"Luck counts."

"Maybe it shouldn't."

"You did good."

Tracy lingered for a moment then went out to gather wood for the fire. There was a ledge beneath the cliff where they could sit out of the weather and cook. Wilhelm had brought a camp stove but they hadn't unpacked it. They'd been there for five days. Tracy had mostly given up on seeing anything but once the snow had started the elk began to move, just as Wilhelm said they would, and he'd been waiting.

The bull had come down through the drainage, moving fast and with very little sound. It stopped in the clearing and raised its head. Tracy was under the hanging bows of a pine with his back to the trunk. He raised his rifle and shot before considering what it meant. The bull leapt into the air and ran in a zigzag, kicking up fans of dirt and snow then his legs went out and he pitched forward and his rack dug in and his neck was wrenched horribly. Tracy came out from under the tree, his heart hammering in his chest, and chambered another round. As he started toward the downed animal it stood and staggered another ten or fifteen yards then stopped and turned broadside. Without hesitating for more than a second or two, Tracy shot him again and he went down, gently this time, like he was getting up in reverse.

He relived the moment over and over as he snapped twigs and stacked them in a teepee shape in the firepit. Putting pressure on the trigger, actually pulling it; he couldn't remember. How far had the shot been? He didn't know. Both shots had been good. The first one had killed him, the second had only sped it along. Maybe he would go back and look over the ground tomorrow so he could be sure what had happened. It seemed like it had been a close shot but it couldn't have been. How big did the bull look when he shot it compared to when he stood over its body? He felt uneasy because he couldn't piece it all together. The bull was dead. Shame wasn't right. He didn't feel shame. Wilhelm thought that he was scared, but it wasn't that easy, was it? He needed to know what he was thinking when he pulled the trigger but the fact was that he hadn't been thinking anything. He'd simply done it.

He lit the fire and tossed dead pine needles on top of it then larger limbs. There was dried blood smeared into the cracks in his hands and under his nails. He left the cliff shelter and washed his hands in the dry snow until they ached from the cold. The shadows of Wilhelm and the boys moved inside the tent. He could hear them talking but not what they said. The night was full of snow and in the firelight everything looked festive and warm. He spent a few moments looking at the elk head in the back of the pickup, the meat hanging in the tree. He felt the need for a ritual but didn't know where to start.

Wilhelm was kneeling in front of the kitchen box, digging through the canned food. The boys stood next to him, their stocking feet tapping time gently on the tarp floor. The old man held up one can and the boys shook their heads. He held up another and they nodded. Tracy stood silent and still and watched them. The sound of the fire popping came through the walls of the tent. For some reason he thought of his father pushing him down the road in his wheelchair. He held out his hands and looked at them, some of the blood was still there. He had pulled the trigger. No blame could go to anyone else. He was the only one.

"You all right?" Wilhelm said.

"Sure. The fire's going."

The old man held a can of food in each knobby fist like he might throw them. He told the boys to fetch a pan for the back-strap. "We're gonna eat like kings," he said.

Tracy sat down on his cot and looked at his boots, the snow melting away onto the floor. The boys were clanging away looking for the right pan. Wilhelm was chopping onions. Tracy lifted his pant leg and pulled on his laces. Take your boots off, maybe lie down for a bit before dinner. Just for a little while. The tent was warm from body heat. He lay back. The roof was sagging deeply from the weight of the snow, and there was more coming. He should get up and clear it off but he didn't. He was too tired. He closed his eyes. The sounds of cooking then the smells came to him. He was content, completely relaxed, and sleep came easy.

ACKNOWLEDGMENTS

The author would like to thank the Michener Center for Writers, particularly Jim Magnuson and Marla Akin.

A NOTE ON THE AUTHOR

Born in Idaho, Brian Hart spent years working as a carpenter, welder, commercial fisherman, and framer of elevator shafts before earning his MFA from the Michener Center for Writers at the University of Texas at Austin. He was the winner of the 2005 Keene Prize, the largest student prize for literature.